CHANGE OF HEART

With much grunting and groaning, they were finally able to get Beau seated again. In the process, Shayna somehow ended up in his lap. She closed her eyes, catching her breath. Every muscle and sinew ached. Her back felt as if a thousand-pound man had been stomping grapes on it, and her neck hurt.

She simply couldn't move, and she needed to get her equilibrium back. She had her arms around his neck, heard Beau's heavy breathing, smelled sweat mingling with a spicy cologne. Pinpoints of light flashed behind her closed lids. The room tilted. Her breasts brushed against Beau's chest. He stiffened. She heard his sharp intake of breath.

Beau's arms circled her waist. He covered her face with kisses.

"No," Shayna said, trying to get up. But her protest was cut short by another floor-tilting kiss that made her head spin.

CHANGE OF HEART

Marcia King-Gamble

BET Publications, LLC
www.bet.com

ARABESQUE BOOKS are published by

BET Publications, LLC
c/o BET BOOKS
One BET Plaza
1900 W Place NE
Washington, DC 20018-1211

All Kensington Titles, Imprints, and Distributed Lines are available at special quantity discounts for bulk purchases for sales promotions, premiums, fund-raising, and educational or institutional use. Special book excerpts or customized printings can also be created to fit specific needs. For details, write or phone the office of the Kensington special sales manager: Kensington Publishing Corp., 850 Third Avenue, New York, NY 10022, attn: Special Sales Department, Phone: 1-800-221-2647.

First Printing: October 2001
10 9 8 7 6 5 4 3 2 1

Printed in the United States of America

ACKNOWLEDGMENTS

This book is dedicated to Chris and Stuart, because . . . well, because I forgot you the last time around. Chris, thanks for all the magic tips. Your sense of humor keeps me sane and your dedication to each other is proof that real love exists.

My gratitude and thanks to Dr. Rob Sury, a specialist in rehabilitation medicine. Without Rob's medical expertise, it would have been impossible to write this book.

Chapter One

"Beau! Beau! Beau!"

The chanting made Beau Hill feel invincible. He'd taken the lead, and gold was well within his grasp. He was born to be out here, snow under his skis, the crisp winter wind biting into his face, adrenaline pumping. He sensed the competition closing in. This wasn't just any old downhill run. This was the day America would bring home the medal, the day his dreams would come true.

"Go, Beau! Go, Beau!" the crowd shouted, as he zipped by, spurred on by their adulation.

More adrenaline kicked in. He bent his knees preparing to take the turn. His fans loved him and he loved them. That was the only inspiration he needed. The national anthem already played in his head.

"Oh, say, can you see . . ."

Yes, he could definitely see it. Feel it. Smell it. God knew he'd earned it. All those years of training. Disciplining himself to get up on cold winter mornings when friends were still snuggling in bed. Beau leaned forward, accepting the gold medallion hanging on the end of a red, white, and blue ribbon. In the background the commentator announced his name.

"Beau Hill of the United States, winner of the gold."

Even as a little boy, he'd visualized this moment. He'd known he was destined to be in the spotlight. That he was going to be somebody. Twenty-eight years later, Beaumont Hill was somebody, a champion skier, the USA's only hope for the gold, and according to the paparazzi, one of America's most eligible bachelors. Not bad for a poor black boy born on the wrong side of the tracks.

"Beau, Beau, Beau," the crowd yelled, egging him on. He couldn't disappoint his public. Wouldn't.

Beau's eyelids popped open. He'd been dreaming that dream again. Except now reality had intruded and with it, the nightmare began. Beau Hill would never ski again. Beau Hill couldn't walk. Beau Hill was nothing.

"Beau, my love, it's time for your therapy session," the too-cheery nurse with the chirpy voice greeted. Sister Mary Jane Immaculata, he'd dubbed her.

"What therapy session?" Beau snarled.

"How soon we forget. Yesterday we talked about it, remember? Your physical therapy. I even said the therapist was cute. She's going to help you walk again."

Beau glared at the plump little blonde with the Kewpie-doll face. No matter how nasty he'd gotten, she just became sweeter. Yesterday he'd doused her with a glass of cold water. She'd simply wiped herself off, admonishing him with a "Now, now. Reign in that temper, bad boy."

"Are those teeth brushed, or do you need help?" she chirped, pretending to cut her eyes at him.

Beau scowled at her. "I'm not your child, princess. I'm a grown man. I don't need you to tell me to brush my teeth."

But he did. He hadn't been motivated to brush his teeth at all, though he'd never admit that to her. He'd resorted to gum.

"Temper, Temper," Immaculata said, continuing to smile sweetly.

Her real name was Mary Jane Coppola, and she wagged a finger at him.

Beau tried to sit up but even that small movement caused him pain. He'd survived a broken wrist and back, a fractured tibia, and several cracked ribs. He'd been transferred to the rehabilitation center after three weeks at a hospital and although he kept his drapes closed, the smell of a Colorado spring wafted its way in with every new visitor. People he didn't want to see.

"Are you sure you don't need help?" Sister Immaculata asked, at the ready to assist.

"No, I don't need help," he said, mimicking her. "If I wanted help I would ask for it."

"No, you wouldn't. You're much too stubborn."

Mary Jane, during their short acquaintance, had come to know him well. Beau hadn't always been this foul tempered. This nasty side had emerged since the accident. He gritted his teeth, hoping the pain didn't show. "Can we get this over with?"

She helped him into the wheelchair, settling a blanket over legs that were useless, and smiled at him.

"There, there."

There, there, what? He couldn't walk, much less ski. Life was meaningless. He might as well be dead. Screw the physical therapist and the entire team that had decided to make him their project. He was sick to death of the psychologist, nurses, occupational therapist, and now this damn physical therapist they insisted he see. Screw what everyone said. His life was over.

A flurry of activity at the door got his attention. Chandra, his fiancée, had arrived. She sailed in behind a huge bouquet of red roses and a cloud of expensive perfume. Beau scowled at her. As always, she was impeccably dressed and made up to perfection. Chandra's supermodel status came with such perks as getting to keep the designer outfits she modeled. She unclipped one of those getups, a cape, and folded it over her arm.

"How's my African-American stallion doing?" she purred, blowing him a kiss and setting the flowers down on a chest of drawers to join several other vases.

"How the hell do you think I am?" Beau snorted. "I'm trapped in this blasted chair. My body is useless. My legs don't work."

"Would it help if I kissed you and made you feel better?"

Sister Immaculata chuckled. "Maybe that's just what he needs. I think this is my cue to exit. Don't forget your therapy session." She left, closing the door of the private room behind her.

No sooner was she out of sight than Chandra unbuttoned the top three buttons of the elegant silk blouse she wore. As usual she went braless. Two firm breasts the color of golden melons were tilted his way.

"These need attention, baby," she said, cupping them.

It was her lack of inhibition that had gotten his attention in the first place. On their first date she hadn't worn panties and, boy, had she let him know it.

Beau turned his face away. Those perfectly shaped lobes, tantalizing as they were, needed to be left alone. Why start something he couldn't finish?

"What can I do to make my baby feel better?" Chandra asked, raising her skirt an inch.

Beau closed his eyes. "Button yourself up and stop acting like a fool."

Chandra managed to look hurt. "Okay, used-to-be stud, if you don't want them someone else will."

That one hurt. She was right. Who in their right mind wouldn't want a beautiful, rich, and intelligent model? Temperamental though she was. Those qualities had once excited him. There had been a time when he would have leaped at her invitation. But how could he now, when he wasn't even sure if the equipment worked though he was much too proud to tell her that. Their relationship had never been based on conversation but on some deep level he understood her, even cared.

Chandra now gave him her full attention, making sure her assets were still in full view, inches from his face. In slow motion, she buttoned her blouse.

"Be that way," she said.

"We're late," Immaculata yodeled, sticking her head through a space in the door. "Oops. Would you like me to put those in water?" She pointed to the roses.

"Take the flowers home with you," Beau muttered, ignoring Chandra's thunderous glare. "They're setting my allergies off. Looks like a funeral home around here anyway."

"I couldn't do that. Enjoy your flowers. I'll get a vase."

"I want you to take them. There's no space."

"Fine." Mary Jane placed her palms on the handles of his chair. "You're already fifteen minutes late for your therapy session. We need to go." To Chandra she said, "You're welcome to wait, but this will take at least an hour."

"I've got a luncheon appointment," the model said, picking up her cape. "I'll try to stop by later." She blew kisses at Beau. He flashed her a smile that didn't quite reach his eyes.

"Later."

As soon as she had exited Immaculata started in.

"Ready to take off, bad boy?"

Beau grunted at her. "Might as well. I have nothing else to do."

Five floors down in Denver Rehabilitation Center, Shayna DaCosta tapped an impatient foot. She hated to be kept waiting. Time was money. She'd heard this new patient was a bear, and she wasn't looking forward to working with him. Forget his superstar status. It was common knowledge Beaumont Hill was known to throw food and tantrums. Rumor had it he'd gone through a dozen nurses at Denver General, and in the few days he'd been there he'd already upset a few. She wasn't about to put up with his nonsense.

Ever since his accident, Beau Hill had apparently undergone a rapid personality change. Denver's darling had grown fangs and now bit. Beau had been the all-American boy, a successful athlete who'd never forgotten his roots. He'd pumped money earned from endorsements into numerous charities and had even funded a recreation center in his hometown. Hill Of Dreams provided a place for the poor and troubled to meet, play, and eat.

Would the real Beau Hill do his photos justice? Shayna wondered. He'd endorsed everything from Chapstick to a popular cologne. That sexy smile, white against ebony, had set more than one Denver female's heart a-flutter. It should be a crime to look so good.

"Your patient's here," Mary Jane Coppola yodeled, in the chirpy voice Shayna had come to recognize and love. "Now see, didn't I tell you she was cute?"

Beau Hill appeared to be assessing her. He was dark

in complexion and had that lean and hungry look some women found endearing. A gold stud glistened from one lobe. He had that bad boy thing going on, a shaved head like Michael Jordan, except he was much better looking. Shayna would hazard a guess his hospital stay had caused him to lose at least twenty pounds. That weight loss only made him seem more mysterious.

It was his slate-gray eyes that got to her, filled with hostility and brimming with hurt. Beau Hill had taken a beating mentally and physically. She sensed he needed repair. Shayna recognized that look of defeat. Smelled his fear. She'd been there, boy, had she been there. It had been an uphill battle to recovery but she'd been determined to survive.

"Cute is as cute does, my mother used to say," Beau Hill answered, bringing her firmly back to the present. His deep, throaty voice, inspired chills. It reminded her of a cool winter's wind blowing against her cheeks. Biting, yet at the same time invigorating. It was the kind of voice a woman wanted whispering in her ear when the temperature soared, and even air-conditioning wasn't enough. When it was just you and him.

What on earth had gotten into her? Beau Hill looked nothing like the sex symbol he was purported to be. He was unshaved, unkempt, and wasn't even gracious.

"Hi, I'm Shayna," she said, squatting her under five-foot body to his level, making sure to keep her hands off his wheelchair.

"Immaculata already told me who you are," Beau snarled. "Can we get down to business?"

"Who's Immaculata?"

"That would be me." Mary Jane smiled at her from her spot off to the side. "I'm off. See you two later."

"As for getting down to business," Shayna continued when Mary Jane had left, "that depends on you."

He was an unpleasant man. Who could blame him? At twenty-eight he'd been one of the oldest skiers on the US team. Money had been bet on him. He was a certainty to bring home the gold. One unfortunate accident had cost him that medal. Except for the grace of God he might have died.

"You look about sixteen," Beau continued rudely, letting his gaze linger on her, making her flush. "Hardly old enough to do this type of work."

"I assure you I am a lot older than I look," Shayna answered, her words measured. No need to tell him she would be twenty-seven in a few months. "Even more important is that I'm experienced. I have a long list of successes behind me."

She would not let him bully her. He was used to lots of attention. Getting his way. People fawning over him. Not her. She knew his type. Didn't particularly like it.

"Go ahead, work your magic on me, princess. I need a whole lot of whatever you're smoking."

Beau's gray eyes searched hers, his jaw tightened. Not a hint of a smile to be found.

Wound like a spring, Shayna thought, understanding his bitterness. Back then, when she'd had her accident, she'd been young, optimistic, full of dreams. Naive, some would call it. Things had turned out all right, but at the time, she'd thought her whole world had ended. And in some ways it had. Now she'd learned to adjust to her new life, even enjoyed it.

Beau Hill was still staring at her.

"Is something wrong?"

"You look familiar."

"Do I now?"

Shayna never volunteered personal information. When she'd been a gymnast she'd worn her hair in a sleek top knot. Today it was natural and cut close to her scalp.

She'd gained a good twenty pounds these last few years. Now she tipped the scales at barely one hundred. Two Olympics ago, she'd been one of America's most promising athletes, a talented gymnast, slated to take the world by storm. Her face had smiled from popular cereal boxes. She'd competed against the best. Been the best.

"Shall we begin?" Shayna asked, glancing at his chart and frowning. He should have been further along in the recovery process, a sure indicator that his mental state was not good. Shayna had planned on putting him through a series of exercises. Now she abandoned that plan. Beau Hill would have to let go of that anger or they weren't going to get anywhere.

"Do you read?" she asked.

Beau snorted. "Read? Hate it."

"What do you do all day?"

He slanted his eyes at her, his inner dialogue evident. He must be thinking she was one crazy chick.

His laughter was ugly. Bitter. "What does a man with a broken back, wrist, and fractured tibia do all day? Lie on my back, watch television, eat. Recount memories. Hopes. Dreams." She heard the bitterness in his voice. The smile he flashed her way didn't quite reach his eyes.

"How about you start reading? I have a list of books I can recommend. They might help pass the time."

"What does reading have to do with my therapy?" He eyed her warily. "I thought we were here to work, get these legs functioning again."

"Before we can do that, I need to get to know you, and you need to get in touch with the person you used to be. The real Beaumont Hill."

"Pure mumbo jumbo. I already have one head doctor, I don't need another." Beau spat a crude epithet at her. With some difficulty he managed to wheel himself over, closer to her.

He smelled of hospital, but even so, the scent of man was evident. His heady musk titillated her senses and fed her imagination. *Easy, Shayna, he's your patient. Don't get taken in.*

"I won't let anyone into my head, princess, so don't even try." Beau's gray eyes flashed dangerously. Shayna's pulse pounded.

"Then you won't ever recover," she said. "You'll be dependent on that contraption for the rest of your life. At best you'll be tied to a cane. Just think, the great Beaumont Hill, lame. Do it my way and you'll ski again."

Shayna turned her back on him and began sorting through the books on a nearby bookcase. At last she found the one she was looking for, *Turning Hurts Into Halos*. She turned back to him. "If you want to leave here walking you might try reading this."

Reluctantly Beau took the book from her. "You drive a hard bargain, princess."

"And another thing," Shayna said, refusing to soften, "I'm not your princess. My name is Shayna. I call the shots. You listen, and there's a pretty good chance you'll be on your feet in a couple of weeks. Understand?"

Beau muttered another expletive. Visibly disgusted he thumbed through the pages. "No. But I don't have anything else to lose."

"Exactly." Shayna reached for the phone.

"What are you doing?"

"Session's over. I'm calling a nurse. Next time we meet, we'll discuss that book."

Beau glared at her. "We'll see, prin . . . We'll see."

"That we will," Shayna said, punching in the numbers.

Chapter Two

Bored with the game shows on television, and having no interest in soap operas, Beau returned to the book open on his nightstand. *Turning Hurts Into Halos*. What kind of name was that? Grumbling all the way, he'd flipped through the book last evening, and after ten minutes, tossed it aside. He'd never had tolerance for psycho-babble.

Beau snapped the television remote and groaned. He was faced with talk show guests espousing the mind's power to heal, how important mind over matter was, and good energy versus bad. It would be his luck that Shayna DaCosta was one of those spiritual types who believed in holistic healing. That touchy-feely stuff. What he needed was results. To be made whole again.

Beau hated to admit it but Immaculata was right. Shayna was cute in an offbeat kind of way. If he could stand up, she would come up to his shoulder, maybe. But tiny as she was, she had a big woman's personality, and was bossy as all hell. Her elfin haircut made those huge almond-shaped eyes look even larger. The knowledge in their depths ran way beyond her years. He hadn't lied when he'd told her she looked sixteen. Beau imagined she would appeal to a certain kind of man. The protective type. Little would they guess that under the fragile exterior was a woman of steel. It would be an interesting several weeks working with her.

"How's my patient doing?" Immaculata stuck her head in the open doorway and smiled at him. It grated on his nerves that nothing seemed to ruffle her. No one could be that upbeat all of the time. No one.

"Lousy as always."

"Get over it. What are you reading?" She pointed to the book in his hand. "I've never seen you read."

Beau mumbled something he preferred she not hear under his breath. "Got to be a nut to believe in this stuff." He flung the book halfway across the room, breaking the spine.

"Now look at what you've done." Immaculata bent over to retrieve the book. She read the title out loud. *"Turning Hurts Into Halos.* Shayna must have lent you this. You'll have hell to pay when she gets it back in this condition."

"I'll deal with it. I'm supposed to read this garbage and discuss it with her next session."

"Isn't that tomorrow? Will you be finished by then?"

Beau shrugged. "I'm not worried. What's she going to do? Refuse to work with me?"

"She just might." Immaculata checked his chart. "Yep. Your second session's tomorrow. How did the first go?"

Beau propped himself on his elbows and scowled at her. "How did you expect it to go?"

Mary Jane beamed at him. "Did you like Shayna?"

Beau longed to wipe that ever-present grin off Immaculata's face. It was sometimes difficult to remember that he actually liked her. Bringing his chart with her, she took a seat in the adjacent chair, crossing her legs at dimpled knees.

"What's there to like?" he grunted.

"Everything. She's beautiful inside and out."

Beau made a rude sound. "Is she legit? Does she get results? Since she works for Denver Rehab, I'm going to assume she comes with credentials and a degree. Never mind that she looks like a child."

"A beautiful child who has brains and lots of successes under her belt."

"Her personality needs work. She's hell on wheels."

Immaculata chortled. "And you aren't?"

Beau blushed. He had reason to be ugly. Shayna DaCosta didn't. She had two fully functioning legs and had a fairly lucrative career from what he could see. Whereas he was about to lose all his endorsements. None of the major companies would want a cripple representing them.

"What's Shayna's story?" Beau reluctantly asked. Something about her had captured his interest. Call it insatiable curiosity. Call it whatever you wanted. He suddenly needed to know.

Mary Jane's smile widened. "You're interested in Shayna. This is the first time you've asked me about anyone on our team. Anything in particular you'd like to know?"

What was it he wanted to know? Why the sudden curiosity, or interest, as Immaculata called it? He'd met the physical therapist once, briefly. They'd exchanged pitifully few words. The few they'd exchanged had been heated. Still, if he was about to turn his body over to her, he needed to make sure that she was experienced, well thought of, and could deliver.

"How long has she been doing this?"

"Rehabilitation therapy?"

"Yes, physical therapy."

Immaculata leaned forward as if she was about to reveal a confidence. "Shayna came to us less than a year ago. She moved here from Seattle. Rumor has it—"

There was a commotion at the door. A light-as-a-breeze fragrance mingled with hospital smells.

"I'm here to see my Beau-Beau," Chandra announced, bouncing into the room and nodding at Immaculata dismissively.

Mary Jane took the hint. She rose, brushing herself off. "I've got patients to see. Have fun, you two."

Chandra plopped herself down on his bed. Beau winced. No matter how many times he'd begged her not to just plant herself down, she always claimed to forget. Beau had decided it was easier to grit his teeth and bear the pain. A much better alternative than getting into a fight with Chandra.

"I'm off to Milan tomorrow," she announced. "Baby, I'll miss you so much."

"Milan?" Beau inhaled a huge sigh of relief but was careful to keep his expression neutral. "How long will you be gone?"

"Don't know. Two weeks. Maybe three." Chandra twisted his top sheet between perfectly manicured nails. The five-karat emerald-cut diamond he'd given her sparkled from her left hand. "Well, that's the thing. The client wants me there at least three weeks. As spokesperson for the Bellissima line, I'll be shooting commercials and making appearances."

Three weeks without Chandra's whining and hounding him for sex sounded like heaven to him. A month was a long time to expect her to go without sex. But she professed to love him, even though time and time again, he'd offered to let her out of the engagement. That she'd declined surprised him. A woman like Chandra would have no trouble finding someone to take care of her needs. Someone who could walk, and was fully functional.

Glad for this unexpected reprieve, though he would never tell her that, Beau hastened to reassure her. "I'm going to miss you like crazy, babe."

Yeah, he'd miss the unexpected visits. The nagging for sex. Lately she'd taken to dropping by the hospital at the most inopportune times, always outside of visitors' hours. Usually when he'd taken a painkiller and was groggy and nonfunctional, or after he'd been up all night haunted by those unpleasant dreams. She would park herself on his bed, taunting him, when he could do nothing about it.

"So what about you giving me a good-bye gift?" Chandra asked, slowly hiking her skirt up and demonstrating that she'd come sans underwear. There was a time when just the sight of her honey-colored skin, her carefully trimmed mound, would have had him foaming at the mouth. Not now. Not when he lay in bed helpless.

Chandra straddled him, at the same time working a couple of buttons open. Beau, despite the discomfort of having her on top of him, obliged her by taking a bare breast into his mouth. Chandra's skirt settled around her hips. Beau heaved a sigh. He'd given in to temptation and couldn't finish what he started. Didn't even want to try. Why embarrass himself?

"My parents will be here any minute," Beau said. "Wouldn't do for them to walk in and see us like this." He kissed her soundly.

Reluctantly Chandra tugged down her skirt and pouted. "Screw your parents. Why can't we make love like we used to? It's been over a month. If this continues much longer I'll shrivel up and die."

All of Beau's pent-up fury came to a head. He'd cut back on the painkillers, and so far the horrible temper tantrums and ugly mood swings had lessened. But Chandra's sniveling set him off.

"Look, I'm not keeping you bound to me," he snapped. "I've offered you your freedom numerous times. If sex is more important to you than my getting well, then let's call our relationship off until you get back from Milan. I won't ask you what you did over there, if you promise not to ask me what I did here. Deal?"

Chandra raised her long neck. Her eyelashes swept her cheeks. The tears flowed freely. Crocodile tears. Still, he hated that he'd made her cry. Any man would be crazy to let her go.

"I'm sorry, Beau-Beau," she said, looking up, brown eyes brimming. "I'm just so horny."

"And I'm giving you the opportunity to resolve that issue. You have three weeks to do as you want. If at the end of that time you decide you still love me and want to make it work, we'll talk about it." With the back of his hand, he wiped the tears away. "Go to Milan. Have fun. Send me a present."

"I'm not happy about this," Chandra sniveled. "Next you'll be asking me for the ring."

Her ring, platinum setting and all, had cost him a bundle. "Wearing it on your right hand might not be a bad idea until we get this thing resolved," Beau suggested.

"You bastard."

Just like that, her mood shifted again. Beau barely dodged the pillow she threw at him. The quick movement made his ribs ache. He'd like to believe Chandra's reasons for sticking with him had to do with loyalty and love. But he wasn't so sure of that. If he was truly honest about why he was still involved with her, he would be forced to admit she was right. He was a bastard and maybe he was using her for arm candy. Having a fiancée as good-looking as Chandra helped to validate what was left of his existence and made him feel alive.

Yet a nuzzle here, a nip there, and lots of stroking didn't cut it with a woman as highly sexed as Chandra. Never mind that even those few meager attempts had caused him agony. He knew he would have to do something about Chandra, and soon. Marry her or let her go. Right now marrying her didn't hold much appeal. In the meantime, he would try doing things Shayna DaCosta's way but that didn't mean he had to be charming. Three weeks should give him enough time to know if he would ever walk again.

There was a soft tapping on his door. Beau scowled. His agent had said he'd stop by. Usually that meant he'd heard from another company wanting to get out of their endorsement contract. He couldn't deal with more bad news.

"Go away," Beau shouted.

"We wouldn't think of doing that," his mother's voice called.

Chandra scooted off the bed, but not before showing him the full moon. "See what you're missing?"

Beau sighed. She buttoned her top buttons and straightened her skirt. His mother, Victoria, had that effect on her, turned her into an immediate lady. Beau hid a smile. His first since he'd been brought in by ambulance to Denver Rehabilitation Center.

"Hello, Mr. and Mrs. Anderson," Chandra greeted. She'd become the picture of decorum, even turning to smile at his parents as they entered. Arms open wide, she moved forward to kiss them. Victoria took a step back, skillfully evading her.

No love lost between the two, still Chandra had always bent over backward to make a good impression with his parents. Beau didn't know why. She made little effort to be gracious with anyone, unless she benefitted in some way. Beau had often thought it might have something to do with the Andersons' social status. They knew everyone there was to know and were frequently featured in the *Denver Times*.

Victoria didn't need to work but she dabbled in high-end real estate, making huge commissions. Ed, one of the city's more prominent criminal attorneys, had earned a name winning some tough high-profile cases. While most of their money had been inherited, they'd made another small fortune through wise investments.

Victoria now flashed Chandra a tight smile. "How are you, honey?" She stood safely out of reach.

Ed, the more susceptible to Chandra's charms, embraced her in a hug. "How's my daughter-in-law to be?"

Chandra sniffed. Her eyes brimmed over. "Beau's trying to dump me."

"Beau?" His father shot him a questioning look. "What's this?"

Victoria simply shook a full head of blond hair out of her eyes and secured it back with one of her headbands. "You're still wearing Beau's ring," she said pointedly.

"That she is," Beau confirmed, omitting that soon it would be on her right hand. He would have to do some serious thinking while Chandra was gone.

An awkward silence descended.

Beau used that time to reflect on how charmed his life had been ever since the Andersons had rescued him from that awful foster home, one of many he'd lived in. They'd adopted him at the ripe old age of ten, no easy feat for a white family with two kids of their own. The system being what it was, kids were usually placed with parents of similar race. But the Andersons had argued relentlessly that they had the desire and where-withal to adopt a child, and didn't care whether that child was pink, white, or green. Luckily they had the contacts and money to make Beau happen.

He'd been one angry little boy when they'd first gotten him. He'd used his fists to settle most fights, and had a tendency to run away. As his scrapes became legendary, the Andersons kept getting summoned to the private school where he was enrolled. Finally they took the advice of his gym teacher and signed Beau up for skiing lessons. All that misdirected rage finally found an outlet. Beau, natural athlete that he was, mastered the sport and the rest was history.

"Mr. and Mrs. Anderson," Chandra said, bringing him firmly back to earth. "Beau wants to put our engagement on hold until I get back from Milan."

Victoria's eyebrows shot to the ceiling. "You're going to Milan and leaving Beau in the state that he's in? No wonder he wants to . . ."

Chandra bristled, a first for her in his mother's presence. "Beau doesn't seem to have a problem with me going." Another slew of tears threatened to ruin her perfect makeup job.

"A little separation might not be a bad idea," Victoria said, her mood lightening considerably. His mother seemed happier than when she'd first arrived.

"It might be good for you both," Ed said, picking up on his wife's cue.

Although Chandra's look was murderous, she held her tongue. She was not a stupid woman.

Victoria began to talk nonstop. "Kelly and Jason send

their regards, Beau. They're both coming home to see you soon."

Beau grunted. "That would be nice."

"Nice, nothing. They're your brother and sister. They care about you."

Kelly, his older sister, had married a Japanese businessman and relocated to San Francisco. Jason, the perennial bachelor, was a successful investment banker who'd made Manhattan his home. Both had managed a visit occasionally, and were now overdue.

"I've got to go, Beau-Beau," Chandra piped up, twirling her fingers at him. She leaned over to plant a big wet one on his lips. "Love you." The diamond twinkled on the finger of her left hand.

Chandra plunged her tongue into his mouth but not before Beau noticed his mother's twinge of pain. He nibbled gently, then put her firmly away from him.

"I really will miss you, Beau-Beau," Chandra said, staring at him as though he was the one. The only one.

"Me too," he said begrudgingly.

His mother looked as if she were about to have an attack of apoplexy, and his father's glasses had fogged up. Shell-shocked was the only way to describe the look on the older man's face. Beau guessed they had gotten an eyeful of Chandra's bare bottom and more. The lecture would come later from his mother. He couldn't wait.

Chapter Three

Shayna glanced at the wall clock. Time ticked slowly by. Very slowly. Beau Hill was her next patient. She could hardly wait.

She'd tried to liven up the vomit-green walls of the place with motivational posters. She'd placed potted plants in strategic positions, and added colorful cushions to the few pieces of furniture there were. Her goal had been to create the illusion of an upscale spa, but nothing could hide the ugliness of functional parallel bars, weights, and pulleys.

Thank God for those lovely window walls. Shayna had rolled the blinds high, letting in the awesome outdoor scenery. Green at their base, the mountains remained snowcapped even in spring. That was Colorado for you.

"Good job, Gail," Shayna called, as Gail Mahoney, aided by a walker, slowly crossed the floor. The old lady was doing well but needed lots of stroking.

Shayna continued to put Gail through her routine,

observing her slow but steady pace. It was rewarding watching a patient progress from standing on her own, to taking her first tentative steps, unsteady and painful as those steps might be. Gail had never forgotten that precious moment and neither had Shayna.

Shayna's mind returned to Beau Hill. Beau would win no awards for congeniality. Prickly as the athlete was, he had piqued her interest. Call it her love of a good challenge, or call it a complete understanding of what he was going through. She knew his abrasive personality was a shield to hide the fear deep inside that he would never walk again, much less ski. An athlete as active as Beau was bound to be devastated by this new sedentary life.

Eight years ago Shayna had found herself in a similar position, faced with a brutal reality. Doctors had told her that she would never walk again. She'd been determined to prove them wrong and read everything she could on the subject of holistic healing. In the process she'd stumbled across a book, entitled *Turning Hurts Into Halos*. That book had changed her life. While she'd never again compete as a professional gymnast, she could walk. And she could walk without even the faintest trace of a limp.

"Your hour's up," Shayna announced, as a huffing, puffing Gail Mahoney continued to take painful steps back to her.

"Whew," Gail said, sinking tiredly into her wheelchair. "So how did I do today?"

"Terrific. Wonderful. Better than wonderful." Shayna kissed the older woman's cheek. "We'll have you out of here in no time. Just keep doing the exercises I taught you. Keep pushing yourself."

Gail beamed at her. "Did I tell you my grandson wants to meet you?"

"Hundreds of times." They'd turned it into their little joke. "Why would some twenty-one-year-old stud want to meet an old bag like me?"

Gail harrumphed. "Old bag nothing. You're young, beautiful, intelligent."

"Did I hear you say you were old?" Mary Jane Coppola called from the doorway. She'd come to deliver Beau. She arched penciled-in eyebrows. Shayna turned to acknowledge the new arrivals. "Hello, Mary Jane. Beau. I'll be with you in a moment."

The wheelchair's brake clicked into place as Mary Jane parked Beau. "Are we too early?"

"No. Right on time."

Shayna proceeded to wrap things up with Gail. The senior citizen's attention was completely riveted on the new arrival. "You're Beau Hill," she gushed, eyes widening at the unexpected bonus. "Yes, you are. You're the skier. Denver's darling, a one-time gold medal hopeful. There was something fishy about your accident if you ask me."

Beau took his time raising his shaved head. His ego had just been trampled on. His gray gaze rested on the old lady. For one fleeting moment his hurt was palpable, and then the mask was put on.

Shayna knew what he must feel like. It wasn't easy accepting the fact that you were a has-been. She wondered what Gail meant about something being fishy about Beau's fall. She made a mental note to go to the library and read up on the event. Call it her insatiable curiosity.

Gail continued. "I heard you'd been admitted. News travels fast in this facility and the nurses like to talk. They said you were good looking, but, young man, you need a shave."

Shayna waited for the explosion but Beau just continued to stare at the old lady. Not the least bit intimidated, Gail stared back. She was off and running.

"I saw a replay of your accident on TV. The newscaster said something about you falling out of your skis. That's why you took that nasty tumble. Don't worry, you'll walk again. You're a resilient bunch. Look at your dad; he's worked to keep our streets safe from crime. He's a tough attorney, but a fair one. That kid in his recent case who beat up that woman should be tried as an adult. Hopefully your dad can make that happen."

Beau grunted.

"Young man, you disagree?" Gail waggled a finger. "I wouldn't be in this predicament if it hadn't been for some hoodlum. The man yanked my purse off my arm and knocked me to the ground, breaking my hip." She fumbled in her new purse, removing a notepad. "Would you mind autographing this? It's for my grandson."

Shayna tuned into the conversation more intently. She wondered if it was for the same grandson Gail kept pushing on her. Gail had made it sound as if Beau's father was some kind of celebrity. Shayna had lived in Denver less than a year and was still trying to figure out who was who.

While Gail's comment had piqued her interest, at the same time it saddened her. Her brother, Reggie, was out on bail for a crime he didn't commit. The attorney representing the woman that had been burglarized and beaten was called Anderson. Edward Anderson He couldn't possibly be Beau's father. He was as white bread as they came.

Shayna watched Beau awkwardly sign his name on the pad Gail provided. When he was through, he returned it to the old lady, who clutched it to her breast.

"Thank you. Thank you. My Timmy's going to be thrilled."

Mary Jane had already taken command of Gail's wheelchair. They headed off with Gail still clutching her notepad as if it were the winning Lotto ticket. "Bye, Beau-Beau," Mary Jane said from the doorway.

Beau raised his head and glared at the nurse. "Don't go there."

Shayna swore his lips twitched. Must be a private joke between them. Those intense gray eyes now assessed her. Feeling warm all over, she quickly opened a window, letting in the crisp spring breeze. It ruffled the daffodils on her desk and brought with it an incredible outdoor smell. Fresh, invigorating, biting as well.

Shayna inhaled deeply. Was that freshly mown grass she smelled?

"I love the spring, don't you?" she said, walking over to him and attempting to make conversation. Beau sat slumped in his chair. Shayna squatted down to eye level. Hmmm, he was wearing cologne. "So how are you?" she asked.

At first she thought he wasn't going to answer. He stared at his hands, at his wrist still wrapped in Ace bandages, and eventually grunted, "I'm alive. I suppose."

"Did you finish your homework assignment?"

"I read what I could stomach."

That wintery voice made her shiver. There were actual goose bumps on her arms. She noticed he hadn't brought the book with him.

Shayna ignored the fact that her heart was pumping furiously and her breath was coming in little bursts. Beau was talking. Now if she could only keep him talking. His haunted eyes scanned her face, assessing her, taking her measure. He must think she was a BS artist, a fraud. He probably didn't believe he would ever walk again. It was her job to make him believe.

"Give the book a chance. Read it. What else do you have to do on a nice spring day? Try wheeling yourself outside, finding a nice shady tree, breathing the mountain air. Why hide in a dark room, TV remote in hand?"

"Immaculata's been talking to you?" Beau growled, his eyebrows rising suspiciously.

"What if she has? She's concerned for you. Thinks you're a great guy. Why is beyond me, given how poorly you treat her."

The muscles in Beau's jaw worked. "She's all right. Just pushy. Now can we get on with my exercises?"

"You're not ready yet. You need to read that book."

"I told you I don't read."

"There's always a first time for everything."

He narrowed his eyes at her. "Obviously you've never been told you might not walk again."

"Don't be so sure." She didn't bother to remind him his was considered an incomplete spinal injury. He had weakness in his arms and legs but there was hope.

"Is that a yes?" He shot her a skeptical if curious look.

What harm would it do to provide Beau with the edited version of her life? He didn't need to know that she too had been an Olympic hopeful. That she'd taken a fall, breaking both hips. No one in Denver would ever associate little Shay DaCosta with the woman she was today, a rehabilitation therapist, living a simple life.

"I was told I would never walk again and if I did I would limp."

"But you don't," Beau confirmed, assessing her with that lazy gray-eyed gaze, his eyes shifting from her face, working its way down her body. Slowly, deliberately, missing nothing.

The goose bumps popped out again. She was glad she'd chosen the cream silk blouse, coupling it with a jaunty scarf at the neck; glad she'd worn the pencil-thin black skirt that stopped at the ankles, and the flat comfortable shoes that shouted business. Even so, she felt naked under his gaze. She doubted Beau Hill, disinterested as he appeared, missed the slightest bulge.

She continued. "It took a lot of work and desire on my part to get well. I had to search deep within myself and find a reason to want to heal. Mentally and physically."

"You were motivated. I'm not."

He'd put into words what she'd feared. Like him she'd lost her motivation, her passion for life after the accident. Shayna again debated whether to level with him. How would he benefit if she shared her shame for failing her family, the United States, the world, herself? She couldn't divulge all that she'd been through, not with a patient. It would be unprofessional at best.

Not that she'd deliberately set out to keep her past a secret. If a person found out she found out. Admittedly, this new life was certainly more fulfilling than the old, but even so she'd had her difficulties transitioning. She'd had to come down off her pedestal, get an education, learn compassion. More important, she'd had to learn to like herself. It had proven to be a huge challenge. Even greater than Beau Hill.

Shayna touched Beau's shoulder. Electric shocks ricocheted off his skin and right onto hers. She'd never seen anyone more wired.

"Beau, what do you recollect of the day you had the accident?"

He rolled his eyes. "That shrink you people insist I see keeps asking me that. That's not important. Bottom line, I can't walk."

"Okay. Then let's talk about Beau Hill."

He snorted. "What's to tell about Beau Hill? There's nothing left of him that's worth talking about."

"So Beau no longer has a life? A family? A home? A recreation center he's proud of?"

He shrugged. "Sure I have a home. A huge one, an expensive one, an empty one. As for family, I have parents, a brother and sister. And Hill Of Dreams does exist."

"What about a girlfriend?" Shayna asked, noting that his hands were free of rings. She'd heard the scuttlebutt from the staff that there was a woman in the picture, and that their relationship was tumultuous. The staff often heard them screaming at each other.

A long pause ensued. Shayna thought he wasn't going to answer.

"My relationship with Chandra, though it's none of your business, is on hold right now," he said.

"What about friends?"

Beau snorted. "Friendships don't amount to a hill of beans."

"Everyone needs friends."

"Not fair-weather ones."

"So I'm gathering your buddies no longer visit?"

Beau made a crude sound. "What buddies?"

"Your evil behavior drove them away?" She arched an eyebrow at him.

A colorful oath rolled off his tongue. "I don't have to take this."

"And I don't have to take your foul mouth. Wheel yourself away. Go back to your miserable room and sulk," Shayna taunted. She'd heard from the nurses that he'd stubbornly refused to learn how to propel his wheelchair.

"I think I will," Beau said, awkwardly attempting to maneuver his chair.

Silently she applauded him. He got halfway across the room before she stopped him.

"Now was that difficult? Yet you were content to let those gorgeous muscles atrophy."

He glared at her. "What's the point of maintaining muscles when you'll never use them?"

"You mean ski again?" Ignoring the way he looked at her, she crossed the room to stand beside him. "How did someone so unmotivated come up with the idea for Hill Of Dreams?" she muttered loud enough for him to hear.

"Have you ever been abandoned by family? Lived in foster homes? Had no place to go?" Beau gritted out. "No, you wouldn't know anything about that, Miss To The Manor Born." He eyed her elegant getup.

He was right. She and Reggie had been raised by normal middle-class parents. Her mother was a teacher, her father, a gym coach. Even so, her teenage brother would probably benefit from a place like Beau's. Reggie had been involved in more than his share of trouble, and he had parents who loved him.

"No," she said, shaking her head slowly. "Can't say I have."

"Well, I have, and it's not pretty. You're unwanted. Tolerated by the families who take you in. Frustrated because you feel you don't belong. As a result you act out."

Keep him talking, Shayna. Keep him talking. "Okay, so you came up with the idea for the recreation center. Did you fund it or get investors?"

"My parents helped. They're well connected and were able to put me in touch with the right people. I ended up donating some of my own money but every penny's been well spent."

"When was the last time you visited Hill Of Dreams?" Shayna asked, an idea slowly beginning to percolate.

Beau shrugged. "It's been at least five to six months. First I was busy training; then the accident happened . . ."

"How about you and I visit?"

"You've gotta be kidding."

"Hey, you two. Hour's up," Mary Jane called. She beamed at them from the doorway. "Ready, Beau-Beau?"

Beau cut his eyes at Mary Jane. "About time you got here," he grumbled.

Shayna tabled the discussion for another time. She'd gotten Beau talking. That, in and of itself, was progress. He glanced over at her as if he was about to say something, then changed his mind. "Let's go," he said to Mary Jane.

"We'll talk more next session," Shayna said. "By then you should be finished reading that book."

As Mary Jane placed her hands on Beau's wheelchair Shayna heard him say, "I can manage perfectly well, thank you."

"You can?" The nurse's eyes were the size of saucers. She shot Shayna an incredulous look. "He can?"

Shayna hid a smile as Beau took control of the wheels of his chair. He lurched forward and zigzagged his way toward the exit.

Beau Hill didn't know it yet but in a few weeks he would be up and walking.

Chapter Four

"Hey, watcha reading?"

The voice came from somewhere up above. Beau shook the fog from his brain and opened his eyes. The recreation room gradually came into focus. Familiar-looking patients sat in groups playing cards or board games. Some simply read. Subdued chatter slowly filtered in. What had he been reading? Who was asking?

Beau glanced down to see *Turning Hurts Into Halos* resting on his lap. He'd managed to make it through four chapters before falling into a trance. He still didn't know what to make of the book. Beau flipped it right side up and focused on the peculiar-looking man standing above him looking as if he'd won the 200-yard dash.

"Interesting title," Beau said.

His new acquaintance didn't look like any patient he remembered. He wore a Dr. Seuss hat, the wide brim partially obscuring his face. He twisted one waist-length lock and gawked at Beau.

"You're Beau Hill, right?"

Oh, no. Not another autograph seeker.

Beau grunted something unintelligible and tried to wake up. He'd been having a dream, one of those fantasies, a vision occurring when you're halfway between sleep and wakefulness.

"I'm Lenox Frasier," the man said, bending over and holding his palm up for a high five. "I'm the drummer for The Springs."

Beau slapped his palm against the drummer's hand. He recognized the name of the popular hip-hop group. They played at some of the better watering holes and had a devoted local following. From what Beau could recall of the drummer he was pretty good.

"I'm visiting my friend Earl, over there." Lenox gestured with his chin. "My boy had a horrible car accident. We're hoping he regains the use of his limbs."

Beau's eyes looked over Earl, taking in the hulk of a man seated in a monstrous wheelchair. An ugly apparatus assisted him to breathe; nevertheless, he acknowledged them with a blink of his eyes. Beau nodded back. He wondered what the agenda was. Obviously both men wanted something.

"I never did get to meet you," Lenox said, "and now here I find you in the most unexpected of places. I heard about your accident. I'm sorry."

"Did we have a meeting set up?" Beau asked, curious, despite the fact that he just wanted to be left alone. Bad enough he'd been evicted from his room by the ever cheerful Immaculata, who'd insisted that his occupational therapist wanted him to spend at least an hour in the recreation room. It seemed bull to him but he'd been getting cabin fever.

"No, man, we didn't. But I used to hang out at your place."

Beau narrowed his eyes. Please, God, not another overzealous fan or scam artist. Not another person looking for him to invest in some cockamamie scheme.

Lenox continued. "I'm talking about Hill Of Dreams, my man. A little over four years ago Earl and I were homeless. We had no prospects. Nothing. Someone told us about your facility, Hill Of Dreams, boy, was that place ever a godsend."

"How did my place help you?" Beau asked, his interest actually piqued.

Lenox tugged on the brim of his hat. "How did it help? It gave us a place to go. Kept us fed, occupied, and out of trouble. I did a lot of reading while I was there. You know that music room you have? Well, that's what inspired me to take up the drums again. Earl's got a great voice. He sang. I accompanied him. We even harmonized together, though my voice isn't as good as his.

"We used your place to clean up. After a while we were able to pick up a couple of gigs, him singing, me on drums. Nothing that paid a lot of money, but it sure helped get our self-esteem back. Now I work for UPS in their offices. I still play drums at night. We're grateful to you, man. Bad as Earl's outlook is, he would never have realized his dream if it hadn't been for you. Neither of us would. He'd like to meet you, Beau."

Damn, there it was. Everybody pulling on him, wanting something. Chandra wanting his body. His agent wanting him to hold on to endorsements and companies threatening to sue when all he cared about was that he might never ski again. Immaculata pushing him to get out of his room, to go out and mingle, and pretend everything was right in his world. Even Shayna DaCosta wanted something. She wanted him to read this stupid book. The only people that didn't seem to want anything from him was his family.

Beau debated about going over. His conscience kicked in. What could it hurt? This man was far worse off than he. He had difficulty breathing on his own and all he was asking was an opportunity to meet him. It would take a little effort to wheel himself across the room and say a few words, but his dexterity was improving. He owed it to these men who were proof positive that Hill Of Dreams worked.

"Okay," Beau grunted, awkwardly maneuvering his wheelchair, attempting to follow Lenox. He kept his eyes straight ahead, acutely aware of the other patients staring, of the whispered conversations as his wheelchair lurched and wobbled. He focused his attention on the man sitting in the monstrous wheelchair, head back, eyes riveted on him.

"Hi, Earl," Beau said when he was almost there.

Lenox was crouched down next to his friend, talking to him softly. Earl managed a gurgling sound that Beau interpreted as a greeting. He was a big bear of a man, dark skinned, and with a neatly trimmed beard. Even in his incapacitated state his eyes still twinkled. What did he have to feel good about?

"Lenox here tells me that you're a Hill Of Dreams graduate," Beau said, attempting to keep things light.

Another gurgling sound escaped as Earl attempted his version of a nod.

Beau struggled for something else to say. What did you say to a man whose recovery looked hopeless? He was no doctor but it was evident from Earl's appearance, and labored assisted breathing, his situation was far more serious than Beau's. For the first time Beau silently thanked God for being alive. Seeing Earl in this state had reminded him of his own mortality. He suddenly wanted to get away.

"Take care, man," Beau muttered. "And good luck to you." He nodded to Lenox, pushed the joystick of the mobilized wheelchair in place, and headed out.

As he wove his way down the hallway, barely escaping bumping into walls, it occurred to him that for once he'd no desire to return to his room. He took a quick left, barely missing colliding with a nurse's aid and muttered a hasty "Excuse me."

He continued down a long hallway hoping that he was heading in the right direction. On one of the rare occasions he'd peeked out of his window he'd spotted an outdoor terrace filled with flowering plants. He was determined to find that terrace. Meeting Earl had made him realize how lucky he was. He had a lot to think about.

Chandra had been gone a full two days, and he still hadn't heard a word from her. That, in and of itself, was unusual. Truthfully he couldn't say he missed her. It felt good not to be under pressure, to have space, to be able to think. Chandra's continuous whining, her demands only served to agitate him. He was tired of her sailing into his room, regaling him with stories of her glamorous life, and the shallow people in it, when he was no longer a part of that life.

Beau lurched to a full stop in front of huge French doors. Unlatching them would pose a problem.

A familiar female voice came from behind him. "Can I help you with that?"

Beau squelched his initial annoyance that Shayna would catch him at such a vulnerable moment. He managed to angle his wheelchair so that he could see her and grunted a halfhearted hello. Even so he couldn't stop himself from gaping.

Shayna Da Costa was a major babe. In her skimpy athletic getup she radiated energy and confidence. Beau couldn't take his eyes off her compact little body. Black biking pants molded around strong thigh muscles. She'd coupled those pants with a hot-pink, midriff-baring top. A fanny pack was snugly fastened around her slim waist. A gold stud peeked from her belly button and her tiny feet were encased in Nike sneakers. Size five if he had to guess. Hot-pink socks with a crocheted border were cuffed around her ankles. She reminded him of Jada Pinkett Smith. A cute chocolate Barbie doll, sleek, but still scrumptious enough to eat.

"Heading out to read, are we?" Shayna asked, eyeing the book in his lap, broken spine and all. She made a *tssk*ing sound. "Looks like you've actually been reading, or should I say throwing?"

"Just help me with the door, prin. . ." Beau snarled.

"Shayna," she said through clenched teeth.

She stood back to the door. Her crossed arms and raised eyebrows said it all. "There's a magic word."

Beau felt the heat creep into his cheeks. Better to ignore the smirk on her face and the dressing down she'd not so subtly given him. He had to admire her brass. She was not easily intimidated by him and that was refreshing. Not that there was reason to be awed these days. Beau Hill, the skier, was washed up. A has-been. An overnight wonder who'd never ski again.

"Please, since you insist," Beau mumbled, reining in his temper.

"Now that's more like it."

She blew him a kiss and opened the door, standing aside until he wheeled himself through. She had the tightest butt he'd ever seen on any woman. The most perfect shape. Compact yet womanly. It was her smile that got to him, insincere as it might be. What was wrong with him? The woman was a witch. He shouldn't be having this reaction. He shouldn't be thinking of sex.

"Now what comes after please?" Shayna said sweetly, eyelashes batting.

"I don't remember."

Beau twirled the gold bob in his ear. Irritated as she'd made him, he liked sparring with her, matching wits. It helped perk up a boring day.

"Tsssk. Must be all the medication you're taking."

"You really are an annoying woman," he snapped.

"No more annoying than you."

Touché. He hoped she hadn't noticed she'd gotten to him in her skimpy attire. How hot and bothered he'd now become. Those uncontrollable hormones. Everything inside him pulsed. A fire had settled deep in his loins that needed stoking. He hadn't had feelings like this in eons. Not since the accident. No, even before the accident, sex had become a mechanical thing, a reaction to stimulation.

Hope sprung anew. He was alive down there. Beau Jr. was responsive. Shayna, without even trying, had achieved success where Chandra had failed. She'd made Beau Jr. budge.

"Do you have a second job moonlighting as an aerobics instructor?" Beau asked, openly eyeing Shayna up and down. He couldn't take his eyes from her body, her face. Curiosity had momentarily pushed aside churlishness. He wanted to know why she was dressed that way. Where she was going. Rehabilitation therapists didn't look like that. Act like that.

"I'm going for a walk if you must know," Shayna answered, bouncing on her tippy toes, excess energy apparent.

"In the middle of a workday?"

"Two of my outpatients canceled. My next sessions aren't for a while. I'm at loose ends. Want to join me?"

Beau knew she could be a witch but never thought she'd be that cruel. He gave her the full effect of his stony gaze. He wouldn't let her know how much her off-the-cuff invitation hurt him.

Shayna's expression softened. "Oh, come on. We'll explore the grounds. Smell the flowers. Feel the spring." She flexed her arms. "Stay put. I'll go get my weights."

Beau tried to regain control even as Shayna retraced her steps and disappeared through the same French doors they'd come through earlier. Breathing in the crisp spring air sounded tempting. He'd almost forgotten what it was like to be outdoors.

Feelings of nostalgia washed over him as a light breeze danced across his cheeks, making his shaved scalp tingle. God, but he'd almost forgotten what it was like to inhale fresh air. He'd forgotten he had a life. Albeit a sedentary one. He could use these few solitary moments to sort out his feelings for Chandra.

You were supposed to miss the woman you were engaged to. The woman you planned on having a future with. Beau Hill, champion skier, and Chandra Leon, supermodel, were supposed to have been the ideal couple, set for a life of happily ever after. They were the beautiful people. Perfection personified. Yet if he were honest he'd admit he'd fallen out of love with Chandra. She'd become a habit, a person simply to endure.

His disenchantment with her had happened long before the accident. One day he'd simply woken up to the realization that she was all glitz and little substance. Yet he'd hung in there, convincing himself this too would pass, that they were well suited and could make it work.

He and Chandra had one thing in common, the need to succeed. He'd been determined to bring home Olympic gold while Chandra had set her sights on being a supermodel of godly proportions, the face of the new century. Chandra still had her hopes and dreams. He had nothing.

Beau vaguely remembered hearing the newscasters' speculations. Then he'd been angry, hurt, and resentful. Too bitter to really listen. His coach and agent had shared the rumors with him, but he'd found it difficult to believe that anyone would want to sabotage him. Yes, he knew the competition was fierce. The gold medal coveted. But he was one of the more popular skiers. The guy everyone liked, even the competition.

"Ready?" Shayna asked, returning, weights strapped around her wrists.

"How did I get myself into this?" Beau mumbled.

"No excuses. Let's go."

Shayna was already striding ahead of him, leaving him to awkwardly maneuver his wheelchair down the ramp. He was determined to keep up with her and despite the willfulness of his chair, made it to her side. She whistled and applauded despite the thunderous look he threw her.

Rolling green lawns now faced him. Seated under several shady trees were patients he recognized. Many had visitors. Beau suppressed a moment of panic. It had been months since he'd been outdoors and the space seemed wide and unending. Everything seemed foreign but familiar at the same time. Scary yet new. He'd been so self-focused he'd forgotten the world existed. He'd lain there content to waste away.

Shayna led the way to a paved pathway running the length of the property. She began to bounce on the balls of her feet. "Time to show me your stuff, big boy," she said, curling a finger at him.

Swinging her arms, she took off, lengthening her strides until she found a comfortable rhythm. Beau tried his best to keep up with her, but he still wasn't completely comfortable maneuvering his chair, and it wobbled right and left. With some difficulty he avoided colliding with others, then eventually caught up.

His competitive nature kicked in and he pushed himself. "This place is huge," he puffed, sweat beading his brow, his arm muscles aching.

"Fifty acres exactly."

"Tell me we're not going to explore the entire fifty acres?"

"Not unless you insist."

The two had covered an equal distance but she didn't appear warm or moist, nor did she show the first signs of slowing down.

"Do you always power walk around these grounds like someone's in hot pursuit?" Beau panted, barely keeping up with her.

Shayna tossed him one of her enchanting smiles. That smile went right to his heart. Kaplunk.

"Not these grounds," she explained. "A girl does what she has to do to maintain her shape."

"Your figure needs little maintenance," Beau said dryly.

"That's your opinion."

Shayna had slowed down enough for him to catch his breath. The thought occurred to Beau that she'd done so more for his sake than hers. She must sense that all of his atrophied muscles ached, that his upper arms felt leaden. She must see his sweat. God, he might even have to ask her for help on the way back. He would die first.

"Mr. Hill? Mr. Hill?" A woman's strident tones called from behind him.

Beau turned to see a nurse's aide running toward them. She brandished a cell phone.

"Phone call, sir," she shouted, getting closer. "The woman insists it's an emergency."

Beau's heart practically stopped. His first thoughts were of his parents. It was not uncommon for his dad, criminal lawyer that he was, to receive death threats. Had something happened to his mother, Kelly, or Jason?

"Who is it?"

"Your fiancée, sir." The aide thrust the phone into his hand. "She insisted I find you."

Shayna smirked. "Fiancée? Didn't you say you'd broken up?" He could tell she was doing her utmost not to laugh. He could do without her listening in.

Beau covered the mouthpiece. "Chandra is no longer my fiancée," he said with finality.

"Could have fooled me." She guffawed. "That hasn't sunk in apparently. I've been reading up on you. Your engagement was front-page news. You were America's most high-profile couple."

"What's my personal life have to do with you?"

"Everything about you is now my business. You made it my business when you hired me. You'd be surprised how much it can affect one's progress. You've become my pet project."

Beau harrumphed. "I'm no one's pet, princess. Like I told you before, things are on hold between Chandra and me. Our engagement is temporarily off."

"Then why is she hunting you down?" Shayna challenged, her skepticism showing.

"Because we're still friends."

"Right. You're single, just not available." Her laughter was a throaty sound. It mocked him. He had the

sudden urge to kiss her and shut her up at the same
time.

"Don't even go there," Beau snapped, turning away
to speak into the phone.

Chapter Five

Milan was Milan. What could Chandra say? The city was upscale, glamorous, thriving, much like her. She was the center of attention here. She was wined, dined, and admired by the gliterrati, though not necessarily in that order. All that was lacking was a man.

Even as a child Chandra had believed she was special. She'd convinced herself that a case of mistaken identity had left her one of seven siblings. The poor farmhands that called themselves parents were caregivers, she'd decided.

She'd been aware of her unusual looks when at the tender age of twelve she'd successfully seduced the farmer's son. The teenager had been blond-haired, blue-eyed, and eighteen and had somehow managed to forget that she was jailbait.

Their torrid affair had lasted a full two years until she'd met Elan. He was a scout for the Ford modeling agency and she'd met him at a concert. He'd spotted her and literally stood there and gaped. It was she who'd approached him, knowing the effect she had on men, knowing that before the evening ended, he'd be eating out of her hand. They'd had a whirlwind courtship and despite her parents' protests she'd gone with him to New York.

There she'd become an expert at turning her exotic good looks into big bucks. After Elan had been Drew and she'd kept using every bit of ammunition to get her way. Now seven years later she was a household name, her face gracing some of the more upscale magazine covers. Anyone who didn't know who she was had to be born under a rock and needed an education. Chandra Leon planned on taking the world by storm. She planned on being bigger than Tyra, Iman, or Beverly. Poor Beau, useful as he had been or might still be, providing he regained use of his legs, wasn't to be considered. What was she going to do about him?

Chandra looked up from the book she was signing and flashed her cover-girl smile her fan's way.

"Your name?" she asked the pretty Italian girl outfitted in Versace.

"Anna Maria. Please write something nice."

Chandra graced her with another phony smile and hastily scribbled *Stay Beautiful, Anna Maria.*

At the same time she spotted an elegant man in an expensive suit. Chandra tossed her full head of hair and turned the wattage up. He was an important man, she sensed. Not only important but monied. Somebody. The cut of that suit, the way he held himself, the entire package spoke to her. The brief eye contact they shared had communicated interest. He'd reacted, his color heightening, the light in his eyes signaling she turned him on. Time to pounce before someone else did.

Chandra turned her attention back to the book signing. It was a Bellissima-sponsored event and had been set up in the fragrance and cosmetic department of one of the swankier stores. A nice-sized crowd lured by free fragrance samples and her name, of course—Chandra preferred to think it was her name—had turned out to stand on a line that wrapped twice around the floor. Already she'd sold more than a hundred copies of *Chandra's Kind of Beauty*. She could sell more.

"How are you?" Chandra asked, turning her attention to the next person in line and accepting the book the middle-aged woman proffered.

She threw the mystery man another smile, mindful that there were only three women between them. The man's arms were loaded with books. Her books. Chandra wondered if he planned on giving copies to all of the women in his life. She cast him a Mona Lisa smile and he held her gaze. She completed her business with the three women rapidly and faced Romeo.

She upped her smile another watt and twirled a lock of hair. "That's quite the pile you have," she said.

"So I've been told."

The voice was accented. Italian. He was about as brazen as they came.

"I'm not here to talk about books, bella," he continued. "You are a delight to look at. Bee-au-tiful. Perfect."

His liquid gaze and that heavily accented voice were a turn-on. She smelled the testosterone coming off him. She wanted to jump his bones. Chastity was for the birds.

Chandra's new acquaintance set the entire pile of books down in front of her, and placed his palms on the table, leaning in. He smelled of an expensive and erotic fragrance. Familiar yet foreign. Walking, talking sex.

"Shall I autograph those for you?" Chandra said,

enjoying the way his eyes caressed her as they shared secret looks. Looks that clearly said he wanted her.

She counted at least a dozen books in his hand, translating the amount from lira into US dollars, and silently whistled. You had to be well heeled to spend $600 on books.

"My name is Franco Santana," he said, presenting a well-tended hand that was obviously used to manicures.

Santana. She'd heard that name before. It clicked. She'd hit the jackpot. "Franco, how manly. What does it mean?"

"In Eeeenglish it's Frank. It means Frenchman."

"But you're not?" With slightly parted lips she looked to him for further explanation.

"I am as Italian as they come," he said. "I am also heir to the Bell-eee-see-ma fortune. But I can tell you more about that over dinner."

A flash of white teeth indicated he was certain her answer would be favorable.

She did not disappoint him. "What time will you be picking me up?"

"My man will come for you in a black limousine. We will be dining at my vee-lla."

He extracted a Mont Blanc pen from his inner pocket, scribbled a note on a piece of paper, and turned it over. "My address."

Chandra quickly scanned the note. Address? A likely story. He'd written:

Dress comfortably. Don't make it difficult for me. Tonight we start something new.

Chandra eyed him ruefully. Darn sure of himself, wasn't he? Beau Hill was now a thing of her past. Franco Santana was her man. He could do something for her. Boy, could he do something for her.

* * *

"You've missed your curfew and tomorrow's a school day," Shayna greeted, as Reggie slunk in. "You're grounded."

Reggie hung his leather jacket on the coatrack and muttered, "Sorry, something came up."

"Sorry isn't good enough," Shayna said, getting in his face and blocking his progress. She waved a hand, fanning her nose. "Wheeew. You've been drinking."

"Have not."

Shayna grabbed a fistful of Reggie's Tommy Hilfiger shirt. "Don't lie to me. I can smell the beer on your breath. You're seventeen. You have no business drinking."

"Come on, sis, give it a rest." Reggie yawned, clearly bored. He tried to get around her but she hung firmly on to his shirt. What did it take to get through to him? He was an all-right kid. He just didn't exercise good judgment and was easily led. Lately he'd started hanging with the wrong crowd.

Shayna tried another tack. "Look, you've got a court case pending. Till then it's imperative you keep your nose clean. I can't have you wandering the town, in and out of bars, involved in another scrape. I don't want my brother in jail."

"Come on, Shayna, you know I was set up. I'd never break in to someone's place and steal their stuff. I'd never hurt anyone. My lawyer believes me, why can't you? He says I probably wouldn't even have to do time. Maybe some community service but I have no past criminal record."

"He was making you feel good. We're all worried. You aren't exactly squeaky clean. There was the time you got caught red-handed with Mrs. Lewis's purse . . ."

"That was a prank. I didn't steal the old lady's money.

I gave it back to her. Can I go to bed? I'm exhausted."
He belched loudly.

Shayna sighed. What was the use in reasoning with
him? Her parents had all but given up, washed their
hands of Reggie. His antics had made them prematurely
gray. They'd been delighted when she'd moved to Denver and taken him with her.

"Fine," Shayna said, moving aside. "But you'll be up
at six. The bus arrives promptly at seven. You'll want
breakfast and I want you on that bus." She hoped to
God he wasn't cutting school, that he would graduate
and go on to college.

"Yeah, yeah. Right." Brushing her aside, he raced up
the stairs of the rented condominium and headed for
his room.

Shayna plopped down on the chocolate leather couch
that had been the first piece of furniture she'd bought
since moving to Denver. She rested her feet on the
antique chest serving as both coffee table and storage.
What was she to do with Reggie? Teenagers came with
their own set of issues, and Reggie's were no different.
Her job, energy draining as it was, required compassion
and patience. Playing parent to Reggie on top of that
was wearing her down.

She debated turning the television on, then decided
against it, opting instead to light an aroma therapy candle. She picked up the scanned newspaper articles she'd
brought home from the library, and began to peruse
them.

The soothing scent of eucalyptus relaxed her, and
she slowly began to focus. She'd read everything she
could about Beau Hill. His accident still didn't make
sense. Why had the man become an obsession? Some
might even call him a worthy or unworthy pastime. She
continued to read about Beau's many accomplishments,

the charities he'd donated to, his involvement in the community, and began to get a very different picture of the athlete. Would the real Beau Hill emerge eventually? How could she reach him?

Shayna had heard from others, and now the newspapers confirmed, Beau had been an all-around nice guy. A down-to-earth type, friendly and open. He'd been referred to as charming. That description certainly didn't fit the man she knew. Beau was belligerent, cantankerous, and determined to make the staff's life hell.

Shayna visualized that rare smile she'd been the beneficiary of. Could anyone who looked as good as Beau be all bad? She read on. Beau had been one of the more popular athletes, a certainty to bring home Olympic gold. An experienced skier, completely at home on the slopes. He'd been a shoo-in to win the downhill. Yet one fluke accident, a faulty binding or something like that, the papers speculated, had caused him to topple.

Some reporters had alluded to sabotage. Many speculated that an envious teammate, or one of his competitors, might have tampered with his bindings. Some even fingered the winner of the downhill, a German man, allegedly a bigot, as the responsible party. That was as far as it had gone. There had been no formal investigation. No one named with certainty.

Shayna rose to the challenge. She had a certain responsibility to put Beau back together mentally and physically. From experience she knew his healing could only come if he let go of his anger and focused on walking again. She'd hoped he'd read *Turning Hurts Into Halos*, knowing that would help.

The ringing phone got her attention. Who would be calling this late? She reached for the receiver and said somewhat impatiently, "Hello."

"Hi, honey, how are you doing?"

Her mother on the other end, thank God. Shayna cradled the receiver between chin and shoulder and made herself more comfortable on the couch. "Hi, Mom. I'm doing okay. Just tired. Reggie's wearing me out."

"That boy needs discipline. I told you we should have sent him to military school. Can we talk about something else for a minute? Have you met anyone in Denver?"

It was an old question, one her mother continued to ask. She'd been disappointed when Shayna broke up with Michael. Little did she know the scum had cheated on her.

"I've told you I'm not looking for a relationship, Ma. I'm putting all of my efforts into my career."

"Oh, come now, every woman's looking for a relationship. If you're open to it, the right one will come along. You're in a new city, forget about Michael and move on."

Shayna had dated Michael for two plus years. He'd been someone she thought she loved and might still love. Except Michael hadn't been ready to commit. She'd found out she was one in a series of women he'd led on. Armed with that knowledge Shayna had tossed him to the curb. Moving to Denver was supposed to help put him behind her.

"Michael's my past, Mom," she said, with some finality. "As I mentioned before, I'm focusing on work. Want to hear about my new patient? He's a challenge."

"You've always liked a challenge," Kara DaCosta answered. "I remember you at age three, eyes glued to the television, imitating everything those gymnasts did. You'd tumble. Do back flips. Scared us to death. We decided to enroll you in gymnastics school. You just loved it and we knew you were special."

"My patient's an athlete," Shayna said quickly, aborting the stroll down memory lane. "He's extremely high profile and temperamental as all hell."

"Reminds me of the way you used to be," Kara muttered.

"I wasn't." Shayna filled her mother in on Beau's antics.

"He sounds full of himself. A real egotist," Kara said. "You'd have to have an abundance of patience to deal with that nonsense."

"But it's a front. A facade to hide his pain."

"Whatever. Sounds to me like you're more involved than you need to be." Kara's voice was heavy with skepticism. "Do you like him?"

Did she like Beau? Was she more involved than she needed to be? Nah. She cared for her patients. Challenged them to give her their best. Beau was attractive but she had no desire to take advantage of a patient. Especially a patient as prickly and vulnerable as the skier could be.

"If Reggie gets to be too much," Kara said, changing the topic, "send him back to us after the hearing, provided he gets off free." Her voice caught. "We'd take him now, but he's not supposed to leave the state." Her voice caught again. "God, Shayna, what will we do if they lock him up?"

"We'll deal with that if it happens," Shayna said firmly.

Colin Johnson, the attorney they'd picked, had come highly recommended. Shayna hoped Reggie had told him the truth about what went on that night. She made a mental note to see Colin and get an update. She'd find out if he'd come up with a witness that might help their side. As it was, he was costing them a bundle.

She wasn't a quitter. Never had been. Giving up on

Reggie would mean admitting defeat. She didn't plan on sending him home.

"You and Dad are still coming for the trial, right?" Shayna asked.

"Yes. We won't miss it."

"I'll send you airplane tickets."

"No need to. Your dad's got that covered."

"I want to. That's the least I can do."

"Shayna! Shayna! Come up here." Reggie's shouts interrupted, putting her instantly on alert.

"Got to go, Mom," Shayna said. "I love you."

She slammed the receiver down and took off. "What's wrong, Reggie?" She called, taking the stairs two at a time.

"Edward Anderson's on TV. Just look at that mean son of a bitch."

Shayna entered her brother's room to see Edward Anderson's face plastered across the TV screen. He looked huge and intimidating, definitely not someone you wanted to mess with. Shayna's heart sank. Could Colin Johnson take this man on?

Chapter Six

Edward Anderson spoke into the microphone the reporter held under his nose.

"There's a whole new breed of thug out there. Generation-Y kids who come in every color, class, shape, and size. They're unconscionable and downright evil. Their primary focus is themselves."

"Don't you have generation-Y kids, Mr. Anderson?" the television reporter asked.

"Three of them. And they're all law-abiding citizens. Victoria and I raised them right."

"All of them?"

There was a pause before Anderson smoothly interjected, "All of them. My youngest went through the usual growing pains, but he turned out all right. Made a name for himself."

"Mr. Anderson, are you saying this seventeen-year-old kid that beat up your client should be tried as an adult?"

"What do you think? People of Denver, what do you think?"

The smooth politician that he was, Edward Anderson spread both arms wide. He peered over half-moon glasses at the television audience. Shayna's heart sank to her stomach. In a few weeks Reggie and his attorney were about to come up against this man. This tough adversary, from the old school, rigid and unbending. At least he didn't appear to be a bigot. He'd admitted that the criminal element encompassed all colors and classes.

Even so, Ed's physical appearance intimidated. He was a huge, ferocious-looking man with a ruddy complexion, and a balding dome for a head. He'd scowled his way through the interview, peering over those half-moon glasses. His speech patterns shouted upper crust. White bread.

Reggie's eyes were fixated on the screen. Shayna sensed, though he would never admit it, he was scared. His jaw was clamped so tight she feared he would crush his molars. She ached for him and, though he was innocent, hoped that this was a lesson he would never forget. Reggie would face serious jail time if he was convicted. He'd done some pretty stupid things in the past but she couldn't imagine him hurting another human being.

Shayna had read up on the crime. The victim had been found tied to a chair, bludgeoned and bloody, her house ransacked and valuables taken. When the cops were called, Reggie and a carload of his buddies were picked up on a surrounding block. During a lineup the woman had picked out Reggie and the driver. Both boys had sworn up and down that they'd never even been on her block. They'd stuck to their story relentlessly and even though all their friends had supported that tale, they'd been taken in and arraigned. Would that have happened it they weren't black?

The DaCostas had paid big bucks to bail Reggie out and get him the kind of lawyer he needed. They'd been forced to take out a second mortgage on their home. Even now, Shayna couldn't control the anger and outrage that surfaced when she thought of the injustice of it all. Why were her folks forced to come up with money they didn't have? Reggie had been in the wrong place at the wrong time and for that he had suffered.

Shayna's attention returned to the television screen. Edward Anderson was no longer on camera but the reporter continued to pontificate.

"There you have it, folks. Our very own Edward Anderson, encouraging us to rid our Denver streets of crime. To take a hard line, put the riffraff that continues to move to Denver behind bars."

Shayna viewed that comment as a direct dig against Reggie. What had happened to objective reporting?

"Time to turn in," she said to her brother. "You need to be up at six."

"Yeah, yeah, yeah," he grumbled.

"I want you on that bus," Shayna admonished, closing the door firmly behind her.

"I got a call from the Sports Authority's attorneys," David Mandel, Beau's agent, said, flexing and unflexing his hands, a sure sign he was agitated.

"Yeah?" Beau focused his attention on the TV's remote, continuing to channel-surf, listening with one ear, wishing the dull pain in his gut would go away.

"They're angling to get out of their contract. They're claiming that your, uh . . . incapacitation held up the film shoot and print ads they had hoped to run."

"That's bull. We weren't supposed to do anything with them until the fall."

"You and I know that."

"What's our attorney say?"

Beau's father had made him retain a sports and entertainment attorney, familiar with exactly this sort of thing. She was supposedly one of the best.

"Laura's fighting with them, arguing that they've acted prematurely. She's told them your prognosis is good, and you could make a full recovery."

Beau settled on a channel and lay back on his bed, trying to get comfortable. "Even I don't know that."

"You've given up?" David said, shaking his head. "Where's that fighting spirit gone? You're content to lie back or sit in that stinking wheelchair all day." He pointed to the empty chair. "For Christ's sake, man, don't give in to this thing. You'll walk again, maybe even ski."

How could he not give in when he felt so hopeless? When he couldn't even wiggle his big toe. He wouldn't admit that he was scared to death, that the tingling in his toes made him wonder what else was wrong. He'd been afraid to ask the doctor what that meant. He wasn't up to more bad news.

"You and my physical therapist are a pair," Beau joked. "You're starting to sound the same."

"Maybe we both believe in you. Your energies should be focused on finding out the real reason you fell. Everyone thinks the whole incident smells, Beau. That gold medal should have been yours. Why are you willing to let whoever did this to you get away scot-free?"

Beau didn't want to think about that right now. "It's all speculation," he said. "Why would someone do this to me?"

"Because they're jealous. Plain old envious."

"You're speculating."

"Didn't one of the guys claim he saw someone nosing around your equipment hours before the race?"

"I don't remember. How come he hasn't come forward?" Beau raised his eyebrows, skeptically.

"He might have been uncomfortable. Nervous about saying anything."

"Right."

Immaculata chose that moment to stick her blond head through the door and say, "You've got physical therapy in exactly ten minutes, Beau-Beau. Do you need me to take you down?"

"No, I don't need you to take me down. I'm perfectly capable."

Immaculata's eyebrows rose to the ceiling. Her smile was miles wide. "Good. It's what I like to hear. If you change your mind, buzz me."

"Who's that?" David asked when she'd left. "I like her style. Is she single or married?"

"One of the nurses, and I don't know whether she's available or not."

Beau didn't have a clue, nor had he thought to ask. He'd been totally self-absorbed, focused solely on his problems. So focused, in fact, that he'd never viewed Mary Jane Coppola as a person. She'd become a necessary evil, someone to endure. While she'd grown on him, and he'd come to accept the fact she took care of him, he still viewed her as his keeper.

"I'm going to shove off," David said. "Think about what we talked about and do a little investigating for me. Find out if that nurse is available."

"Right."

After David had left, Beau heaved himself into his wheelchair. He didn't want to think about the implications if what his agent said was true. How could anyone be that vindictive, that evil? It was only a competition. *Yeah, a competition with winner take all.*

He had to admit that it was odd that a binding would be defective. It was even stranger that his skis were nowhere to be found. He'd repeatedly given himself a verbal flogging for not checking and double-checking his equipment, making sure it was sound.

No time to think about that now. In a matter of minutes he would see Shayna again. He'd made it halfway through *Turning Hurts Into Halos*. The book had an interesting premise but he wasn't fully convinced that a positive outlook had anything to do with speedier healing, or being able to walk again. But he wanted to discuss the book with Shayna, hear her perspective on things.

Beau wheeled himself to the elevator, actually managing to nod in the direction of the nurses' station. Ignoring the muffled whispers behind him, he continued to the bank of elevators. His dexterity had improved and he was more in control of his chair, he no longer wobbled all over the place. Practice made perfect, he supposed.

When Beau entered her room, Shayna was totally absorbed in whatever she was reading, her face obscured by a newspaper. He sat silently, observing her, watching those slender, perfectly shaped legs in black hose bounce to an unheard rhythm. The woman was walking sex.

He hesitated. Should he call out to her, disturb her reading?

Shayna must have sensed he'd come in. She lowered the newspaper and tried to quickly put it away. She wasn't quick enough. He'd already seen the photo on the front page. Why didn't it surprise him?

"Mind if I look at that?" he asked, holding his hand out.

"If you'd like." She made no attempt to turn it over.

He could tell she was uncomfortable being caught. Maybe she suspected he'd seen the photo and her discomfort stemmed from wanting to protect him. Or maybe she was simply embarrassed for having been caught reading about him.

"The paper," Beau insisted, holding a hand out and scooting closer.

"Here." There was a haughty tilt to her head as she turned the newspaper over.

Beau took his time shaking it out, smoothing out the creases. He stared at the photograph on the front page of the Living & Arts section and couldn't resist a smirk.

"This didn't take long."

"Oh, Beau, don't do that to yourself. Would you like some water?"

"No. I'm a big boy."

"Would it help you to talk?"

"No." He dismissed her with a nod of his head, and turned back to the newspaper, his eyes focusing on the caption again.

PARALYZED SKIER DUMPED FOR BELLISSIMA HEIR.

Such bull.

Splashed across the front page was an oversize photograph of Chandra looking exceedingly chic in a bright red catsuit. A pair of dark glasses were perched on the end of her nose. Her wild mane of hair had been carefully spritzed and tousled. She was being helped from a limousine by a dark-skinned man who could easily have been a cover model himself. The man's suit was impeccably cut. Armani, Beau would guess. A tie completed the high-powered look. He too wore sunglasses.

Beau's photograph, juxtaposed next to theirs, wasn't

exactly flattering. It was an aerial view of himself in his wheelchair, taken the day he'd been sitting on the patio waiting for Shayna.

"Beau, are you sure you don't want to talk?" Shayna asked, touching his shoulder gently.

He was still too humiliated to say a word. How dare the press make fun of him? Chandra pictured with that man could be innocent enough, but what did they have to gain by making these photos public and holding him up to ridicule? Why be so brutal? He'd always made time for reporters. He'd patiently answered their dumb questions. Beau read the accompanying article.

Franco Santana, heir to the Bellissima line, was Chandra's constant companion. These two beautiful people were taking Milan by storm. They'd been seen at the more upscale eateries, been shopping together, and frequently seen at the designer showings. They'd made a big splash at a recent soiree, arriving in his and her tuxedos.

The reporter, tongue-in-cheek, questioned whether it had been love at first sight, or an arrangement made in Fragrance heaven. Whatever, Chandra had just thrown down the gauntlet and sent Beau a definite message. She was parading her newfound freedom for all to see, and it had been assumed he'd been cast aside. Her blatant disregard for his feelings made him decide it was over with. Permanently.

He would maintain a "to hell with them" attitude. What hurt wasn't seeing her with another man, but rather the hypocrisy of it all. She'd made such a fuss when he'd suggested they put things on hold. And every few days she'd called, terrorizing the poor nurse's aid, demanding to speak with him. She'd filled his ear with tales of having missed him. My, how quickly things changed.

"I'm sorry you had to find out this way," Shayna said, coming to kneel beside him. "It was insensitive of me to flaunt your fiancée's betrayal in your face."

"She's no longer my fiancée," Beau said gruffly. "She can do whatever the hell she wants."

"Be that as it may, you still hurt. That headline was awful. No one likes being made fun of."

Beau grunted. "There's been a lot worse said about me."

"And there's been a lot of good said. I've been reading about you."

"Obviously."

She smiled and touched his hand. "I like to get to know my patients. I can help them better if I know what makes them tick."

"I'm halfway through your book," Beau said, deftly changing the subject. "I'm not sure I'm getting it though."

"Keep reading and you will. Shall we try something a little different today?"

"Like?"

"Like fitting you with ankle weights. Like having you work out your legs."

"All right, if you think it would help." He was tempted to tell her about the tingling sensation that he was experiencing. That it started in his toes and slowly worked its way up his legs. Was that a good sign? Would she know? He'd been nervous when it first happened, still was. Yet some sensation was better than the oppressive numbness. The dead weight.

Shayna crossed over to a cabinet, fumbled around, and selected the weights. She hefted them in one hand. "Yes, I think these will do."

Returning, she bent down next to him, strapping the weights on his ankles. He resisted the urge to reach out and touch her hair, stroke the naked nape of her neck, caress her coffee skin. She was wearing some type of perfume that was fresh and outdoorsy. It reminded him of orange blossoms.

"I think you should be discharged," she said. "It will make you much more self-sufficient. You've been here almost two weeks, and you were in the hospital longer."

"I'm not ready."

"You'll never be unless someone kicks you out."

Beau felt himself beginning to panic. His psychiatrist had said the same thing. They were conspiring against him. In a structured environment he could cope. Sending him to the outside world was another matter.

"You'd benefit from being an outpatient," Shayna said. "You're too dependent on the staff."

"Hey, I thought you were on my side," Beau joked.

"I am, that's why I'm recommending this."

He couldn't tell her he wasn't ready to face the real world, much less navigate his spacious home alone. He wasn't ready for people. Friends. The few that still came to visit made him uncomfortable. They hadn't known what to say. How to act. They weren't even successful at hiding their looks of pity, their discomfort at seeing him in a wheelchair.

Beau had read somewhere that people had a tendency to look through disabled people. Pretend they didn't exist. How would he adjust to that type of inattention? How could he have gone from boy wonder to an object of pity in a matter of months?

He needed to convince Shayna that he was better off here in Denver Rehabilitation Center with others like him. No press hounding him. Family fussing over him. All that stuff.

"I live alone," Beau said. "My place has two stories. It's going to be difficult getting around."

"You'll have to make accommodations. Check with your insurance company. I'm sure they allow for an aide to come in. The quicker you can assimilate yourself back into society, the better chance you have for recovery. You have limited mobility and with work your strength should improve. Let someone who really needs your bed have it."

"My occupational therapist thinks differently," Beau said quickly. "What about personal hygiene, dressing myself?"

"That's what an aide is for. I'm sure your friends and family will help."

The thought of rattling around in his huge house, alone, didn't hold much appeal. This home he'd wanted, had custom made, meant nothing to him now, though at one time it had been his pride and joy. He'd viewed it as a status of his achievement. His refuge. A place to get away from it all, where he could ride horses and explore.

What was the point of having all that space when you couldn't truly enjoy it? What was the point of going home not knowing if a wheelchair would become a way of life? He'd have to start thinking about ramps. Accessibility.

"Stop wallowing in self-pity, Beau, flex your legs," Shayna ordered.

With some difficulty, Beau attempted to do just that, even though it seemed as if bags of cement weighed down his legs and heart.

"Good. Better than good. Great effort." Shayna applauded. "We'll get you walking yet."

All he'd done was make a feeble effort to pick up his feet, and he hadn't been that successful. Yet Shayna's cheering had made him feel like a million bucks, as if he was capable of doing almost anything, including getting on a ski slope again. How could one petite beauty have that ability?

Lowering his eyelashes, Beau slanted a look Shayna's way. It was a mistake. He suddenly felt flustered and out of sorts. The weights on his ankles were heavy. What did she think of him? Today he'd taken time to clean himself up. He'd even been motivated to brush his teeth and put on a brand-new sweat suit. With some assistance from Immaculata he'd managed to shave. And for what? He couldn't be interested in Shayna, nor she in him. He didn't go for the waifish type. He liked his women model-tall. Elegant. Commanding. Women like Chandra.

Chapter Seven

"Are you telling me the absolute truth, son?" Colin Johnson, Reggie's attorney, shot him a look that clearly stated he wasn't buying any bull.

"Look, man, if you don't believe me, why are you representing me?" Reggie rose, sending the chair behind him toppling.

Shayna interceded quickly before things got out of hand. It was exactly that hot temper that often got Reggie into trouble. She got up and faced her brother. "That's enough, Reggie. Colin is simply trying to obtain the facts. Answer his question and stop being rude."

Colin remained where he was, his fingers steepled. He regarded Reggie through shrewd brown eyes. "It's exactly that kind of attitude that's going to land you in jail," he admonished, in a slow, lazy drawl. "You'll need to answer the questions in modulated tones. If you appear testy or belligerent it will work against you. Don't forget, you're fighting a stereotype."

"You mean you want me to lie down and die? Sell out?"

"I'm not asking you to do either. You're in a lot of trouble, young man. Being respectful and not losing your cool couldn't hurt. The jury's bound to be more sympathetic to a polite kid than the thug the prosecution will describe. It's up to you to help them change their minds."

Shayna listened intently as Colin continued to reason with Reggie. She'd driven her little brother to the attorney's office after work. With only a few weeks to go before the trial, Colin had wanted them to meet and go over their defense once again.

Even though Colin appeared outwardly calm, she could tell he was worried. They were up against the powerful testimony of the victim, Mrs. Simpkins. She'd been beaten up pretty badly, and her appearance alone assured her sympathy. Shayna had also learned of an eyewitness who'd come forward claiming that the boy's Saturn had been seen casing Mrs. Simpkins's block. It had been parked on a corner for a considerable time. Reggie, when confronted, had insisted it was a lie. He'd stuck to his story about looking for a McDonald's.

Colin had insisted they hire a private eye. He'd hoped to find a witness to substantiate Reggie's story. If this person came forward confirming the time the boys were in McDonald's, the case would most likely be dismissed. So far they'd come up empty, but Colin remained optimistic.

"The prosecuting attorney's going to play hardball," he said to Reggie, capturing Shayna's attention again. "He's going to paint you as the worst kind of monster. A beast that should be put away. Your job, and mine, is to make the jury think otherwise. To create reasonable doubt."

"Why is it always harder for black people?" Reggie asked, his youth and naivete showing. "That lawyer on TV looked like a redneck. He spoke all proper and stuff. Yapping on about me being the new breed of thug."

Colin's white teeth were prominent in a face that was almost coal black. Shayna wondered what was so funny about Reggie's remark. There were elements of truth in what he had to say. Although she'd never considered Reggie's attorney a handsome man, when he threw his head back, cognac eyes sparkling, she saw what others must see, an attractive and very virile man.

He'd come highly recommended by their family attorney. The two had gone to law school together. What she'd been told by the very proper Rita Pinkett Meadows, esq., was that Colin Johnson was the best lawyer that money could buy.

Shayna noticed his ringless hands and wondered if he was married. Not because she was particularly interested in him, but because it had occurred to her that she hadn't met an available man since moving to Denver. What was it? Eight, nine months ago? Actually that wasn't true. She'd met Beau, though she would hardly call him available.

"Ed Anderson, a bigot," Colin repeated, when he'd stopped laughing. "Far from it. He's tough but fair. He enjoys defending the underdog."

Shayna remembered something the reporter on television had said. He'd implied that one of Anderson's sons had been a problem.

"I understand Ed Anderson's got kids of his own," she said, joining the conversation.

"That he does. One of his sons is famous. You might have heard of him."

"Can we stick to my case?" Reggie said, bouncing on the balls of his feet impatiently. "I'm meeting the guys to play basketball in exactly one hour. I don't have a lot of time to waste. So fill me in on what's going on. Tell me how you're planning on getting me out of this mess."

"There's that attitude again." Colin jabbed a finger at Reggie. "Next time check it at the door or you'll need to find a new attorney. You'd better check it at the courtroom or there's not a damn thing I'll be able to do about getting you off."

Colin returned to his notes and continued to brief Reggie. When he was through, he placed a hand on Shayna's elbow and pulled her aside. "Reggie, will you wait outside for a moment? I'd like to speak to your sister," he said.

Grunting something unintelligible, Reggie loped off. He had a ticked-off expression on his face, and grumbled something about not being part of the conversation.

Shayna smiled politely, waiting for Colin to say what he had to say. Hopefully it was not more bad news. She just couldn't take it.

"Are you available this coming Saturday?" he surprised her by asking.

"I might be," Shayna said evasively. She hated making commitments until she knew what she was getting herself into.

"I was thinking we'd get a bite to eat at one of the trendy restaurants in LoDo."

Theirs so far had been a business relationship. But he was one of the rare single men she'd met since moving to Denver. Besides, one date did not an emotional attachment make.

She was familiar with the lower downtown area. It had recently been gentrified and several trendy boutiques and small businesses had replaced the warehouses. Overnight, it had become Denver's answer to New York's Soho. When she'd first moved here she'd considered renting a loft in the area.

"Great. I'll look forward to it," Shayna answered.

"Shayna," Reggie called from outside. "Are you almost done? We need to go."

"We're wrapping up," she shouted back, rolling her eyes. "That boy's a handful."

"He's a teenager." Colin's strong fingers circled her forearm. "I'll pick you up Saturday, say around eight."

"Let me give you my address. Phone number."

"I have it all here." Colin released her to tap a fat folder on his desk. "I'm really looking forward to our date, Shayna."

"Likewise."

She followed him out. While it wouldn't be a love connection, a date would help break up the monotony of another Saturday night.

Beau wasn't ready for this, the vast outdoors surrounding him, wide-open spaces, no evident boundaries. Sunlight poured through the open van windows as he sat huddled in his seat, trying to forget how exhilarated he felt out on the slopes, the cool mountain air blowing against his face.

He slumped in the back of a leased van, his father in the driver's seat, his mother beside his dad. Immaculata and an assortment of medical personnel waved to him from the front steps, his occupational therapist among them, but no Shayna.

"Bye, Beau-Beau, don't be a stranger," Immaculata called, waving to him. "You come by and visit when you have therapy, or there'll be hell to pay."

Beau nodded at her but didn't trust himself to speak.

He flipped her the thumbs-up sign and choked back the bile that was beginning to rise in his throat. His safety net had just been pulled out from under him. Denver Rehabilitation Center had represented organization and structure. It was safe. There, he wasn't an oddity, just another patient with special needs.

So many here were in far worse shape than he. But thanks to Shayna and that pushy psychologist, he was being thrust out into the world of able-bodied people. A world that viewed the disabled as not quite human.

His mom would be staying with him until he settled in. His dad, busy soul that he was, would remain in his own home but there would be frequent visits. Then Kelly, his sister, was flying in from Seattle, to take over. His brother, Jason, still hadn't made it to Denver. And in between, Beau would be interviewing a succession of aides, hoping for a good fit.

Beau's bedroom had been relocated to the first floor. Makeshift ramps had been built to accommodate his chair, the presumption being he'd be nonambulatory the rest of his life. He would prove them wrong. He was determined.

"How are you doing back there?" his dad asked, placing the van in gear.

Beau grunted something unintelligible, continuing to scan the crowd on the front steps. Where was Shayna? He'd hoped she'd be there. As Ed steered the van out of the driveway, Beau acknowledged he would miss many of the staff—Immaculata, whom he'd heaped abuse on, Shayna, who'd abused him, pushing him past his limits, forcing him to do things he didn't think he'd ever do again. He'd see her again in a couple of days. He'd be back for outpatient therapy.

Meanwhile, he'd send Immaculata and Shayna flowers. They deserved them for putting up with his foul temper, and it was the right thing to do. Thank you had always been difficult for him to say.

Beau fingered the partially read book on his lap. Maybe he could finish *Turning Hurts Into Halos* in two days. That way he would have something to discuss with Shayna the next time he saw her. Reading would keep him occupied.

Ed parked the van in the driveway and announced, "You're home, son."

Towanda, Beau's housekeeper, wore an earsplitting grin that was forced, no doubt. But Beau felt as if he were on a movie set, starring in a bizarre show, waiting for his cue to go on. What role did he play? Home owner? Disabled hero? He didn't know.

His dad opened up the van doors and began unloading the luggage. He secured a ramp so that Beau could wheel himself down.

"Ready, Beau? Do you need help?" he asked.

"I can handle it," he answered, gruffly. He would never be ready for this.

With some difficulty, and a last-minute need for assistance, Beau made it safely to the ground. Tears ran down Towanda's cheeks when she greeted him.

"Hello, Beau."

What did she have to cry about? It was he that had been hurt. He that ached inwardly and might never have legs that functioned again.

His mom went to Towanda's side, embracing her, speaking with her softly, probably coaching her to put on a bright face. He might be disabled, but he was back and he was the same person.

Little did his mother know how he looked at the world now. It was an effort to smile and stay positive. When he'd built Hill Of Dreams he'd wanted to turn lives around, to show the poor and disadvantaged that there was hope. If he could be somebody, so could they. How would he cope now that skiing wasn't a part of that life?

Beau squeezed his eyes shut as the memories threatened to take over. He'd been healthy, happy, alive, and engaged. One visit to Salt Lake City, Utah, had changed all of that. He'd been so certain he would return home a winner. The money gained from endorsements he planned on pumping back into the recreation center, giving people opportunities they would never have had. He'd employ experts to teach skills. Skills like operating a computer.

Instead, he'd ended up in a Denver hospital, his body and psyche broken. Later he'd been transferred to the rehab center and worked with a team of medical professionals who'd tried to put him back together again. Could be worse. He could be like poor Earl. The quadriplegic's eyes still held a twinkle and he had no reason to be hopeful.

Beau wheeled himself up another makeshift ramp giving him access to his front door. He sat in the vestibule trying to get his bearings. His parents flanked him. Towanda still sobbed though his mom tried her best to shush her.

Ed laid a hand on his shoulder, squeezing gently. "It'll take a bit of getting used to, son," he said, his voice rough with holding in his emotions.

It was all familiar, yet surreal. He felt as if he were in the twilight zone. Nothing in his life would ever be the same again. Not his home. Not his friends. Nothing. He couldn't even begin to think how he would put the pieces back together again and achieve some sense of normalcy. Would he ever find the type of woman who would understand that he was still a man? A man with needs?

An image of a petite woman with a commanding voice filled his vision. Even if he was interested, he had nothing to offer Shayna DaCosta beyond the material, and even that wasn't a certainty now. Not if he lost most of his endorsements. While finances, or the lack of them, should certainly not come into play in a relationship, they did.

"Beau, honey, would you like to go to your room and rest?" Victoria asked.

"Maybe later."

He now regretted having told his agent he needed a couple of hours to settle in. Having David here would have alleviated any awkward moments. They would have talked about the mundane, strategies to ensure his contracts were maintained. David would have kept him focused, not tripping down this dismal path of memory lane.

How did an experienced skier just fall? He wanted to know. He'd been in denial too long. Purposely ignored all the whispers. How arrogant of him to think that no one would ever intentionally want to hurt Beau Hill. That he was too popular an athlete.

In retrospect, Beau now saw why he might have been the prime target of envy, hostility, and rage. He was a young black man destined to make history. He'd already won some of the more challenging downhill races, including the giant slalom. He'd gone where no African-American man had dared to go before, dominating a sport customarily won by whites. It was expected of him in track and field, basketball even. But not skiing.

"Son?" His father tapped him on the shoulder. "Sure you won't be more comfortable in the bedroom?"

Reality returned. Beau focused on the butter-soft leather couch with its satin pillows and exotic tassels arranged in a row. Rare and expensive artwork, acquired from his travels, covered the fabric walls of a two-story living area. African artifacts were aesthetically positioned so the eye could enjoy. The house was his reality. Could he adjust to a life lived primarily indoors?

"Are you hungry, Beau?" his mother asked, flicking a handful of blond hair out of her eyes and adjusting her headband.

Why did he feel like a teenager who was about to be sent to bed with the flu? He used to enjoy being pampered, knowing that it was only temporary and would end once he wasn't ill. These last few months of confinement, staring at four walls, had changed all that.

"I'm going to my den," Beau said, wheeling himself away. He needed the space and the tranquility to acclimate.

The phone rang as he took off.

"Should I get that?" Towanda asked. She'd finally stopped crying.

"I'm only taking calls from David. Tell anyone else I'm resting."

Towanda picked up the receiver. "Hello? Yes . . . uh . . . no. Mr. Beau's resting." She mouthed the word "Shayna."

Beau waved his hands, signaling frantically to her not to hang up. Using the joystick on the control of his chair, he broke a new Special Olympics record to get to Towanda.

"Give it to me," he demanded, tugging on his housekeeper's arm.

An infusion of warmth suffused his body, making him feel giddy and off-kilter. He growled, "Hello."

"I thought you might be resting," Shayna said.

"I'm not."

By calling she'd more than made up for not being there at the center to see him off. He'd felt let down and abandoned. Now he was happy to hear her voice. Delighted that she'd been thinking about him.

"I'm sorry I didn't make it back before you left. I had to go to my brother's high school. I'd like to stop by with my farewell gift for you."

She'd bought him something. But instead of expressing his delight, he asked, "You have a brother?"

"Yes. A teenager and very difficult. He wants to be a man."

"When would you like to come by and bring the gift?" Beau asked.

"How about after work?"

He gave her directions.

The quiet on the other end was deafening. Beau was conscious of the others listening to the one-sided conversation. Of his mother's sharp intake of breath. Of the fact she beamed at him.

"All right. I'll come over, but only for a brief moment," Shayna said.

Beau's heart soared. He forgot that his parents were hanging on to his every word, that Towanda stood quietly listening. All he cared about was that he was going to see Shayna soon.

Chapter Eight

Shayna hung up the phone angry at herself. She was acting like a teenager with a first crush, manufacturing reasons to see the object of her desires. Shame on her. It was unprofessional to go to a patient's home. She didn't do house calls. Granted, she had bought Beau a present, but she could give it to him at the next therapy session.

Half of Shayna's morning had been taken up meeting with Reggie's guidance counselor. She'd been summoned to the high school and told that her brother had been skipping classes. If he didn't shape up he would not graduate.

God, what was she to do? Reggie was rapidly whirling out of control. She'd tried lecturing, taking away his privileges, nothing seemed to work. Maybe she should ask Beau to put him to work at Hill Of Dreams, she thought, half jokingly. If he was kept busy, focused on something other than himself, maybe, just maybe, he'd come around.

Gail Mahoney was Shayna's next patient. She clomped in on her walker. Gail was making remarkable progress and Shayna had hopes that soon she would be up and about. After that, Shayna worked with a double amputee whose goal was to participate in the Paralympics. She was bound and determined to have him realize his dream.

Checking her schedule again, Shayna noted she also had a session with Earl. The quadriplegic was the patient with the most spirit. He could be an example to them all. If only she could take some of his optimism and rub it all over Beau.

The remainder of the day raced by. At five, Shayna gathered her things and made a quick call home. The phone rang and rang. Reggie, rather than attacking his homework, must be involved in one of those never-ending basketball games with the guys. Good. She didn't have to hurry home and start dinner.

Shayna picked up the gift she'd bought Beau and carefully placed it in a carton to keep it steady. Smiling to herself, she rested it on the sports utility vehicle's floor. What would he think of the offbeat gift? Removing the paper where she'd scribbled the directions to his house, she set it on the console where she could see it, and put the Explorer in drive, following Beau's directions. They led up a winding mountain road, the air getting thinner the higher she went.

Beau lived approximately twenty-five minutes outside of Denver, in one of the fancy, smansy, suburban areas, where the houses sat on a minimum of one acre. A pretty pricey neighborhood, she would guess.

Maybe he was just feeling insecure and needed reassurance. Oh, who was she fooling? This growing attraction between them defied explanation. Besides, she wanted to see his home. A person's home often mirrored his true personality. And she sensed that Beau's prickly personality masked a sensitive, caring man. You'd have to have qualities like that to create Hill Of Dreams.

Shayna glanced at the directions again as she made a right up another steep incline. The road twisted and turned and the houses became sparser. She steered the Explorer up a steep driveway, then came to a full stop in front of a sprawling brick home with huge window walls. Behind it the Rocky Mountains made an attractive backdrop.

She got out of her vehicle, removed her carton from the floor, and quietly assessed the home. It was a huge place for one person to reside. The sounds of neighing from someplace in the back got her attention. Beau had horses? Curious, she followed the sound. Sure enough, set back from the house were stables. How lucky could one person be?

"Are you Ms. DaCosta?" a woman's voice called from behind her.

Shayna turned to see a plump light-skinned woman dressed in a swishing skirt and cherry-red top following her. The woman eyed the carton she carried.

" I am," Shayna confirmed, embarrassed to be caught snooping. "I thought I heard horses, and figured that Beau wouldn't mind if I looked."

"I'm Towanda Brooks, Beau's housekeeper," Towanda said, extending a hand.

Shayna grasped the woman's chubby hand, surprised by the firmness of her grip. Beau had a housekeeper? Stables? He was more loaded than she'd thought. He must have invested wisely.

"Mr. Beau's waiting for you inside," Towanda said,

her gaze still fastened on the cardboard box. "That's different." She pointed to Beau's gift.

"I thought it would be something he would enjoy."

Towanda stared at her. "I didn't expect you to be so attractive. You're a physical therapist?"

Shayna smiled and raised a brow. "Physical therapists aren't supposed to be attractive?"

Towanda colored. "That's not what I meant. I was expecting someone older. Miss Victoria said you—"

"Is Beau's mom here?" Shayna interrupted.

"Mr. Beau's parents were both here, up until a while ago."

There was no point in encouraging the housekeeper to gossip but she might as well know what she was walking into. "Who left?"

"The mister. He had a meeting. But David, Mr. Beau's agent, is here. Come on, we'll go inside."

They came to an imposing wooden front door inset with copper. Off to the side, blue columbines peeked from behind a rock garden. The housekeeper pushed down on one of the copper handles and waited for Shayna to enter.

Shayna's first impressions were of wooden cathedral ceilings and a living area that ran two tiers high. Artwork covered every inch of wall space, and artifacts the likes of which she had never seen before were strategically placed throughout the house. A winding wooden stairway provided access to both floors.

Shayna's initial thought was that no way would Beau be able to navigate both floors. Then she noticed that movable ramps had been built to accommodate a wheelchair and give him access to most rooms. While she hovered at the entrance, a handsome blond woman came flying across the room, arms open wide.

"Shayna? I'm Victoria. Beau's mom. Isn't this a gorgeous house? Beau got really lucky. It was a foreclosure. I helped him snap it up."

"It's great to meet you, Victoria."

Shayna, cardboard box and all, was enveloped in a huge hug. Water sloshed over the rim of the container she carried. Shayna tried to gently disentangle herself. Her gift was still intact, thank God.

"Oh, my. Now look what I've done. Towanda, we'll need a mop and some paper towels."

Beau's mom. The words slowly registered. This blond-haired, blue-eyed creature looked nothing like Beau. Yet she'd identified herself as such. It didn't make sense unless of course Beau's father was black.

Shayna set her carton with its precious cargo on the floor and gave herself time to think. She hadn't been prepared for this. Not that she had a problem with interracial marriages. She straightened and accepted the napkins Towanda handed her, dabbing at the blue silk blouse. There would be a huge water stain left, no doubt.

"So how do you think my boy's doing?" Victoria asked, her tone lowered so Towanda wouldn't hear.

"If Beau continues therapy and allows his muscles to get stronger his coordination should get better."

"No promises, then?"

"No promises, but lots of optimism. I've worked with people far worse off than Beau and they made a full recovery."

"You're so young. Familiar looking too."

Brow knitted, she stared at Shayna.

Would Beau's mom remember that eight years ago she'd been little Shay DaCosta, the media's darling?

"Mom, is that Shayna I hear?" Beau called. His voice came from someplace in the rear of the house.

"Let's go find my son," Victoria said, waiting while

Shayna scooped up her box. "He and David are out back, talking shop. Can you stay for dinner?"

Could she stay for dinner? Dinner hadn't been a part of the plan. She'd come to drop off Beau's gift and see how he was doing.

"I . . ."

"You what?"

"I'm supposed to have dinner with my little brother."

"Is he old enough to drive? Call him. Have him meet you here. If not, I can send Towanda to get him. We're having barbecue. Beau's agent David's manning the grill."

Shayna thought about it for a moment. It might actually be good for Reggie to meet Beau. It would give him bragging rights with the boys. Still, having dinner with a patient could be construed as crossing the line. But she wouldn't just be having dinner with Beau, Shayna reasoned, she'd be sharing a meal with his friends and family. What could be wrong with that?

"Get the cell phone, Towanda," Victoria ordered.

The housekeeper went scurrying off, and Shayna was left to follow Victoria's brisk lead to the outside patio.

Beau and David were in the middle of a heated argument when she joined them.

"How can I commit to shooting a coffee commercial in three weeks when I can't even walk?" Beau questioned defensively.

David, seated on the redwood chair across from Beau, leaned in closer, his freckles prominent. "But that's exactly it. Drinking coffee doesn't require standing. Your attorney checked. The scene calls for you and an attractive young woman to be seated around a fireplace at a ski lodge. You'll be sipping java and gazing into each other's eyes. If the company tries to weasel their way out of our agreement, arguing that you're paralyzed, we'd sue their pants off."

"The public is expecting a virile man."

"And you're not? Where's the confidence?" David's freckles almost popped off his face.

"The client hired an athlete, a hotshot skier. Doesn't the voice-over say something like 'real men drink coffee on their downtime'?"

David laughed, then chugged his beer. "I'm glad you still have your sense of humor. That's more like my old cocky Beau."

Beau's colorful expletive shut David up.

"Okay, boys, clean up the language," Beau's mom called. "We ladies are about to join you."

Shayna followed his mother, heading his way. Boy, did she look good enough to eat. Beau wasn't sure how much of the conversation she'd overheard. He'd taken time with his appearance, ditched his comfortable old sweats, and put on a designer polo shirt and loose-fitting chinos. The outfit made him feel more like his old self. Although the crisp evening air lent itself to a sweater, he'd draped one over his shoulders, looping the sleeves around his neck.

Shayna was wearing a stylish pair of capri pants with a matching jacket. The jacket hung open and under it was a sky-blue camisole. She'd opted for flats and looked tinier than ever. Again he had this huge urge to protect her. But Shayna didn't need protecting. She could hold her own with the best of them. The carton she carried looked as if it might have survived a spill. Beau wondered what was in it.

"Hi," he greeted, and quickly introduced David.

Shayna set the soggy box down on the patio table and accepted the hand David offered.

"I've heard a lot about you," David said. "Beau just never told me how pretty you are."

Shayna batted her eyelashes, flirting back. She still hadn't paid Beau much attention. He noticed that she scanned the surrounding area. He'd often heard it said that his home was impressive. That the view from the patio was something that one would expect to see on a movie set. Shayna obviously thought so.

"She is, isn't she?" his mother interjected. "Beauty and brains, a lethal combination. I'm trying to convince her to stay for dinner."

"Can you?" Beau heard himself ask. Having Shayna for dinner would be an unexpected bonus.

"I've made plans to have dinner with my brother," Shayna answered.

"But you were going to call and invite him to join us," Victoria reminded her. "Where is Towanda with that phone?"

"Here, use mine," David offered, removing a cell phone from his pocket and flipping it open.

Shayna promptly dialed. She held the phone to her ear for what seemed an eternity and ended up leaving a message.

"He's not there," she confirmed, returning the telephone to David.

"Good, that settles that. You're having dinner with us." Victoria flopped onto one of the vacant chairs. "I'm glad you offered to help Towanda barbecue, David. I'm exhausted."

"What's in the box?" Beau asked, changing the conversation.

"Oh, I almost forgot." Shayna crossed over to the table and gingerly picked up what looked like two vases. Out of the tops of each, healthy-looking greenery grew. Swimming around their bases were two colorful betas.

"What's this?" Beau asked, looking at the swimming fish, who didn't appear overly happy.

"That's Salt and Pepper. They needed a home. I thought, who better to care for them than you? Fish are very therapeutic and soothing to the nerves."

"They're cute. I take it you think my nerves need soothing?"

Beau found himself exchanging looks with Shayna while David sat quietly, observing them both.

"Now did I say that?"

"You didn't have to."

"My nerves need soothing," Shayna muttered.

How different she was from Chandra. Chandra would never have thought to bring him fish. Chandra, rather than joust, would probably have started a screaming match by now.

"Children," Victoria called, "you're beginning to sound like an old married couple. Before you really go at it, can I convince one of you to help David barbeque?"

Shayna immediately volunteered. Beau watched as she and David collaborated on how best to cook beef and roast potatoes, and deal with the portabellos. Had things been different he would have been up there helping them. He used to make a mean barbecue.

As Shayna joked with his agent, Beau realized how easy she was to be with. Under different circumstances he and she might have had a chance but they'd started off on the wrong foot. Besides, he needed to remember that Shayna was his therapist. He had little to offer her now.

Even as a boy Beau had hated the idea of asking for help. Now it had come down to this, his being dependent on a therapist to show him how to walk again. He despised having to open up, let another human being in, have someone see how helpless and vulnerable he was.

Towanda brought out napkins, cutlery, and plates, and quickly set the table. The tantalizing smell of barbecued beef filled the air as huge portions of food were forked onto each plate. David guzzled another beer while everyone else settled for iced tea. They'd asked Towanda to join them, but she'd declined.

Sunset coated the mountains in pinks and corals, turning what was left of the day a delightful pinky hue. Beau had missed this. Missed being home. A feeling of peace and contentment wrapped itself around him like a well-worn blanket. He heard Vodka, Scotch, and Whiskey neighing in the background. Tomorrow he would get himself down to the stables. His horses had probably forgotten him. Finally he began to relax.

"Who's overseeing Hill Of Dreams these days?" David asked, after coffee was served, and an incredible-looking carrot cake placed before them.

"My dad, and the fellow I hired on as a manager."

"How's it going?"

Beau shrugged. He really didn't know how it was going. He'd trusted his dad to ensure the place ran smoothly. There'd been frequent updates but he hadn't paid attention.

His mother came to the rescue. "It's going really well. 'Course the staff and people frequenting the center miss Beau's monthly visits. I've assured them that once he gets well, he'll be back."

"Why don't you visit?" David asked.

"We said we would, didn't we?" Shayna turned to Beau. "I've heard so much about Hill Of Dreams, I'd really like to see it."

David and Beau's mom stared at Shayna openmouthed, then quickly recovered. "What a great idea."

"Do volunteers work there?" Shayna asked, an idea beginning to percolate.

"We exist because of volunteers." This came from Beau's mother. "Yes, I think you should visit. It's always a good idea to see firsthand the work we do."

"Let's set a date then. How about Monday? We'll substitute that for your normal therapy session."

Victoria placed a hand on Beau's shoulders, squeezing gently. "My son was put on this earth for a purpose. Ed and I knew it the moment we laid eyes on him. That's why we wanted him so badly."

Beau grunted. Shayna was probably exercising every ounce of restraint not to ask for clarification. Her brain must be going a mile a minute trying to figure out what his mom meant. Shayna was a bright woman. It shouldn't take her long to put two and two together unless of course she thought he was the product of a mixed marriage.

Shayna seemed to come to her own conclusion. She was looking at them with interest. Speculatively. Curiously. She seemed to be about to ask a question, then snapped her mouth shut.

Chapter Nine

"How's your stewed duck?" Colin Johnson asked. His own veal and pasta dish sat in front of him untouched.

"It's absolutely delicious. Thank you for bringing me here."

"You're very welcome. I knew you would enjoy the food. The ambience isn't too bad either."

The congestion in the LoDo area had been prohibitive on a Saturday night. They'd attempted to brave the traffic and after a while, frustrated, Colin had gotten out his cell phone and canceled their original reservation. He'd then called the Barola Grill, where they'd been lucky enough to get a table. Now he was seated across from Shayna.

The Sixth Avenue eatery was often referred to as a chichi farmhouse because of its upscale countrified look. Arrangements of dried flowers filled every available urn and basket, and hand-painted porcelain pieces adorned the nooks and crannies. Where as other establishments strived to impress with opulence, the Barola catered to romance: those on a first date or about to pop the question. Several couples were engrossed in conversation or staring into each other's eyes. Shayna thought a violin player would pop out at any moment crooning syrupy love songs. The Barola was an incredibly pretty restaurant with truly wonderful cuisine.

"Do we have any witnesses?" Shayna asked, trying to keep the conversation strictly business.

Colin, who'd been about to spear his veal, laid down his knife and fork and flicked an imaginary crumb off his monogrammed cuffs. He regarded her intently. Shayna was conscious of the stir he'd caused. Several women stared at him. In a city where relaxed western chic prevailed, Colin Johnson, in his starched, business look, stood out.

"Our PI found an eyewitness who saw the boys gassing up when Mrs. Simpkins claimed they were in her house."

Shayna sucked on her bottom lip. As it got closer to the hearing she'd become increasingly more nervous. What would she do if Reggie was incarcerated? Her parents had trusted her to watch over him. Reggie would do something stupid soon, he was getting more and more antsy as each day went by.

"Tell me a little about the opposing attorney?" Shayna asked.

Colin sipped on his red wine and eyed her over the rim of his glass. "I'm not sure what there is to tell. I've known Ed Anderson for years. He has a reputation for winning tough cases. I just happen to think I'm better."

Shayna smiled at his arrogance, clinking her wineglass against his. "Hey, that's why we hired you. You did say Anderson had children. One of his sons was a problem child?"

"That would be Beau. He's since turned himself around

and is quite the big name. You've heard of Beaumont Hill, the skier? The guy who took a pretty bad fall at the Olympics. We were so sure he would win a gold medal."

Shayna almost choked on her own wine. "Beau Hill," she jabbered, dabbing at her mouth with a napkin, while trying to regain her composure. "Beau Hill is Edward Anderson's son?"

Colin shoved her glass of water at her. "Easy now."

Shayna did a quick recovery. Her lungs still felt compressed and her breathing constricted. "Beau's a patient of mine. How could he and Ed Anderson be related? They look nothing alike."

"Ed adopted him. He raised Beau as his own. Do I detect some interest there?" Colin's cognac eyes twinkled. He leaned across the table and looked directly at Shayna. She refused to believe he was flirting. "How come you've never mentioned you were Beau's therapist? Is he my competition?"

Shayna ignored the latter part of the question. "I'm not in the habit of discussing my patients," she said. Her mind raced a mile a minute. Beau related to Edward Anderson. Ed Anderson's son.

Colin's fingers circled the stem of his wineglass. He continued to stare. "It would be difficult to work with the son of a man determined to put your brother behind bars."

"I'd never let my personal feelings get in the way," Shayna got out.

A hundred thoughts milled around in her head. Beau had been adopted by the man out to get her brother. She struggled with the dilemma of turning him over to another therapist. It was the right thing to do. But she hated backing off from a challenge. Maybe she could make this work to her advantage after all. This could well be her opportunity to assure her brother a viable future.

"Wouldn't it be easier to have another therapist work with Beau?" Colin asked, echoing her initial thoughts.

"I'm a professional. I can handle this," Shayna answered, more haughtily than she intended.

"You're human," Colin countered, covering her hand with his. "It's natural to feel resentment. Beau's father is convinced your brother's a criminal."

Reggie was no criminal. Stubborn at times, prone to poor judgment, but a criminal, no. It would kill her if Reggie was put away for a crime he didn't commit. Worse, it would kill Reggie.

Blinking back tears, Shayna said, "You wouldn't let Reggie go to jail. Would you?"

"Not if I can help it. I'm a damn good lawyer and I believe in your brother's innocence. I'm also attracted to you."

With that, Colin picked up his knife and fork and began attacking his veal. Shayna nibbled on her duck, discovering she no longer had an appetite. She used her napkin to wipe her mouth and then rearranged the cutlery. How did her life all of a sudden get so complicated?

"Do you know why the Andersons chose Beau?" Shayna asked, scrambling for something to say. "Most white families want kids who look like them. They could have picked any kid."

"I can only tell you what I heard. Beau was ten years old when the Andersons adopted him. He'd been living in a bunch of foster homes. Edward Anderson had handled his parents' estate as a favor. He took an interest in the boy. They'd been big-name athletes themselves, and had lived a pretty wild life."

"Beau's real parents are dead then?" she asked, suddenly fascinated by the story. Everything to do with Beau had begun to fascinate her lately.

"Killed in a car accident. Rumor had it they'd been partying. They did a lot of that."

"Sounds like the poor guy's had more than his share of hard knocks."

"Don't feel sorry for him. He's a pampered, rich athlete. Can we talk about something else, like you and me?"

Here it came again. Shayna was so astonished by the resentment in Colin's voice, she simply gaped at him.

"Come on, Shayna, I told you I was interested in you."

What did she say to that? She'd had no idea of Colin's interest until he invited her to dinner. She'd justified the invitation as his needing to talk to her about Reggie's case. She didn't want to hurt his feelings, but she felt no love connection here. She'd gone out with him because it had been a long time between dates. The fact that he was articulate, debonair, and good looking was a bonus.

"You hid your interest pretty well," Shayna began, chuckling softly, figuring she would handle his interest with jest.

"We were usually discussing Reggie," Colin reminded her. "You were this no-nonsense, focused, business-woman. I was intrigued and wanted to get to know you better."

"And now you have. Why are you interested?"

"Because I like what I've come to know. I remember seeing you on television years ago. God, you were a joy to watch on those parallel bars. My entire family rooted for you. We all thought you were going to win a medal. When you got hurt, we said, she'll be back next Olympics, and then you weren't. Having you retain me is karma. You've been my fantasy for so long."

Shayna took a long draft of wine. This was too heavy duty for her. She didn't want to be any man's obsession. She was surprised Colin knew about her past. He'd never mentioned it before. Time to switch the conversation back to Beau.

"When I take on a patient, I like to find out what makes him tick," Shayna said conversationally. "I've been reading up on Beau and his accident. Everything seems to point to sabotage. Did anyone investigate the accident or question the competition?"

"I don't know. What's more I don't want to talk about Beau Hill. I'd rather talk about you and me."

"Perhaps we shouldn't talk about us right now," Shayna added evasively. "Let's get through the trial first. Things will only get more complicated if you and I start dating. Emotions tend to get in the way."

Boy, did she know that. Emotions were already clouding her good judgment when it came to Beau.

"Shayna, are you putting me off?" Colin said, confronting her. "We're two levelheaded people. To use your own words. We're professionals."

Their waitress interrupted. "Can I get you anything else? Wine perhaps?" She pointed to the empty wine bottle.

"More wine would be nice, thank you," Shayna said before Colin could speak up.

The waitress departed to get another bottle and Shayna turned her attention back to Colin. "You're accomplished, smart, have a great reputation as a lawyer. Where did you go to school?"

He fell for the bait and she listened as he went on about himself. It would be a long night she sensed, but Colin wasn't exactly boring.

* * *

Chandra lay buck naked in bed contemplating her hot-pink toenails. She'd spent the entire afternoon at the salon, getting a massage, lounging in an invigorating sauna, then having her hair and nails done.

In another hour, Franco would be sending a limo to pick her up. They'd been invited to a party on a friend's yacht. It wasn't any old party either. She was to be introduced to Carlo Mancini, the famous movie producer. This type of soiree deserved a new dress and Franco had bought her one, costing mucho lira. He'd been buying her expensive baubles, explaining that Bellissima wanted to keep its most beautiful spokesperson happy.

The dress was purposely cut low, exposing more than ample cleavage. But a girl needed every advantage she could get. A movie contract might be hers for the taking. She wanted to follow the path of the other big names: Renee, Andie, and now Vanessa. She'd show the world she wasn't just the flavor of the season. Franco could help her go places. He wasn't the lover Beau had been, but he was teachable and could be trained. If she married him it would be an incredible coup. Chandra Leon, African-American beauty, capturing Italy's most eligible bachelor. Let the naysayers thumb their noses at her then.

And there had been plenty of those. The paparazzi for example. They'd considered her Franco's bella negra. His temporary diversion. An exotic arm decoration that would soon be replaced. Boy, would she show them.

Time to get up and get dressed, but not before giving Beau a quick call. Their relationship wasn't over by a long shot. She still had his engagement ring. With no firm commitment from Franco, it wasn't smart to let Beau go. A bird in the hand was worth two in the bush.

Just her luck that Beau might have a full recovery, and regain the use of his legs. Those lucrative contracts with the cereal manufacturers and athletic gear companies were worth millions of dollars. Not exactly chump change. Beau was probably the most beautiful man she knew and at one time he did fulfill her every need.

How would he have found out about her involvement with Franco? Milan was a continent removed. The American press couldn't have gotten wind of the heated affair with Franco. Even if they had, she would deny it. It wasn't as if the media was credible.

Just thinking of Beau made her hot. Chandra's fingers circled her nipple. Making love to Beau used to be a gratifying experience. She picked up the phone and punched in Denver Rehab's number. Six rings later a female picked up.

"Denver Rehabilitation Center."

"This is Chandra Leon. Connect me to Beaumont Hill's room now."

The operator grunted something that didn't sound very complimentary, and put her on hold forever.

She returned to say, "Mr. Hill's no longer with us," her voice so saccharine sweet that Chandra wanted to punch her.

"Find out where he is," Chandra demanded.

"I'm an operator, not a fortune-teller, hon."

"A soon to be unemployed operator," Chandra railed. "Get me your supervisor."

The phone clanged in her ear and Chandra was left with the dial tone.

A series of colorful expletives filled the hotel room. Infuriated, she punched in the numbers once again. This time a different operator answered.

"I need Beau Hill," Chandra demanded, listening for a moment before snapping, "What do you mean he's no longer a patient here?"

"He was discharged several days ago."

Discharged, and Beau hadn't called her? Her head reeled. What woman had taken her place? Beau had wanted to put their relationship on hold. Had her trip to Milan provided him the perfect excuse to end their relationship? Nah, who would want a cripple? She laughed derisively.

"Where did he go?"

"I don't have that information, miss."

At least this one called her "miss." Chandra slammed down the receiver only to pick it up again. This time she punched in Beau's home number.

A woman's voice eventually answered. Must be his dumb ox of a housekeeper.

"This is Mr. Hill's fiancée," Chandra announced. "Get him for me."

"Fiancée?"

"Honey, just put him on the phone, especially if you value your job."

"Who may I say is calling?"

The ox was dumber than she'd thought. "Chandra Leon."

"Oh, Chandra, I should have known. Only you would call at this hour." The person on the other end yawned in her ear. "Are you still in Milan?"

"Just wake up Beau, and get him on the phone, you stupid servant," Chandra thundered.

"I'm not a servant," the woman on the other end enunciated. "This is Victoria, and I most certainly will not wake up my son. He can call you tomorrow if he chooses."

She'd blown it this time. Her other personality to the rescue.

"Mrs. Anderson," Chandra said in her most conciliatory voice. "I'm sorry. Why didn't you identify yourself? I was upset. I heard my Beau-Beau's been discharged. No one's telling me anything, like if he's even walking again."

"You'll have to ask him that tomorrow," Victoria said firmly. "Good night."

The phone thudded in Chandra's ears. Beau's mother had never been particularly fond of her but she'd never openly been rude. If she and Beau patched things up Victoria would have to go. She'd see to it.

Chandra glanced at her watch. Not much time left to bathe, dress, and get pretty. Not much time at all.

Chapter Ten

"I've heard the name Shayna DaCosta before and I've seen that face." Victoria straightened up from helping Beau tie his shoelaces.

"Mom," Beau argued, "you're in the real estate business. You meet tons of people every day. Didn't you say after a while everyone starts looking alike?"

"True. But this isn't the case here. Shayna was in the public eye. I know it. She's too petite to be a model. I see her skinnier, with longer hair. That smile melted hearts."

Still does.

"Skinnier than she already is? Shayna's a bone. A shapely bone, mind you."

"I'm surprised you noticed. I thought you were immune."

The remark was said tongue in cheek.

Beau decided to ignore it. He hated being this helpless, dependent on his mother to help tie his shoes. It had taken what seemed hours to dress and he'd had to endure the persistent tingling in his legs and feet. The constant feeling of being on pins and needles. He would have to speak with his doctor about this. Maybe even speak to Shayna. What if it was worse news?

Beau did up the buttons on his shirt while his mother droned on about his brother's visit being further delayed. Jason had been called away on business.

"Bet you're looking forward to visiting the center," Victoria said.

He dreaded it. Dreaded answering questions. What could he say to all those hopeful people when he'd given up hope? How did someone like him give a pep talk with any kind of conviction? Visiting might not be such a good idea after all.

Beau wheeled himself across to his desk and cooed to the two betas. Salt and Pepper swam blissfully in their separate vases oblivious to his inner turmoil.

"You two don't have a care in the world," he said, as they swam off in opposite directions.

Victoria tossed him a speculative look. "Those critters are unique. That Shayna's got a good sense of humor. You've done far worse than her."

"Cut the matchmaking, Mom," Beau growled. "Stop taking digs at Chandra."

"Speaking of the lady, she's called," Victoria said.

"When was this?"

"Some ungodly hour this morning. She mistook me for Towanda and read me the riot act when I refused to wake you up."

"Sounds like her."

Beau had once found that witchy side of her personality amusing. Not anymore.

"Did she leave a number?"

"Nope."

"Then I'll have to wait until she calls again."

"I'll bring the van around," Victoria said, touching his shoulder. "Sure you're ready for the center?"

"Ready as I'll ever be."

Left alone with his fish, Beau confided, "What do you think, boys? Would Shayna consider dating a cripple?"

The fish whose gender remained a mystery gulped at him. Beau quickly wheeled himself out. Time to take the advice he'd read in *Turning Hurts Into Halos. Reality thinking is not why me? Reality thinking is now what?*

Now what? What steps did he need to take to get his life back in gear? In just a few minutes he would be meeting with people financially far worse off than he, a positive attitude would go a long way when greeting them. Their lives were miserable enough, and he had an opportunity to change their thinking.

Victoria waited out front. Beau, as quickly as he was able, wheeled himself up the ramp. He was getting used to it. Victoria, who'd taken two weeks off from her real estate business, deftly pulled out of the driveway. They were on their way. Twenty minutes later, they were stopped in front of a long, low, brick building.

With some assistance, Beau was able to get out of the back of the van. The front door flung open and several employees flanked him. Most were volunteers he recognized. People who'd dedicated themselves to working with those less fortunate. There were hugs and kisses all around.

"Beau, you're back. We missed you."

"Good to see you, Beau."

"Mr. Beau," a large woman in an apron greeted, enveloping him and his wheelchair in her ample arms. She kissed him all over.

"Easy, Penny," Beau said, when his air supply was almost cut off.

Penny was the center's cook. At one time she'd been homeless. But she'd made a remarkable turnaround, and now she shared her story of redemption freely. She'd been another one of the lost souls Hill Of Dreams had saved.

"Did I hurt you, Mr. Beau?" she queried. "I forget you're no longer the big strong man you used to be."

So much for his ego. The hell he wasn't. He'd show them.

"I'm fine, Penny. Give me another hug. Just go easy this time."

Ten minutes later, feeling as if he'd been hugged to death by three-quarters of the staff, and almost all of the inhabitants, Beau wheeled himself inside. The one thing he'd insisted on when the building had been constructed was that it be fully accessible. Boy, was he ever glad he did.

Inside, Victoria was already in deep discussion with Mohammed Llewellyn, who managed the place. Mohammed was another Hill Of Dreams graduate. Spotting Beau, Victoria ended the conversation. "I'll pick you up at three," she said.

After she'd left, Mohammed punched his arm and leaned in, confiding, "We missed you, man. The place just hasn't been the same without you popping in."

"I couldn't get here sooner," Beau mumbled.

"We're just glad you got here. Ms. DaCosta's looking around. She brought a young man with her. You know what you're doing, I assume?"

Beau frowned. "Why? Because I let Shayna talk me into visiting?" he asked.

"No, because you let her bring that hoodlum."

"Huh?"

"So what would you like to see first?" Mohammed

asked, "Game room? Library? Gym? Lunch will be served in half an hour."

"Let's find Shayna, then decide."

"Did I hear my name?"

Shayna blew into the room like a breath of fresh air, bringing all that pent-up energy with her. Following sulkily in her wake was a lanky young man with his cap on backward.

"You made it," she said, bending to kiss Beau's cheek.

That intimate greeting took him by surprise. She'd never done this before. He breathed in her scent. She smelled heavenly, like a fresh spring day that had just been rained on. The tingle in his toes turned into a full-fledged throb, settling in his groin. How could one chaste kiss arouse him so? Even his trousers had shifted.

"Who's this?" Beau asked, eyeing the young man with her up and down. Silly as it was, his testosterone pumped. No one should have Shayna's attention except him.

Shayna pushed the youth forward. "Beau, I'd like you to meet my little brother, Reggie. He was so excited when he found out you were my patient. He's been a huge admirer of yours."

Judging by the kid's expression he seemed anything but excited. In fact he didn't even seem the least bit impressed. "How ya doing?" he drawled.

"I hope you don't mind me bringing Reggie," Shayna added hurriedly. "We've been looking for a black-owned organization where he could volunteer since we moved to Denver. Hill Of Dreams seems so perfect."

"We can always use volunteers," Beau said pleasantly. "The more the merrier. When are you free?"

"Mostly weekends. Maybe one day after school," the boy grunted, taking a protective stance next to his sister.

"Great, we'll take whatever you can give us. Won't we, Mohammed? Now onto the game room."

Just as Mohammed was about to place his hands on the bars of his wheelchair, Beau scooted out of his reach. "I can manage."

High-pitched conversation floated down the hall as they approached the very popular game room. Beau visualized the scene inside. There would be fierce competition on every Ping-Pong table, dartboard, foosball machine, and computer game. Primarily alpha males and a handful of females would watch TV, commenting raucously. More importantly, the place would be vibrant. Alive. Forgotten would be the daily woes. Men and women succumbed to fantasy here.

They entered the noisy, crowded atmosphere and were instantly absorbed in the fray. High spirits and unbridled gaiety abounded. Spontaneous laughter ricocheted off the walls and people called to each other in high-pitched voices. There were few rules imposed at the center. The important one being that personal hygiene had to be maintained at all times. Anyone arriving unwashed was handed a change of clothes, bar of soap, and towel, then led to the showers. If they refused, they would be diplomatically asked to leave. Few did. A free four-course meal was the reward for cleanliness.

Beau hunkered down in his wheelchair silently observing. He was not the only nonambulatory person in the room. Several people in wheelchairs sat playing board games and chatting quietly. For a while he went unnoticed.

Shayna was drawn to the pool table where two beefy types played a strategic game cheered on by enthusiastic onlookers. Her presence made the men preen and show renewed interest in the game. Who wouldn't react when Shayna was there acting as if you were the only one that mattered? Her scent still lingered in Beau's nostrils and the spot where she'd kissed him tingled. Reggie had plopped down in front of the TV, where a small crowd watched a highly overrated talk show. No one even looked at him, they were so used to a transient crowd.

Mohammed clapped his hands and magically the room came alive. All attention was now focused on Beau. An off-key version of "For He's A Jolly Good Fellow," followed. In came Penny, wheeling an elaborate sheet cake that could easily feed fifty that she'd baked and iced herself. Colorful skis were mounted on the snowy white icing and the wording read:

Welcome Home, Beau.

We missed you.

He missed them too. They'd collected money for cards and flowers, showered him with their love. He was patted on the back, thumped on the arm, and embraced by men and women alike. Many of the regulars had come out to wish him well. Even so, he sensed their unease, felt their forced heartiness, and hoped that soon they would be their old argumentative selves with him.

Even Cody Cayote, his favorite senior, the first ever to patronize his center, wasn't his ebullient, posturing self. The psychologist at the rehab center had prepared him for this, but it still hurt.

"Can I have a word with you?" Mohammed whispered, when the festivities quieted down enough so that he could be heard and Penny and his cake departed for the lunchroom. The cake would be dessert.

"Sure."

Mohammed waited until the room emptied before finding a place where they could converse. Shayna was still speaking to one of the women and seemed oblivious to the goings-on around her. Reggie's attention remained with his talk show.

"You know I normally support whatever you do," Mohammed began. "Our board does as well."

"Get to the point."

Mohammed jerked a thumb in Reggie's direction. "You're crazy to have him work for you."

"You've been alluding to that from the time he arrived. I'd think you'd be thrilled that a high school kid wants to do something worthwhile. Most don't give a damn. They're totally self-focused."

"That kid doesn't want to volunteer. His sister's volunteering him," Mohammed said, dryly.

"What's with the animosity? We're hurting for volunteers and the young man comes highly recommended. His sister's my therapist."

The veins on Mohammed's neck bulged, matching his eyes. "Why would you want to hire a kid your father thinks is incorrigible? Why, Beau? Why? You'd have him a week or two, then off to jail he'd go. Especially if he's being tried as an adult."

"What are you talking about? Is he in some kind of trouble?"

"Where have you been, under a rock? Oops, sorry, man. You dad's about to hang and quarter him for breaking and entering, and beating some woman up."

Mohammed proceeded to fill him in. Beau listened intently. He felt duped. Why hadn't Shayna said something? She must have known the prosecutor was his dad. Mohammed had told him the crime made all of the major newspapers. Of course, Beau had been too busy wallowing in self-pity to notice. According to Mohammed, the teenager had a history of minor scrapes with the law but no arrests.

Why would Shayna deliberately bring Reggie here in search of a job? What would she get out of deliberately deceiving Beau? A part of Beau wanted to believe that she hadn't made the connection. That she didn't know who his father was. That her sole mission was to keep Reggie busy and off the streets.

Wasn't that one of the reasons he'd created Hill Of Dreams? It was supposed to be a place where indigents and troubled souls found solace. Now he was thinking of turning one away. It wasn't as if he didn't have staff members with less than perfect records. He prided himself in giving the underdog a chance, in trusting those others considered untrustworthy. He'd vowed on his biological parents' grave to help those who needed help.

"Beau, I have to tell you I'm impressed," Shayna said, speaking quickly in her excitement. "This is a wonderful concept. You've got every ethnic group represented under one roof. I've heard the most delightful stories of how this center saves lives. I've heard the most wonderful stories about you."

Beau grunted, hoping his stretched lips could be interpreted as a real smile. He was rapidly processing information. Shayna had an agenda. What was it?

"Let's tell Shayna about our scholarship program," Mohammed interjected, coming to his rescue. "We'll discuss it over lunch. Hey, Reggie, are you hungry?"

"Yup." The teenager shuffled to his feet and slowly made his way over to them, rubbing his stomach. "Hope that woman can cook."

"Reggie!" Shayna admonished, giving him the benefit of a raised eyebrow. "Isn't the center wonderful? You checked out those awesome basketball courts and that running track goes for miles? There's even a meditation room." Shayna's eyes were round in excitement. She exuded energy and life.

"Cool," Reggie said with little enthusiasm.

Mohammed led them to the dining room. Beau made a mental note to call his dad and find out all about

Reggie's case. Armed with information, he could figure out if he was being used.

"We'll need a recommendation from a teacher," Mohammed said, draping an arm around the still sulking Reggie. "We'll also need a phone number where we can reach you."

Mohammed handed the teenager a pen and paper. "Here, write them down."

As Reggie scribbled, Shayna leaned over and kissed Beau's cheek.

"Thank you, Beau," she said. "I owe you big time."

"No. It's more like the other way around."

Chapter Eleven

"Damn it, Shayna, I don't have time for this. Why did you go shooting off your mouth, telling that man I would volunteer at his home for losers?"

Shayna snapped the dated copy of the magazine she'd been reading shut. "Don't give me lip, child. You should be counting your lucky stars you're not arrested. You need every edge you can get. Volunteering at Hill Of Dreams just might provide you that."

Reggie pouted. "What's volunteering at your boyfriend's place going to do for me?"

"Beau's not my boyfriend."

"Could have fooled me. You get all nervous and jittery when the cripple's around. You start fluffing your little bit of hair and fooling with your jewelry. You've got a thing for the man. It wouldn't be so bad if he was still somebody. I could say my brother-in-law was still skiing."

"Shut up, Reggie. If you must know, Colin suggested it wouldn't hurt to keep your image squeaky clean right now. Volunteering at a place like Hill Of Dreams couldn't hurt."

"Why couldn't we have picked some other place to volunteer? Why does Beau Hill have to own the place? I get to work with all those smelly, homeless people that can't find their way in life. Be their baby-sitter, while you're making time with Beau. You talk about the guy all the time. Even now you're reading some stupid article about his accident. He had a lousy downhill run and he's washed up, a has-been. He's not even particularly nice to you. All he does is sit in that chair looking like he's carrying the weight of the world around, and talk to his manager."

Why couldn't she have picked some other place indeed? She could have, but what she'd said to Beau and Mohammed a few days ago was true. It was hard to find a black-owned organization like this one in Denver. One that was clearly not for profit, that truly wanted to help the underprivileged succeed.

If she were truly honest she would admit that she did indeed have an ulterior motive. She'd hoped that word would somehow leak out to the public that Reggie was working there, that Edward Anderson was bent on prosecuting a volunteer at his son's place. That kind of news was bound to generate negative PR for the prosecution. There would be overwhelming sympathy from the public, which would work in Reggie's favor. Her brother would not be painted as all bad if he was shown as volunteering at a place where underdogs and misfits found a haven. This wasn't using Beau. She was doing what any concerned sister would do for a brother she loved more than anything in the whole wide world.

When Shayna looked up, Reggie had already stalked off to his room. She returned to the article she'd been reading, frowning as it ended. The more she read about

Beau and his accident, the more certain she was that it wasn't an accident. Why hadn't someone investigated it? Why hadn't the competitors been spoken to? Beau had been the favorite, the contestant slated to win gold. Sure he was coming up against other good skiers, great ones actually, but based on his record alone, this should have been a pretty easy race.

Lars, the German skier, had won the World Cup and Goodwill Games previously, but that was only because Beau was recovering from a bad sprain and broken collarbone during that time, according to the article. The Swiss skier, Jan, had been bragging all along that the medal was his. Nothing and no one would stop him from winning. Even Beau's American teammate had had several scuffles off the snow with anyone who even doubted his ability to place. Ironically, Joshua Vanderhorn, the American, had placed second, the German first, and the Swiss third. Shayna made a mental note to talk to Beau and find out if he had at any point left his equipment unattended.

She snapped the magazine shut and headed off to make dinner. In the midst of seasoning chicken, the phone rang.

"I'll get it," Reggie shouted from upstairs.

"Fine."

It was probably just another of Reggie's noisy buddies. She had no real friends in Denver. She hadn't had the time. Most of her acquaintances were people she'd met at the rehabilitation center, women like Mary Jane Coppola, whom she still hadn't taken up on her invitation to go out and have drinks. She would have to remedy that soon.

"It's for you," Reggie called after several seconds had elapsed.

"I'll get it in a minute," Shayna said, carefully washing

her hands and drying them on a towel before picking up the extension. "Hi, this is Shayna."

"How are you?" Colin Johnson asked.

She hadn't been expecting him. The last time they'd spoken was the night of their date when he'd driven her home, settled for a friendly kiss on the cheek, then seen her inside. He'd seemed to be okay about being friends. This call must be about Reggie, she decided.

"Great. But busy. Very busy," Shayna carefully answered. "What's new? Did we get another lead?"

"Yes, we have." We just found ourselves a witness who claims to have seen the boys at McDonald's. He describes them in detail, down to the clothes they were wearing. Could be he's been looking at the news. A word of caution though, he's not very credible. The man has a drinking problem."

"Now we've got two witnesses. Isn't that better than none at all?" Shayna's excitement bubbled. She'd always been an optimist.

"What's your weekend look like?" Colin asked.

What was this about her weekend? She thought she'd made it clear to Colin that she wanted to be friends, at least for now.

She didn't answer right off, and he must have sensed her hesitancy.

"Hey, no pressure, hon. I thought you might enjoy hiking. I'm going with another attorney from the firm and her significant other. The weather this weekend is supposed to be beautiful."

While the thought of getting exercise and being outdoors appealed to her, she didn't want to encourage Colin. If she went traipsing off with him and another couple he might get the wrong message. She didn't want to lead him on.

"I've already made plans for the weekend," Shayna lied. "Maybe another time."

She did indeed have chores, like going to the grocery store, cleaning house, reading up more about Beau.

"You will call me if things change?" Colin said, his tone light. "I'd like to show you another side of Denver."

Shayna thanked him for thinking of her, then went back to her dinner preparations. She'd done the right thing. It wouldn't do to tick off Reggie's attorney, who was definitely making his interest known. She felt no attraction for Colin, so why encourage him?

Shayna thought of the contrast between Colin and Beau. Both men were so different. Colin was suave, well groomed, and definitely a man about town, while Beau, with his one gold earring, marched to a different drummer. Beau was competitive, driven, committed to causes. He had this compelling need to see the underdog succeed. Colin, she would guess, probably donated money to designated charities, but only because it provided him with a good tax write-off. Otherwise he would not really be involved, she sensed.

Shayna placed the chicken in the oven and the phone jingled again. She counted the rings, waiting for Reggie to pick up. After the fourth, she grabbed the receiver.

"Hello."

"Shayna?"

Her heart did a rapid thump-thump and breathing did not come easy. Beau. How had he gotten her number at home? That's right, Reggie had given Mohammed his phone number.

"Anything wrong?" she asked, when she finally found her voice.

"Nothing that two new legs wouldn't fix." He chuckled self-consciously. Shayna waited for him to go on. "By the way, I finished your book."

"Good for you. And how did you find it?"

Was he really calling because he'd finished her book or did he want something else?

"An interesting take on life. You must feel I need motivation. A little inspiration in my life?"

"So the message was lost on you, eh?" Shayna teased.

"Did I say that?"

Reggie came traipsing through the kitchen, tossing her a quizzical look. He headed for the refrigerator, removed a can of soda, and downed it in a couple of gulps. "When's dinner?"

Shayna signaled that dinner would be ready in fifteen minutes.

"Hey, you still there?" Beau queried, his voice bringing her back to the present.

"Sorry. What were we talking about? Yes, the message being lost on you. As the author says, why dwell on why me? Instead, ask yourself what now? Well, Beau, what now?"

"You never let up, do you?" His chuckle came from deep within his belly.

"Just doing my job," Shayna said cheekily.

"Is Reggie there?" Beau asked. "Mohammed's tied up and I have some questions for him. Call it preliminary screening, we need to determine if he's a good fit for the center."

Shayna looked up to see Reggie, openly listening, his back pressed against the refrigerator door.

"He's right here. I'll put him on."

"See you tomorrow at therapy."

Tomorrow they were going to try something new. Aquatic therapy had been successful with so many of her patients. Shayna's breath whooshed out of her lungs at the thought of seeing Beau in bathing trunks. She'd had powerful fantasies of seeing him naked. This was the next best thing.

"Beau wants to talk to you," she said, holding out the receiver to Reggie.

"More likely he wants to talk to you. I'm just the excuse," Reggie muttered.

Shayna ignored him, concentrating on the appetizing aroma wafting its way from inside the oven. Glad for the convenient excuse to see how her chicken was doing, she practically buried her head inside the open door, welcoming the heat. Just talking to Beau had produced its own glow.

She grabbed plates, napkins, and cutlery from the cupboards and pretended not to listen to Reggie's one-sided conversation.

"Yeah, I suppose I could make it. . . . Yeah, I've ridden before. No, I never worked with adults. . . .Why are you asking why I want to do this?"

Reggie looked frantically in Shayna's direction.

She came to his aid, mouthing words at him. "Because . . . I want to make a contribution. I need extra credits to graduate."

Amazingly, Reggie parroted her. "Sure, I'll tell Shayna," he said before hanging up. He flung himself into a chair, grabbed his napkin, and waited for Shayna to serve him.

"Help yourself," she said, pointing to the kitchen counter, where the chicken, pasta, and tossed salad had been dished out.

Snorting loudly, Reggie lumbered to his feet and heaped his plate full. When he was seated across from her, she asked, "What was it Beau wanted?"

"I'm not sure. I think he was feeling me out. He wanted to see if I was really interested in volunteering. He says we'll talk in person and that we should stop by this Sunday. Since it's easier for me to get around he wants me to come to his house and fill out paperwork. He asked if we liked horseback riding."

Reggie swallowed a mouthful of pasta. "The guy's weird. You think the accident went to his head?"

Shayna laughed at her brother's assessment of Beau. "Not weird, just different. Beau's an original thinker."

"You always stick up for him. Do you two have something going on?"

"No," Shayna snapped.

Trust Reggie to call it as he saw it. She hoped he didn't see the telltale signs of heat flooding her cheeks. "It was nice of Beau to invite you to ride," she said.

"Us," Reggie corrected.

"Whatever. It will give you a chance to get to know each other. He's an interesting man. His legs may no longer function but there isn't a thing wrong with his mind."

"I was planning on playing basketball this weekend," Reggie grumbled.

"You can still play basketball. Just bear in mind you need extra credits to graduate. And you need to stay out of trouble."

"Right, like that would make a difference."

Shayna heard the catch in his voice. The stress was starting to get to him.

"You can't give up hope, Reggie."

"Why not? I'm a young black male. That means I'm trouble. White women clutch their purses, and cross the street when they see me." He continued to shovel food into his mouth, the idea obviously bothering him.

"Maybe volunteering at Beau's will help you," Shayna said carefully. "He's well respected."

"So that's why you're insistent I work for him? You think if I volunteer at Hill Of Dreams, I might get off?"

"That's not guaranteed, Reggie."

Reggie still didn't know about the connection between Beau and Ed Anderson. He would go ballistic if he knew that they were father and son, and that she'd knowingly chosen to associate with Beau. There wouldn't be a prayer in the world of him volunteering at Hill Of Dreams. She'd also hoped that if Beau got to know Reggie he would recognize that under the bluster was just a frightened little boy. Maybe he'd use his influence to come to an equitable solution for all. Even if Reggie was placed on probation or assigned community service, it was better than going to jail.

"If I volunteer at that homeless persons' center it doesn't mean I'd get off," Reggie said, voicing what Shayna refused to even think about.

"Hill Of Dreams doesn't just cater to homeless people," she corrected.

"Could have fooled me. The place seems to have more than its share of displaced homeys. I don't understand why no one believes me. I didn't beat up some old lady, nor did I steal her possessions."

Shayna believed him even if the rest of the world didn't. He was a typical teenager and hadn't exercised good judgment. He hung around with the wrong crowd and had been a magnet for trouble. There'd been that group of boys in Seattle he'd hung with who stole cars and joyrode them out of boredom. Next had been the crowd of thugs who sold herb to their buddies and anyone else willing to buy.

The final straw came when Reggie had been picked up for shoplifting a couple of comics, and a handful of candy bars. The sum total being less than ten dollars. He'd had plenty of money on him. The shopkeeper knew the DaCostas and had declined pressing charges. But the embarrassment had almost killed them. Her parents had kept Reggie on a short leash until he'd been sent off to Shayna's.

"So you're telling me Beau Hill might be my savior, that's why you're so chummy with the guy? He's a patient. Didn't you always tell me business and pleasure don't mix?"

"They don't."

Reggie rose, and taking his empty plate with him, stuck it in the dishwasher. It was the first time since coming to live with her that he'd done that. Must be a good omen.

"I hate it when you treat me like a child," he sulked. "You believe that a few hours of volunteering is going to make a jury look favorably on me. Know what I think? I think you're just using me to get close to Beau Hill. That stinks."

Shayna cut her eyes at him. He was starting to get on her nerves. "You are a child," she said. "One that's costing this family a lot of money."

She'd never spoken to him so sharply.

Reggie's eyes practically popped out of his head. The veins on the sides of his neck bulged. His temper was well known. Shayna braced herself for the explosion but his voice came out deadly quiet.

"Everyone makes mistakes, Shayna," he said, sounding for once like the adult he was on the verge of becoming. "You made a whopper with Michael, but no one keeps throwing that in your face."

He stomped off, muttering something about her expecting too much of him.

Chapter Twelve

"You'll never guess who's been trying to get in touch with you." David's voice boomed through the receiver, forcing Beau to hold the earpiece several inches away.

"Not Chandra?"

He was just about to wrap up an interview with a caregiver, and the phone call had come at an inconvenient time. Beau signaled to Mark, a young blond man, that he would be only a moment.

David guffawed in his ear. "Nah. Your ex has been otherwise occupied. Even you must read the paper. This morning's feature was a doozie."

Beau hadn't seen the morning paper. He'd scheduled this interview first thing, and right after this, he was heading off to the rehabilitation center for aquatic therapy.

"What's Chandra up to?" Beau asked, curiosity actually getting the better of him.

David snickered. "Looks like you've been publicly

dumped, my boy, replaced by Santana, the Bellissima heir. You might think of your engagement as off but the public doesn't know that. This morning's paper was filled with pictures of your ex and Franco looking mighty cozy. The caption read *'Heir to the Bellissima fortune negotiates another successful merger.'* There's speculation an announcement is in the works."

"What kind of an announcement?" The intensity in Beau's tone got the attention of the candidate seated across from him. He studiously examined his nails and pretended not to listen.

"An engagement. Wouldn't that be quite the coup for scheming old Chandra? Got to give the woman credit, under that beautiful exterior has always been a good business head."

"You're right."

Beau tried not to sound sour but it did hurt. Not because his feelings ran deep for Chandra, but because his ego was hurt. No one liked to be used. Chandra had most likely targeted Franco Santana for the same reason she'd initially targeted him. From the PR end of things, Franco would be good for her career and would keep her in the public eye. It didn't hurt that financially she wouldn't have to worry for the rest of her life.

God bless them both. The match was made in Fragrance hell. Beau signaled to Mark that he would be another couple of minutes. He returned to David. "So who's trying to get in touch with me?"

"One of your old teammates."

"And that would be . . . ?"

"Joshua Vanderhorn."

Beau frowned. What would Joshua want with him after all this time? He hadn't heard hide nor hair from him since the accident. But given they'd never been friends, that was hardly surprising. They'd been civil for the sake of the United States ski team.

Both men were from vastly different worlds. Joshua came from old money. A snob from the word *go*. He was blessed with one of those handsome, aristocrat faces, and an athletic body that had women drooling for miles. You could easily picture Joshua with skis slung over his shoulders, blue eyes peering from under a headband. Perfect for commercials. Except Joshua would never sink that low and sully the family name. The Vanderhorns would have a cow. Commercials and endorsements were for the lower classes, skiers like Beau.

From the moment he'd qualified for the ski team, Beau had sensed Joshua's dislike of him. Dislike was probably too strong a word. Disdain or disapproval was more fitting. Joshua would never have expected to ski with the likes of Beau. Skiing wasn't the typical black person's sport. Joshua's exposure to blacks was limited to what he saw on TV and he tended to treat Beau like the stereotype. Beau belonged on a basketball court, not skiing.

Another dose of curiosity prompted Beau to ask, "What did Joshua want?"

"Your home number. Says he just got back from Europe. He meant to call you before, but things got crazy. Yada, yada. You know how he goes on. Now he claims he has something to discuss with you."

"Go ahead and give it to him."

"Why? You sure you want to do this, Beau?" His agent sounded skeptical.

David knew him too well. No, he wasn't sure he wanted Joshua to have his number. But he did want to know what he wanted.

Beau hung up to find Mark's eyes on him. He managed a smile and quickly apologized. This candidate had come with excellent recommendations but Beau no longer felt he needed him. His coordination had improved remarkably and the strength in his arms had increased. He was even able to take charge of his personal hygiene and could almost dress himself. Therapy with Shayna was obviously paying off.

Hiring an aide would mean that he wasn't self-sufficient, that he might never walk again, much less ski. What did William Rudolph, the three-time Olympic gold medalist, say? *"My mother taught me very early to believe I could achieve any accomplishment I wanted to. The first was to walk without braces."* And he meant to walk again, maybe even ski.

Beau smiled at the thought of what Shayna would say if she knew that a quote from this book of hers had popped into his head. Would she understand why he was reluctant to hire an aide? Would she support his choice not to? He'd ask her later.

"I do want to thank you for your time," Beau said, turning his attention back to Mark and shaking the young man's hand firmly. "I'll get back to you. You're very well qualified for the post of personal assistant."

Personal assistant sounded a heck of a lot better than aide. Aide conjured up stark white hospital walls and smells of disinfectant. Pain and despair rather than hope. He was growing maudlin.

Mark stood, briefcase in hand. "What's the time frame, sir? I do have another offer."

"I'll let you have my decision within the week. I'll phone your agency."

"I'd appreciate that."

"Towanda," Beau called, "will you please show Mark out."

"I'd be happy to," Victoria said, materializing from some invisible place. Beau wondered if she'd been lis-

tening. "Towanda's running an errand for me," she said, escorting Mark out.

When she returned, she eyed Beau's designer pullover and pressed chinos. "You're dressed to go to the center? Didn't you say you had aquatic aerobics or some funky stuff?"

"It's called aquatic therapy, Mom, and I'll be changing when I get there."

Victoria raised both eyebrows. "I see. But until then there's someone you want to impress?"

Beau refused to acknowledge the snide remark. His mother was clearly over the sympathy phase. A few weeks of living with him had done that to her. Now she even ribbed him about his disability. In a couple of days she'd be relieved by his sister, Kelly, and she would return to her real estate business and clients. Much as Beau hated to admit it, he would miss her.

Twenty minutes later they were seated in the van heading toward Denver Rehabilitation Center. The windows were open and there was the promise of a lovely day in the air.

Victoria took her eyes off the road briefly. "Did you see this morning's paper?" she asked.

"Should I have?" It seemed as if everyone was bent on telling him about Chandra.

"You had to have heard that your young lady's dating another man," Victoria said carefully.

"Good for her."

His mother tossed another surreptitious glance his way. "I take it that doesn't bother you?"

Beau sighed loudly. "Sure, my ego's taking a beating and I'm disappointed that I could be so easily replaced in her affections, but I'm not heartbroken. I guess it wasn't love."

"Imagine that," Victoria muttered. "A man mistaking lust for love?"

A car tooted behind them. The driver eventually changed lanes.

"Apparently I'm going too slow for him."

Conversation lagged.

Beau brought up the topic again. "You never did like Chandra."

"I didn't dislike her. I just thought you two weren't well suited. May I be frank?"

"Why ruin an impeccable track record?"

"You should be with someone like your therapist. Shayna's got a good sense of self. She's tough but charming. You'd be able to count on her when the chips are down. And she's cute as a button. I just wish I could remember where I'd seen her before."

He and Shayna together? An impossible thought. They'd most likely kill each other after the first couple of dates. Best to say nothing and just let it go.

"Could Shayna have come into your real estate place looking for an apartment?" Beau asked.

Victoria drummed her fingers against the steering wheel. The van swerved. Another car whizzed by them, tooting its horn.

"No, I don't think so. My rentals are pretty pricey." She gazed out the window, making the van veer to the right. The driver in the lane next to them gave her the finger. "No, that face has been in the newspapers, possibly even on television."

When the car in front of them braked, Beau jolted forward. "Keep your eyes on the road, Mother," he cautioned.

Victoria turned and glared at him. "Would you like to drive?"

"No."

"Good, then keep your mouth shut."

"Look," Beau said, "Shayna's brother's in trouble. Dad's the prosecuting attorney. The newspapers and television probably ran pieces on the family, complete with photos. That's probably why you think you've seen Shayna before."

There was a moment of silence while Victoria contemplated. "Which of your father's cases are we talking about?"

Beau repeated what Mohammed had told him.

"You mean that punk Reggie is Shayna's brother? That boy committed a heinous crime. Shayna knows who you are but continues to work with you?"

"I don't know that she does. She's never brought up the case, nor has she said a word about Dad."

"Trust me, as high profile as you and your father are, she's bound to have heard."

"Was," Beau said softly. "I'm no longer high profile."

"Yes, you've turned into chopped liver overnight. Woe is me," Victoria muttered. "Poor Beau."

Beau reined in his temper. Maybe it was time for his mother and him to put some distance between them.

"What would Shayna's motives be for pretending she didn't?" he asked. "Eventually it would have to come out."

"By then my son might have fallen in love with her. He'd be putty in her hands."

"Mother, get off my case."

"We're here," Victoria announced, unperturbed. "Confront your therapist and see what she says. I'll be back to get you in an hour."

Victoria slammed the door of the van after Beau had wheeled himself out.

"I think I'll take a taxi home," Beau muttered.

"Suit yourself," Victoria said, taking off.

* * *

Shayna tapped her foot nervously. She'd been waiting for Beau to get out of that changing room for how long? Knowing she had aquatic therapy scheduled, she'd taken extra special care to select the one-piece bathing suit. Midnight black, and cut high on the thighs, it gave the illusion she had lots of leg.

Shayna smiled. When you were this petite you needed every advantage. Tank suits tended to make her look like a child. She wanted to be taken seriously, to be viewed as a woman. Why was it suddenly so important? Didn't she know who she was?

She tied a towel low on her hips, sarong style, and stretched out on a lounge chair. The pool was hers and Beau's for the next hour, and she planned on putting him to work. He'd been in a strange mood when he'd first arrived and had responded to her greeting tersely. She wondered what that was all about, and had asked if he'd needed help changing, but had been turned down. What on earth had happened to the teasing young man who a couple of nights ago had invited her and Reggie over this Sunday?

Shayna glanced at her watch. Beau was taking an awfully long time to get changed. What was keeping him?

"Beau," Shayna called, "can I do something to help?"

A muffled grunt came from somewhere inside.

"Beau, is something wrong?" Shayna called even louder.

Another muffled expletive wafted its way out. Shayna's heart pounded. Something was definitely wrong.

"I'm coming in on the count of ten," Shayna shouted, starting a slow countdown. "Ten, nine, eight, seven . . ."

More groans. Forget about counting, something

needed to be done. Fifteen minutes had already elapsed since he'd been inside. There would be no one else in the changing room; the place was still theirs for the next forty-five minutes.

"Hold on, Beau," Shayna said, rushing through the curtained entry.

The groans came at her louder now. She picked up her pace. Beau was someplace back there, maybe to the right. She found him facedown on the floor, pants tangled around his ankles.

"Are you hurt, Beau?" she asked, squatting down next to him, and quickly assessing the situation. Determining there had been no harm done to his physical self, she tried to keep a straight face.

He must have lowered his pants, then struggled to get off his pullover. He'd probably leaned forward to remove his sweater and catapulted over. Off to the side his wheelchair sat angled. The scene could have been funny except for the fact that Beau was virtually helpless and sputtering angry words.

Shayna tugged the sweater over his head.

"You didn't answer me. Are you hurt?"

The moment Beau was able to see, he glared at her. Hypnotic gray eyes flashed daggers. "No, I'm not hurt."

"Then you need to thank me," Shayna said when their glances met and held.

"Don't push it."

She'd literally caught him with his pants down. A Kodak moment.

"Need help getting up?"

"I'll manage myself."

A mumbled oath followed, one Shayna chose to ignore. She laid her hand on Beau's bare back. It felt smooth, broad, and muscular, chiseled out of the same stuff

Greek gods were made of. Under his chinos he wore black gym shorts and his legs were covered with smooth dark hairs.

"You need help," she insisted. "And I'm going to get it."

"No. No help."

"I can't pick you up. You're too heavy."

"I said, no. It's embarrassing enough to be found like this."

He was trying his best to roll over, but the tangled material at his ankles got in the way.

"Hold still," Shayna commanded. "Let's at least get your trousers off."

After tugging gently, Shayna was able to get Beau's chinos off. Using his arms to support the bulk of his weight, he was able to half drag, half crawl toward his wheelchair. Shayna, despite feeling awful, couldn't take her eyes off him. The way his arm muscles bulged. The way his washboard stomach was covered with the same curly hair as his legs. Even in this vulnerable position he was tempting as hell. *Help him, Shayna. Help him.*

"Maybe if I pick your legs up, wheelbarrow style," she offered, moving the wheelchair closer.

Beau had somehow managed to seat himself on the floor. "Make sure it's steady," he said, pointing to his chair. "I'll grab on to it and try to hoist myself up."

His muscles had to be aching.

"It would be easier if you'd let me get somebody," Shayna said, checking to make sure the brake was put in position.

"You're the only help I'm accepting," Beau said, grunting and clenching his teeth. Beads of sweat poured down his forehead. "I mean it, Shayna," he said, noticing she'd walked away. He tried to ease himself up. It was impossible.

"Put your arm around me," Shayna commanded, returning and giving in to his request. It would require superhuman effort but she'd try.

With much grunting and groaning, they were finally able to get Beau seated again. In the process Shayna somehow ended up on his lap. She closed her eyes, catching her breath. Every muscle and sinew ached. Her back felt as if a thousand-pound man had been stomping grapes on it. Her neck hurt.

She simply couldn't move and needed to get her equilibrium back. She had her arms around his neck, heard Beau's heavy breathing, smelled sweat mingling with a spicy cologne. Pinpoints of light flashed behind her closed lids. The room tilted. Her breasts brushed against Beau's chest. He stiffened. She heard his sharp intake of breath.

Beau's arms circled her waist. He covered her face with kisses.

"No," Shayna said, trying to get up. But her protest was cut short by another floor-tilting kiss, which made her head spin.

Heat radiated off Beau. There was a pulsing beneath her that reminded her he was still a man, and a very virile one at that. Rough chest hairs grazed her thin lycra suit, creating friction, setting her breasts on fire. Spicy cologne and sweat melded with heat and passion.

Beau is a patient of yours, a little voice reminded her. *This is wrong.*

Then why did his probing kisses feel so right? Why did he have the power to release emotions in her she didn't know existed?

Just give in to the feeling, Shayna. Go with the flow, another voice said.

Beau's hands were on her breasts. A ripple of longing rushed through her as his hungry tongue explored and demanded. Shayna accepted his tongue, joining him in an age-old dance that seemed to promise forever. If only that were the truth.

Kissing Beau was like kissing no other man she'd known before. It was a sensory experience, intimate, yet titillating. She was engaged in artful foreplay. She ignited, sizzled, and burned. Her entire body was on fire. He'd awakened in her a deep desire. But the timing was wrong, the man and place inappropriate.

"Beau," Shayna managed.

"What is it, honey?"

His voice sounded deep, impassioned, throaty.

"We've got to stop."

Had he heard her? The intensity of their kisses increased and his hand slid under the thin material of her bathing suit to stroke an already taut nipple. She groaned. Then good sense kicked in. Shayna fisted her hands and banged against his chest. "Let me go, Beau. Now."

He went deadly still but abruptly released her.

"As you wish."

She knew she had hurt his feelings. Trampled on his ego. But it was for the best. Beau was still a patient of hers.

Chapter Thirteen

Shayna's kisses were like nectar from the gods. Sheer heaven. At first Beau did not register her fisted hands beating a rapid tattoo against his chest. Then he came to realize that the noises he heard were not expressions of passion but gasps of protests. Something was wrong.

No woman had gotten to him as this one had. Not even Chandra, passionate soul that she was. Shayna's kisses were sweet yet sensuous. Her small hands pressed against his chest and her tiny body on his lap made him feel protective and manly. How had it come to this?

Shayna's sharp words penetrated. "Let me go, Beau. Now." He went deadly still. She'd seemed to be enjoying his kisses. His touch. She'd been keeping up with him.

"What's wrong, honey?" Beau asked, holding her slightly away from him.

"I'm not your honey. I'm your therapist," Shayna said churlishly.

"Could have fooled me."

He would never understand women. There she was one minute kissing him as if there would be no tomorrow, now she wanted him to stop.

Shayna slid off his lap and straightened her bathing suit. Her face was still flushed and her eyes slightly glazed from their foreplay. "We've got exactly half an hour left of pool therapy," she said firmly.

"You've got to be kidding?"

"I'm not."

She stalked off. Beau followed more slowly in his wheelchair. He must have done something to turn her off. He couldn't think what. By the time he'd caught up she was speaking into a wall phone.

"I'm going to need one of you to help me get Mr. Hill into the pool," she said to someone on the other end.

How quickly things changed. He was Mr. Hill now. Shayna hung up the receiver, refusing to look him in the eye. He wasn't about to be ignored or put off. He wheeled himself closer.

"You want to tell me what this was about?"

"I've called someone to help get you into the pool. Be sure to hold on to the metal bars at the side when you're in."

Avoidance was going to be her technique. She'd been the person lecturing him about facing up to reality, dealing with what had happened. She'd spoken about moving on, accepting your lot in life and about not becoming complacent. She was the person who'd given him a book to read with motivational quotes like "Yesterday is where it was. . . . Today is where it is. . . . Tomorrow is where it's going to be." Sure looked as though there would be no tomorrow for them.

Beau suddenly felt anger building. How dare she kiss him senseless, then simply brush him aside?

"We need to talk," he said, reaching out for her.

Shayna stepped back, avoiding his reach. "We don't have time to talk."

"Make time. You don't just kiss a man passionately, then order him to stop. You don't get a person going, then expect him to turn it off at a moment's notice. I'm a man, Shayna, a man with needs."

"That you are," she said quietly. "And that's exactly why we had to stop. You're my patient. I almost forgot that. I should never have let it happen."

"So you're saying it was a mistake?" Beau's words were quietly spoken, each word clearly enunciated.

"You can call it that if you'd like. Let's just pretend it never happened." Removing her towel, she dove into the pool.

"Shayna," Beau called, but a loud splash drowned out his words. By the time she surfaced he was shaking with anger. "So that's it then. You dangle the bait at me, offer up your considerable charms, hoping there would be something in this for you. Maybe I'd go home and talk to my dad. One hand washes the other, right?"

Shayna blinked at him and treaded water. Her hair was a sleek wet cap against her head. She looked like one of Neptune's spirits. He wasn't going to bend.

"What can your dad do for me?" she asked.

"Plenty. Your brother's in trouble. My dad's prosecuting the case. You were going to have Reggie volunteer at Hill Of Dreams. Was that a coincidence or had you purposely targeted me? Make Beau want you. Make him believe he can walk again. Have him fall in love with you. Isn't that your game?"

Shayna's mouth opened wide, at first nothing coming out. "You have it wrong," she said quietly, "at least some of it."

Were those real tears in her eyes or was it the effect

of too much chlorine? He waited for her to go on but her attention had already been distracted by the arrival of a burly man with biceps the size of tree trunks. He hurried their way.

"Is this the patient you need help with?" he asked.

"Yes," Shayna said, all business now.

Before Beau could protest he was scooped up and gently deposited in the water next to Shayna. The man did not release him until he was certain he had his balance and a good hold on the bars running around the pool.

"Can I let go?" he asked.

Beau nodded.

"You need anything else, Ms. Shayna?" the man asked, as if she were a goddess and he'd do anything she commanded.

"Thanks for your help. That will be all."

Shayna had that effect on men. This one looked as if she'd wrapped him around her little finger. Thank God he'd found out she was just using him before it was too late. Before he'd done something stupid like fallen in love with her.

After the aide left, Beau faced Shayna. He compartmentalized his emotions and simply followed instructions. All his concentration needed to be focused on walking again. Perhaps she wouldn't think he was a toy to be used and discarded if he were able to walk again. He would then deal with her on equal footing.

The micro brewery was crowded, considering the time of day. A smattering of professionals were hunched on bar stools or crowded into booths. A few blue-collar types tossed back beers while debating the pluses of one political candidate over another.

Beau faced Joshua Vanderhorn across the table. Other than going back and forth to therapy and his visit to Hill Of Dreams, it was his first venture out of the house. He was disoriented and more than a little taken aback by how foreign everything looked.

The last time he'd been to this bar/restaurant he'd come in on his own two feet, planted himself at the bar, and drunk his share of Anchor Steam. Now the beer he sipped, mild as it was, had already gone to his head. He found himself really having to focus.

Thank God you're not driving, he thought wryly, and put down the remaining brew.

Joshua was busy eyeing a shapely redhead that was jammed into too-tight jeans and a cropped top. She wore a cowboy hat on her head. *Old Josh must be looking for a distraction,* Beau thought. *This one isn't the debutante type.* Josh had strolled in dressed in a double-breasted blue jacket and crisp striped shirt, the collar open at the neck. His sharply creased jeans and Bally loafers only added to his look of rich boy out to play. He'd high-fived Beau, inquired about his health, then rambled on about his trip to Europe and about the upcoming ski events.

"Check out those babes," Josh said, eyeing the redhead's more than ample bosom. "Think young Vanderhorn still has what it takes?"

Beau shook his head. "You never know until you try." Beau wished he was up to finishing his beer. An hour with Joshua would be all he could take. He'd instructed his sister to get him promptly, and hopefully Kelly would do just that.

Joshua beamed at him from over the rim of his glass. "I miss you, guy. You're my bud." He raised his glass and sipped on amber beer. "Here's to a speedy recovery. Heard from anyone on the ski team lately?"

Beau frowned. It had been a while since he had. Right after the accident the phone hadn't stop ringing. Everyone had called or sent cards. Some of the guys had even come by to see him, but little by little they'd melted away.

Beau accepted responsibility for driving them off. He'd been angry, and at times downright rude. Abusive and difficult to get along with, some might call it. That reminded him he'd forgotten to send flowers to Immaculata and Shayna. He needed to take care of that business. Soon.

He was still mad at Shayna but couldn't discount that her work had been effective so far. While his legs still didn't work she'd gotten him to the point where he could leave his home and begin assimilating into society again. Mentally he felt better. That, in and of itself, was a major accomplishment.

"So who's called you?" Joshua probed.

What a persistent bugger.

"Several of the fellows," Beau said evasively.

"Peter Turner by chance? I heard he has an interesting tale to tell."

Joshua checked out the redhead again. He caught her eye and smiled encouragingly. Beau found he needed another sip of beer after all. He sat back prepared to listen.

"Do you remember the day we had breakfast together? We'd just completed our practice run," Josh said.

"Sure I do. The entire ski team went to eat in one of those coffee shops in Olympic Village."

"It was packed inside. We left our equipment out front. Your skis, boots, goggles, and poles were next to mine."

"Were they?"

So much of the day had been a blur. He'd awakened early, headed to the slopes with the rest of the guys, and completed his run in record time. Everyone had been excited at the thought of him winning. He'd waited for the rest of the guys to get done and they'd all headed to the coffee shop for a quick bite.

His stomach had been in knots. He'd been wound so tight thinking of the challenge ahead that he could barely choke down a coffee and muffin. The thought of bringing home gold for himself and the United States had had him pumped.

Joshua's voice broke through the memories. "Peter says he'd forgotten his wallet in his car. When he went out to retrieve it, there was a strange guy nosing around. He describes him as having a lantern jaw." Joshua's blue eyes twinkled. "Wonder who that could be?"

Joshua's Colgate smile was wasted on Beau. Better to save it for the redhead that was now ogling him. "Peter says he called to the guy, thinking he was contemplating stealing something. Fans do that sometimes, you know. Wait a minute, hasn't Peter told you this?" Joshua asked.

Peter hadn't. He'd come to the hospital to see Beau on more than one occasion but he hadn't been up to having visitors. Beau had made a mental note to call Peter. This time he planned on following through.

"How come this is surfacing again?" Beau asked Joshua.

Joshua shrugged. "Hey, I've been bumming around Europe. I'm just catching up on all the gossip. Could Lars Schmitt have sabotaged you? He did end up winning."

Beau wondered why Joshua was so interested. He'd placed second and was probably soured and resentful of the winner. Like most people he had an agenda. But Beau was no longer competition, so why would he care?

"What happened to your equipment?" Joshua asked.

"I don't know." After the accident Beau hadn't thought much about equipment. He hadn't really cared. All he'd thought about was that his life had ended, that the sport that he lived and breathed for was no more. Beau made a mental note to have David contact his coach and ask where his equipment was. He wanted to take a look at his boots especially.

"You've given me a lot to think about," Beau said, spotting Kelly heading their way. He reached into his pants pocket and pulled out his wallet.

"I got it," Joshua said, moving the check out of his reach. "This one's on me. Stay in touch. Let me know if you find anything out."

"Sure thing," Beau said, preparing to wheel himself off. Why was it all of a sudden so important to Joshua that they keep in touch?

"Beau," Joshua called after him.

He turned his head. "Yes?"

"I'm sorry you got publicly dumped. Such a shame to have your fiancée flaunt another man in your face, especially Euro-trash. It must hurt to be replaced by the heir to the Bellissima fortune."

Beau decided it wasn't worthy of a response. He wheeled himself in the direction of his sister.

"I'm sorry if I made you mad," Joshua shouted after him.

Beau pretended not to hear him.

"You've got a delivery here at the front desk," the receptionist announced loudly into the phone.

Shayna thanked the woman and hung up. She wasn't expecting a package and right now Gail Mahoney, her next patient, was waiting.

"Sorry, Gail, come on in," Shayna called.

Gail hobbled toward her. The old lady was making terrific progress and had replaced her walker with a cane.

They worked up until lunchtime with Shayna putting Gail through a series of exercises.

"Timmy met a young woman," Gail said when she was done. "You're a better choice."

She was at it again.

"Oh, Gail, you should be happy for him."

"What about that Beaumont Hill?" the old lady persisted. "Are you still working with him? He's cute."

Shayna mumbled something unintelligible and quickly switched the topic.

After she'd said good-bye to Gail, she changed into gym shorts and a tank top and decided to go power walking. She'd pick up her delivery at the front desk on her way back.

Half an hour later, Shayna greeted the receptionist with the elaborately upswept hair. "You've got a delivery for Shayna DaCosta?"

"Dunno," the woman said, chomping loudly on her gum.

"Can you check?"

Shayna wondered who her boss was and made a mental note to find out. She clearly needed polish and was the wrong image for Denver Rehabilitation. In fact she was the wrong person to have at a reception desk.

The receptionist bent over in a too-short skirt and retrieved a basket at her feet. She shoved it at Shayna. "You must have a boyfriend with big bucks. That little nosegay had to have cost a bundle." Chomp, chomp, went the disgusting gum again.

Shayna admired the white wicker basket with colorful tulips artfully arranged. Flowers were the last thing she'd expected. She was apprehensive about what this meant. But rather than being pleased and excited she remained wary. She had a sinking feeling in the pit of her stomach that Colin had clearly not gotten the message.

"Aren't you going to read the card?" the receptionist probed.

"Maybe later."

Carrying the basket, Shayna headed off. She'd have to figure out some diplomatic way of dealing with Colin's persistence.

In the hallway she ran into Mary Jane Coppola.

"Hi," the chipper nurse said. "You got one too." She pointed to Shayna's overflowing basket.

"I'm sorry?"

"Beau's gift. Wasn't that nice of him, and so unexpected? He wrote the sweetest note."

Beau sending them flowers? Just the thought made her heart go thump. He'd said some pretty ugly things about her and maybe this was his way of making up. He'd accused her of withholding information, of using him to help her brother's cause. And he had been right. Once she'd found out about his father, she should have been up front and told him about Reggie.

Shayna looked at her flowers again. The fact that it had been Beau and not Colin made them seem more special. How sweet, he'd thought enough of her to send her flowers. She wondered what his note would say. Would he mention anything about their shared kisses or would he just apologize?

Mary Jane's voice came at her. "Beaumont Hill is the stuff dreams are made of. That prickly exterior is all a front. Just think, some lucky woman, and I hope it's not Chandra, will get to come home to him at night." She sighed. "Wish it were me."

The thought of coming home to Beau wasn't entirely unpleasant. Too bad she wasn't free to pursue him. Any personal involvement would place tremendous stress on the patient/therapist relationship. It already did. Emotions would run high, getting in the way of progress. Then there was the other issue. Her brother was about to be prosecuted by Beau's father. Better not even think about it.

"Shayna, don't you find Beau at all attractive?" Mary Jane asked when she hadn't responded.

"Very much so."

"And now that he's available, are you going to do something about it? You have been reading the paper?"

The only papers she'd been reading were back copies, articles about Beau.

"Why don't you go after him," Shayna challenged, "if you think he's so hot?"

"No. You're more his type. Judging by Chandra, he likes them young and skinny."

"Oh, Mary Jane."

Shayna walked away laughing but something niggled at the back of her mind. There had been something in one of those articles that had gotten her thinking. She made a mental note to reread the articles later. Right now she had more important things to do, like reading Beau's note.

Chapter Fourteen

The weather was unseasonably warm. Beau planted himself on his terrace preparing to enjoy the late afternoon sun. Closing his eyes, he listened to the horses neighing from the vicinity of the stables. How he missed riding, missed the wind whipping against his face, the feeling of exhilaration when his horse cantered.

The fragrance of an unidentifiable flower floated in the breeze, titillating his nostrils, along with Towanda's cooking. Beau suddenly realized that he was hungry. He'd sworn off snacks since too much lounging around had already caused him to put on weight. To distract himself, he grabbed his cell phone, and deftly punched out some numbers, then abruptly changed his mind. Depressing the power button, he closed his eyes and decided not to give in to curiosity. Shayna should be the one calling to thank him for the flowers.

Beau had come to the conclusion that although she'd omitted telling him about her brother it was hardly a crime. He could get over her deception if that's what it was. It wouldn't be the first time a woman had deceived him. Look how he'd been taken in by Chandra.

Reggie was just a kid, a troubled boy who needed direction and should be given a shot. It wouldn't hurt to have him work at Hill Of Dreams. That way Beau could see how dedicated the kid really was and maybe he'd even see more of Shayna .

The phone rang as he was still holding on to it.

"Yes," Beau greeted.

"Beau, is that you?"

The man's voice wasn't familiar. Beau hesitated to confirm who he was. Reporters still called on occasion. "Who's this?" he asked somewhat rudely.

A midwestern voice twanged at him. "This is Peter Turner, a friend of Beau's. We skied together."

"Hi, Peter, this is Beau."

The requisite questions about health and family were exchanged.

"So what else is up?" Beau asked, when the conversation lagged.

"I hoped we could talk in person. Perhaps I can stop by and catch you up. There are a couple of things I want to discuss with you."

"How does Sunday sound?"

Sunday was the day Shayna and Reggie were supposed to come by. Having a crowd over would take the stress off being alone with them. He could always take Reggie off somewhere and talk to him in private. He would invite David to join them as well.

"Sunday, it is," Peter confirmed. "What time would you like me there?"

"How does three sound? Come an hour earlier than my other guests and we'll talk."

Before disconnecting the call, Beau gave Peter directions.

Beau's fingers massaged his temples. A headache was on the horizon, he could feel it. He closed his eyes, contemplating what Peter must want. Why was everyone all of a sudden so anxious to share information with him? It had been months since the accident. Now everyone wanted to talk. The phone rang almost immediately. Forget about lying out and enjoying the sun.

"Hello," Beau barked, his impatience obvious.

"Hi, I got your flowers," Shayna said.

He was suddenly wide-awake and focused, elated actually. "Were the tulips in good shape?" Beau asked carefully.

"Perfect. Thank you."

It sounded so matter-of-fact. She hadn't even said she enjoyed them. "Will you and Reggie be able to make it this Sunday?" he asked.

There was a moment of hesitation on the other end. "I wasn't certain we were still invited."

"Of course you are. I thought you'd enjoy riding the horses and later on we'd barbecue. I'm having a couple of other people over. Reggie and I can sneak away and talk after we've eaten."

Why did he sound so anxious? Needy? Nervous? Why was it so important that Shayna come?

"Are you still angry with me?" she ventured.

Maybe that was what this was all about. The phone call was to test the waters, see if he'd gotten over being upset with her.

"I'm not pleased that you withheld information," Beau said. "But I'm over it. Let's talk about it more in person."

"You did say four, right? We'll be there."

When the conversation ended, Beau found that his

hands were clammy. He'd been on pins and needles the entire time. It had gone way beyond just wanting to see Shayna. He needed her in his life.

Sunday started off rainy and got worse. Shayna managed to get Reggie to church, which in and of itself was a feat. Returning, she placed her wet, open umbrella in the vestibule, while Reggie raced in flopping his damp body in front of the TV.

"Don't even think about putting your feet on the couch," Shayna snapped, as she went off to find something dry to change into. Riding later that day didn't seem a remote possibility unless the rain let up.

Shayna stared into her crowded closet wondering what would be appropriate to wear. Finally she selected jeans and a button-down shirt. If the rain held up she'd wear her boots and the beautiful black leather jacket her parents had sent as an early gift for her birthday.

"Hey, Shayna," Reggie called from downstairs. "How much time are we spending at Beau Hill's?"

"A couple of hours at least. Beau mentioned something about a barbecue afterward."

"Oh, man. Just what I need."

Shayna could hear Reggie stomping around downstairs. She walked out to the landing and peeked over the railing. Reggie, sneakered feet and all, lay lounged on the couch. His one concession to getting dressed for church, his sharp-looking dress pants, were now rumpled. The phone was pressed to his ear and he was yakking nonstop.

"What's the problem?" Shayna called down.

"The guys are getting together to play ball. I need to know when I'll be back."

"Better forget about a game today. Getting hired by

Beau Hill is more important," Shayna said more curtly than she intended.

"Says who?"

Shayna decided to ignore him. She retraced her steps and began laying clothing on the bed. If she wore a jaunty scarf at the neck, it would pick up the outfit and she'd be western chic. That thought made her smile. She was really looking forward to seeing Beau. Maybe the weather would change and they would have that barbecue after all.

Her selection made, she found the folder with the articles about Beau and curled up on her bed. The first magazine had detailed bios of the world's top skiers. Beau's bio was particularly interesting. She hadn't known that he was a college graduate with a major in business. She eagerly read about his involvement in community activities as well as his reason for creating Hill Of Dreams.

Even the numerous downhill events he'd won had all been detailed. He'd been a World Cup winner, won medals at the Winter Goodwill Games, and was considered a very gifted athlete with the ability to make panicfree, on-course decisions, at terrifying speeds. The reporter had also listed his love of horseback riding and mentioned that he spent a lot of his off time teaching disadvantaged kids how to ride. Good for Beau.

Flipping the page, Shayna focused on the biography of the winner, Lars Schmitt. He'd been born in Berlin but educated in California. He was considered a competent skier but Beau was considered the athlete most likely to perform under pressure. Beau was the more consistent skier and the one with style. Lars's hobby was chess. Off the slopes Lars had a reputation for being a renegade.

The other American skier, Joshua Vanderhorn, had

come in second. Joshua's ancestors had come over on the Mayflower. He was the product of old money and had almost literally been born on skis. He'd gone to school in Switzerland and had a reputation for being a fast talker and an international playboy. He'd done well at Vail, placing a respectable third. Somewhere, Shayna had read that Joshua had been involved in a major scandal. The family had successfully hushed it up but it had something to do with date rape.

Another American, Peter Turner, was considered a good skier but had never been a top contender. He was, however, considered an excellent tactician, astute in knowing when to apply pressure to the skis, and when to relax.

Jan Ericksson had been the skier who'd finished third. He was one of the more popular athletes. His infectious dedication and competitiveness had at last paid off, yielding him a spot on the podium. Little was known about his personal life except for the fact that his wife was a champion skater.

In Shayna's opinion either Lars or Joshua could be suspect. But would they risk a man's life for the sake of Olympic gold? Stupid question. She more than anyone knew how fiercely competitive the athletes were. When she'd competed she'd been the topic of ugly rumors that had been gleefully relayed back to her. She was allegedly sleeping with the coach who'd been giving her pointers. It had gone on and on. The goal being to break her concentration, have her perform poorly. Then there was that ugly scandal several years back when one skater's bodyguard camouflaged as a mugger and whacked the competition on the knee. Athletes did indeed go to incredible lengths to win.

Whenever Shayna missed being in the spotlight she reminded herself of the supreme sacrifice she'd made to get there. She'd given up her girlhood. Training had become all consuming. Gymnastics had been everything. She sure didn't miss getting up at the wee hours of the morning, starving herself to the point of anorexia just to maintain an acceptable weight, pushing herself to the point of exhaustion. It had been a lonely and unhappy life and her teammates had had more than their share of physical and emotional problems.

But she did have one thing to thank competitive gymnastics for, her fighting spirit still remained. She felt deep in her gut that Beau's fall had been no accident. That it needed to be investigated. She'd been surprised that he'd so willingly let it go. But a couple of months ago he hadn't been in the mental or physical shape to demand an investigation, or conduct one of his own. Now that he'd made incredible progress, would he be motivated to find out what really happened?

Promising herself to take the matter up with Beau, Shayna continued to read.

Beau waited for Peter in the den. He watched as his teammate's long strides narrowed the distance between them.

"It's been too long," Peter greeted, doing his best not to show how much the sight of Beau in a wheelchair bothered him.

"Much too long."

"It's been months." Peter grasped the hand Beau offered and shook it vigorously. He folded himself into a nearby chair.

The den was one of Beau's favorite rooms. It was open and comfortable. Considering he wasn't much of a reader, books spilled from floor-to-ceiling cases and huge ficus plants created private nooks for those seeking places to curl up with a book.

"Why did you want to see me?" Beau asked, cutting to the chase.

Peter crossed one lean leg over the other. "A couple of things have bothered me for a while."

"Yes, go on."

"Guys, can I get you anything?" Beau's sister Kelly interrupted. She wore jeans and a comfortable-looking sweatshirt. She clutched a can of Coke in one hand. It never ceased to amaze Beau how youthful she looked. Anyone would think she was in her teens as opposed to her thirties.

"I'd love some water," Peter answered.

"Same for me," Beau confirmed.

"I'll be right back. . . ."

Beau suppressed his amusement as Peter openly admired Kelly's denim-clad behind. His sister's bobbing blond ponytail swished as she went off to do their bidding.

"She wouldn't by chance be single?" Peter asked, when Kelly was out of earshot.

"Sorry to disappoint you. She's not."

Kelly was back within minutes carrying a pitcher of water and two glasses. She set the tray down on the coffee table and gave Peter the benefit of her golden smile. "Anything else, gentlemen?"

"N-nn—o, thank you," the skier stuttered. "Beau?"

"I'm all right."

Peter poured water and handed a glass to Beau. He sipped his own water and looked around the room before setting his glass down. "I don't know exactly how to say this."

"Just say it."

Why did he seem so edgy and uncomfortable? He continued to look everywhere except at Beau.

Choosing words carefully, he began. "It's like this, word has it that someone was paid big bucks to put you out of commission."

"Why would someone want to do that?"

"For the same reason that skater had her knee banged in. They're envious and want to eliminate competition. If they paid someone to tamper with your bindings, you wouldn't have a chance of winning."

Beau shook his head trying to compute what Peter was saying. So many people had tried to tell him it was not an accident but he'd refused to listen. "Why would someone intentionally want to hurt me? I don't have any enemies I know of."

"They may have miscalculated, never anticipating you'd be so seriously hurt." Peter was doing everything to avoid looking at Beau in his wheelchair.

"Sounds like you know more than you're letting on," Beau said dryly while eyeing Peter speculatively. "Spill it, man. Are you confessing?" The last was said jokingly.

Peter shifted uneasily in his seat. "I'd never pull something like that, Beau. I'm only repeating what I hear."

"Then speculate with me."

Beau's whole body had tensed up. There was that tingling in his legs again. Except this time it was so intense he feared he might spasm. Why was that happening? He'd meant to talk to his doctor about it, speak with Shayna, maybe. He'd never gotten around to it.

"Come on, man," Beau urged. "Talk to me."

Peter bent in closer. "I heard. . ."

The doorbell chose that inopportune moment to ring. Beau cursed softly, then said, "Talk about bad timing. Looks like more company's here. This will have to hold until later." He moved his chair into position and headed for the door.

"Who are you expecting?" Peter called after him. "Anyone from the ski team?"

"No. Just David, my agent, and Shayna, my physical therapist, and her little brother. Kelly will be joining us, of course, and I invited Mohammed, who manages Hill Of Dreams. My mom might also stop by."

"What about your dad?"

"He's out of town working on a case. Will you stick around until after the barbecue? We can have a more in-depth discussion then."

Peter screwed up his face, seeming to debate. "Normally I would love to, but I have a first date. I want to make a good impression so I'd better be on time. I'll call you and we'll set up another time to talk."

"Let's do that, soon, huh?"

The doorbell jingled again.

Kelly shouted, "I'll get it," at the same time rushing to the door.

The conversation was placed on hold, temporarily. But Beau was left with a sense of frustration. Frustration with the situation. Frustration with himself. Ever since the injury he'd allowed his world to stop while he wallowed in self-pity. So many people had tried to tell him that his accident was no accident, but he hadn't wanted to believe them. It was still hard to believe that someone would intentionally want to hurt him.

Hats off to Shayna for giving him a purpose in life again, in getting him mentally back on track. His self-esteem had risen and with it his fighting spirit had returned. He needed to get his hands on that equipment, examine his boots and skis for himself. He would ask David to take care of that.

David breezed in, Kelly on his heels. His agent had

brought an attractive brunette with him. He introduced her all around.

"This is Alia, everybody."

Peter rose to greet Alia while Beau smiled and waved. She was a petite delicate type, a little taller than Shayna. She had a big wide smile and a warm way about her.

"I've heard so much about you," she said, approaching Beau, hand outstretched.

Beau took the delicate palm she offered. "I trust it's been all good."

"Absolutely," David said, interjecting, and presenting Beau with an envelope. "Your fan mail," he explained.

The doorbell jingled again. The tingling sensation Beau felt in his legs found a home in his arms as well. He was on pins and needles, anxious to see Shayna again.

While Kelly headed for the door, Beau sipped his water. He listened distractedly to Peter and David's conversation. They were talking about the athletes they knew. He sensed Shayna's presence even before she stood before him. Then he smelled her heavenly perfume. She had that surly brother with her.

Shayna's looks were a sharp contrast from Kelly's freshly scrubbed, girl-next-door appearance. But Beau knew that under that cinnamon skin and wide-eyed appeal hid a sexy vixen. While she might look like a cute teenager, she didn't act like a teenager. And she sure didn't kiss like a cute teenager.

"I brought you this," she said, holding out a foil-covered tray to Beau. "Where should I put it?"

"What is it?" Beau asked.

"Brownies. Baked from scratch."

"Yum," Kelly added, "I'll be glad to take them from you."

True to her word, she relieved Shayna of her tray and

immediately lifted the foil, helping herself to one of the heavenly smelling baked goods.

"Anyone else want one?" she asked, offering the tray around.

Peter was the only one to accept. Beau watched in amusement as he flirted with Kelly. He wasn't worried. Kelly would expertly ward off any unwelcome advances. He'd seen her in action before.

Reggie still hadn't opened his mouth. He stood by watching them awkwardly.

"Have a seat," Beau invited, gesturing to one of the comfortable overstuffed chairs.

"First you say hello to everyone," Shayna said, nudging Reggie forward.

Reluctantly he greeted everyone before flopping onto the vacant chair. Big chip on that boy's shoulder, Beau decided. But in many ways Reggie reminded him of himself. When he'd first come to live with the Andersons he'd been in such pain. He'd still been inwardly grieving for his parents but was afraid to cry. Afraid that it would make him appear less of a man. So he'd been surly, obnoxious, and difficult to deal with. Even after the Andersons had adopted him, he'd steadfastly refused to change his last name. It was his legacy, the only thing left of his parents.

"You're looking well," he said to Shayna, who'd taken a seat next to him.

"You don't look so bad yourself. Love the shirt."

He was wearing one of his favorite designers. Hilfiger.

"You look good, period," she continued, smiling at him. Immediately his mood lightened. This afternoon would be fun after all.

"Ready to go riding?" Beau asked Reggie when he noticed the boy was making no effort to join the conversation.

Reggie grunted something unintelligible.

"Why don't we all go riding?" Beau said to no one in particular.

"You're going riding?" Kelly asked, entering the conversation. She set down the tray of brownies on a side table. "This I have to see." She was over treating him with kid gloves.

"Yes, I think I am."

"Interesting." Kelly looked from Beau to Shayna and back again. It appeared she knew a secret.

Shayna placed a hand on Beau's forearm. "Riding's therapeutic. Remind me to tell you how working with horses helped me."

Beau covered the hand on his forearm. "I will," he said, staring at her until she blushed.

The connection was broken when David cleared his throat. "Alia and I will pass," he said. "We'll fire up the barbecue and by the time you guys get back we'll be ready to eat. How about you help us, Peter?"

"I'll gladly act as your sous chef," Peter offered, looking at Kelly as if that wasn't all he had in mind.

"Good. I've got things to attend to," Kelly added. "You three have fun."

"Get one of the guys to bring Vodka, Scotch, and Whiskey around," Beau directed.

Kelly danced off, eyes sparkling. She turned back to glance at Shayna and Beau briefly. Beau could tell she was dying to tell her secret.

Chapter Fifteen

Shayna was surprised at the rapport Beau had with his horses. As everyone watched, he carefully approached from the side, stroking them reverently and whispering softly in their ears. All three seemed delighted to see him, snorting and neighing, vying for Beau's full attention.

She'd read somewhere that coming up directly on a horse was not advisable. Horses had peripheral vision and a head-on approach might spook them. But the obvious trust between owner and equines was hard to miss. Scotch, Vodka, and Whiskey were crazy about Beau.

Bowing their heads, the horses nuzzled him. Beau continued to stroke their manes while cooing at them softly. Shayna was relieved to see the parking brake on his wheelchair was secured or he would have rolled away.

"Hey, bud," Beau said to Reggie. "Come closer, let me show you where my babies like to be rubbed."

Reggie, looking as if he would rather be anyplace but here, was coerced into touching and stroking the horses. Beau told him that even the way one groomed a horse was essential in establishing trust.

Shayna was curious as to how he knew so much about horses. She remembered reading that one of his favorite pastimes was teaching disadvantaged kids how to ride. A versatile, caring person her Beau was turning out to be.

Her Beau! Perish the thought.

"Okay, how about we get in a good forty minutes of riding?" he said.

Shayna nodded her agreement. It had been a long time since she'd been on a horse. Too long. She'd be sore tomorrow.

After some strategizing, Beau let David and Peter hoist him out of his chair and onto Vodka. Shayna, with some assistance, mounted Scotch, and Reggie, who initially refused help, was eventually seated atop Whiskey.

All three horses postured restlessly. They snorted and salivated, tossing their heads from side to side. Shayna wondered if they were being ridden regularly. But she assumed Beau must have that worked out with the stable hands. It wasn't as if he'd been home much, even before the accident.

After Vodka, Scotch, and Whiskey were stroked, soothed, and calmed down, they set off. The threesome trotted down a winding path amid flurries of "Have fun," Beau leading the way.

It was no longer raining, but the soil underfoot was moist, and damp leaves brushed against Shayna's face and arms. For a while no one spoke, and the occasional snort of a horse was the only sound penetrating the

quiet. Shayna followed Beau, staring at his broad back
with its rippling muscles, and his strong column of neck.
His sinewy thigh muscles were what women dreamed
of having wrapped around theirs. He sat tall and proud,
an extension of his horse. A beautiful extension. Shayna's entire body pulsed. Who would believe Beau was
no longer able-bodied?

Reggie rode even farther ahead of them, still gamely
holding on, his entire body flopping from side to side.
Her brother seemed awed by the newness of his riding
experience, but so far he was behaving, and that was all
she asked for.

In the air was an incredible smell of newness. Spring
on the verge of summer. They crunched their way down
another leaf-strewn path and Shayna finally relaxed. She
gave in to the feeling of the horse beneath her and
quickly got used to sitting up high. Silently she began
to count the numbers of Russian Olives they passed. It
was times like these she wished life wasn't so complicated. Why did Beau have to be her patient? Why did
her brother have to be in trouble? And why did Beau's
father have to be the prosecuting attorney? Why? Nothing ever made sense.

Shayna continued to stare at Beau. Beautiful Beau.
Temperamental Beau. Beau whom she loved. The
thought jolted her. When did this happen?

Get off the thought, Shayna. Stick to safe.

"What made you take up horseback riding?" she
called to him, her voice catching in the breeze.

Beau slowed his horse down and slanted her a look
over his shoulder. His shaved dome gleamed with moisture from exerting muscles that hadn't been used in a
while. The gold earring glistened. He smiled at her. A
perfect smile. One that went straight to her heart. All
reservations were immediately placed on hold.

"Probably for the same reason I took up skiing. I didn't have a choice, I was made to," he answered.

"But you're a natural on horseback. It's so obvious you love your horses." She'd caught up with him and they simply stared at each other.

"Had you fooled, didn't I?" Beau said lightly, flashing another wicked grin. "I used to be petrified of horses. They were these huge, intimidating, uncontrollable beasts, I thought." He patted Vodka affectionately. The horse neighed. "Hey, Reg, how you doing?"

Her brother was aggressively charging ahead, forcing his horse to canter.

"I'm managing," he threw over his shoulder.

Barely, Shayna thought, suppressing a grin. Her brother was actually hanging on to Whiskey, letting the horse choose its own path. She could tell behind the brave response lay a terrified child who was simply acting out. Reggie was a whole lot of bluster. An overgrown piece of mush.

"Sit up straight, and get control of your reins," Beau snapped, while demonstrating what he wanted Reggie to do. At that exact moment a cat darted from the underbrush directly into Whiskey's path. The horse was spooked. It railed, then bolted. Reggie's calls for help filled the air. Beau galloped after him, his horse's hooves splattering mud everywhere.

Shayna listened to Reggie's terrified cries for help and Beau's equally loud calls for him to stay calm and hang on. Beau assured him he was on the way. But what if he was thrown? Beau couldn't afford another injury.

"Easy, boy. Easy," Beau soothed, catching up with Whiskey.

It had all happened in a split second. Whiskey bolting, Beau shouting instructions to Reggie, repeating them over and over. Yet her brother had seemed incapable of hearing. All systems had shut down.

Beau was alongside Reggie now, taking charge of the reins. Shayna closed her eyes. *Please, God, let it be all right.* When she opened them again Beau had both horses under control. Thank God.

Shayna cantered toward them. Up close Reggie's pallor was gray and a thin sheen of sweat beaded his forehead and upper lip. He'd been nervous about mounting a horse to begin with. Now that one had actually bolted, how would he handle the rest of the ride?

"Take a couple of deep breaths," Beau instructed. "You're all in one piece. There's been no real harm done. Horses get spooked, you'll have to learn to work with them."

"What are you, some expert?" Reggie snapped.

"Reggie," Shayna admonished. "Beau just saved your butt. The appropriate response would be thank you."

"Thank you," the teenager reluctantly added.

"Ride ahead," Beau ordered, out of the corner of his mouth. "I'll handle this."

Shayna bristled. Why was he dismissing her? She was on his side. She'd insisted he receive the respect he deserved. Served her right for taking Beau's side over her brother's.

The two males began an intense conversation behind her. Shayna couldn't make out the words but sensed the discussion was direct. Heated. Honest. Eventually they seemed to work out whatever it was and had apparently found common ground. She couldn't imagine what they were talking about. Beau was not into basketball as far as she knew. When fifteen minutes elapsed and they still lagged behind, Shayna brought her horse to a full stop and let Scotch graze.

Deep male laughter came from behind her. She'd never understand men.

"Care to share the joke?" she asked, as the men approached.

"Nope, it's private. Male bonding, right, Beau?" Reggie answered.

"Right."

Whatever Beau had said had been the right thing. Reggie's hostility had eroded.

"Well, we sure worked up a good appetite," Beau announced, cantering up to her. "Barbecue certainly sounds good about now. That and a nice stiff drink. How are you holding up?"

In spite of Reggie's recent crisis Beau seemed relaxed and carefree. He obviously loved being outdoors. Loved an adrenaline rush. Shayna could only imagine if he was this exhilarated pursuing a runaway horse what he must have been like on the slopes. She was suddenly determined that he would not only walk again, but he would ski. She would push him.

Feeling more secure now, Reggie cantered ahead of them. He now held the reins the way Beau instructed. "Catch me if you can," he taunted.

"Not a chance, champ," Beau said playfully, deliberately slowing his horse down and allowing Reggie to take the lead. He slanted a look at Shayna. "I'm glad you came."

"I wanted to be here."

"Could have fooled me."

She blushed. "Yes, I know, I should have told you about Reggie earlier. But I wanted to challenge myself that I could still work with you. And yes, I admit there was some deviousness involved. I felt that if you got to know my brother you would know he could never commit that heinous crime."

"Understood and forgiven." Beau reached across and squeezed her shoulder. "There's something even better that came from our association."

"And what would that be?"

"I got to know you."

She didn't want to go there. Not yet. Not while he was still her patient. The house loomed ahead, thank God. Shayna quickly switched the conversation. Beau told her that Reggie had agreed to start working at Hill Of Dreams twice a week after school, and one day on the weekend. Beau had promised he would be there the first couple of times to put him through the ropes.

Shayna calculated. The trial was in three weeks. By then Reggie and Beau should have cemented their relationship. Would three weeks give enough time for her brother to prove he was a committed teenager? Would Beau have had time to bond with him? Would he feel comfortable enough to share his impressions of Reggie with his father?

Shayna was about to put voice to her fears when she realized they were in front of the house. Managing to keep her voice low, she jutted her chin in Reggie's direction. "How did you work this miracle?"

"It wasn't that difficult. I told Reggie that he and I are similar. I shared a little of my life before the Andersons adopted me. Like him I was rebellious and could easily have ended up in jail. A few anecdotes hit home."

The conversation lagged when two stable hands came forward and the two men and Reggie helped Beau from Vodka. Shayna gracefully managed dismounting on her own. Beau seemed pleased.

The party had already moved out back, and the fixings for a barbecue were set up on a long table on the patio. Kelly had chosen festive yellows and blues for the settings: blue plates, yellow napkins, and a mixture of yellow and blue cutlery. Potted yellow tulips were strategically placed in corners and on the round table where they would eat.

Shayna sniffed the spicy aroma of barbecuing beef. She eyed tables filled with mouthwatering salads, breads, corn on the cob, portabello mushrooms, and chicken, eagerly. There were even cherry tomatoes. She was starving and hadn't eaten since breakfast. The housekeeper, Towanda, added a heaping platter of small foil-wrapped objects to the table and Shayna's stomach growled. Roasted potatoes. Yum, yum.

"Hungry?" Beau asked, wheeling himself up alongside her and giving her another devastating grin.

"Starving," she admitted.

"Good. While Towanda continues to set up, how about I get you a drink?"

She followed him in the direction of a custom-made mosaic bar in the same attractive blue and yellow as the settings. A fire had been lit in the open fireplace and the smoky smell of spruce scented the air. Red and yellow sparks shot up the chimney, some actually settling on the tiled floor, raining down on Reggie and Kelly, who warmed themselves in front of the fire. The two sat cross-legged, totally engrossed in conversation. Peter hovered on the outskirts, with eyes only for Kelly. Shayna hoped the drink at Reggie's side held nothing more potent than soda. She wouldn't put it past her brother to try to get over.

Beau's mom had arrived while they were gone and was busy inspecting the spread. Upon occasion she uttered commands to Towanda. She greeted her son with an enthusiastic kiss, and warmly embraced Shayna.

"Nice to see you again. Thanks for taking such good care of my Beau."

"Just doing my job," Shayna said, avoiding Victoria's knowing eyes.

Victoria reached over, tilting Shayna's chin. She stared at her intently. "When are you going to tell him?" she said in a voice only loud enough for Shayna to hear.

"I'm sorry. I don't understand."

Victoria must have decided to let whatever it was go. "You are lovely," she said. "Exceptionally so, and familiar looking, I might add. I wish I could remember who you remind me of."

Shayna's eyes grew full. She wasn't quite ready for a walk down memory lane. She was still trying to cope with her feelings for Beau. It wasn't as though she'd done anything extraordinary for him. She'd treated him like any other patient. No, that wasn't exactly true. She hadn't kissed other patients the way she'd kissed him. And yes, she'd made him work harder. Oftentimes pushing him beyond his limits. She'd challenged his mind. Challenged him not to accept his inert state. The rest was up to him. It was mind over matter.

Shayna blinked hard. "I have one of those average faces."

"Hardly." Victoria took her by the arm, walking her away.

"Mom," Beau cautioned, "don't get personal."

"Mind your business, son. This is girl talk."

"Mom, I mean it."

She and Shayna faced each other. Victoria began, "Beau's got deep feelings for you, Shayna. Don't break his heart."

Shayna gulped. She'd known Beau was attracted to her. They'd shared that earth-shattering kiss and, no denying it, the chemistry between them was alive, palpable, electric. But Victoria made it sound as if Beau had serious designs.

That spelled trouble. She and Beau had already pushed the glue right off the envelope. They'd crossed the delicate line between patient and therapist. And she'd vowed not to let it happen again. Emotional involvements meant trouble. Her ego had taken such a beating after Michael. She'd loved him with her heart and soul, rotten man that he'd turned out to be. The slime hadn't the courage to tell her that he'd found someone else. He'd waited until the other woman had given him an ultimatum. Waited until the whole world knew about his infidelity, except she, then shamed her. It would never happen again. She wouldn't let it. Beau had Chandra waiting in the wings. She wasn't about to let him hurt her.

Shayna resisted the urge to clap her palms over her ears and shut out Victoria's urges to go after her son. Her focus needed to remain on Reggie. On his upcoming case. After that was over with, she'd figure out what to do about Beau, whether to race away from her feelings or give in to them.

"Shayna," Beau called, "get over here." He was seated in his wheelchair next to David at the bar. "Peter, you too."

Victoria chuckled. "Mighty bossy, that son of mine. You'll have to make sure he knows you're an equal partner."

Shayna was only too glad to escape. She joined Alia on a vacant bar stool. Peter explained that as much as he would like to stay he had to go. Beau saw him out.

"How was your ride?" David asked, sliding the bottle of white wine her way.

"Invigorating. We had a wonderful time."

"That so?"

Beau had returned and Shayna felt his eyes upon her.

She hastily filled her glass with chardonnay and took a long sip.

"I'd almost forgotten what it was like to be outdoors on a horse," Beau added. "All that muscle and sinew under me."

He didn't seem to want to share what had transpired with Reggie and she was grateful. It would have only embarrassed her brother and made him belligerent and obnoxious.

"Hey, David," Beau called, "whatever happened to my ski equipment? The stuff I had when I fell. I'd like to have my boots and skis."

David shrugged, knocking back his drink in a quick swallow. "Good question. When you took a tumble we were so shocked, everyone converged on the slope, the last thing we thought about was equipment. There were swarms of people: doctors, medical attendants, teammates, fans. Then a helicopter arrived out of nowhere and you were rushed to the hospital. Things are fuzzy after that."

"You'll inquire about my boots and skis," Beau insisted. "I'd like them as a memento. To remind me of the man I used to be."

"And still are," Shayna said, gently.

"I'll try to get hold of them." David poured himself another drink. He didn't look comfortable. Shayna wondered what that was about.

"That's all I ask."

Alia entered the conversation. "The moment I met you," she said to Shayna, "I said to David, that woman looks familiar." Alia knitted her brow as if contemplating where she'd seen Shayna before.

Shayna steeled herself for the discovery. Here it came. Inevitably it had to come out. It shouldn't matter who she once was. Should it?

"You remind me of . . ." Alia said, her eyes widening.

Victoria interrupted. "My, we're serious. Solving the world's problems, are we?"

"Actually I was just saying Shayna reminded me of someone," Alia said smoothly. "Let me think."

"You too, huh?"

"I know," Alia said, snapping a finger. "That cute little gymnast a while back. She had a terrific smile, was known for her work on the parallel bars."

"Little Shay," Victoria finished. "That teenager got the most amazing coverage. *Time* and *Newsweek* had her on the cover. She had that Romanian gymnast beat. At least in my eyes she did."

"In everyone's eyes she did. Are you Little Shay?" Beau asked, his voice barely audible.

The group grew silent as everyone looked at Shayna expectantly.

Then Reggie's voice boomed at them from across the room. "She is. Though she hates to admit it. She wants to forget about that part of her life. Don't you, Shay?"

You could hear a pin drop in the room. Everyone stared at Shayna. Beau's eyes burned a hole in her face. She was mortified. Wanted to die. For the second time in a short while she'd intentionally deceived him. Would Beau forgive her this time around?

Chapter Sixteen

"Ah, bella, you wear me out," Franco Santana puffed, rolling off Chandra and reaching for the pack of cigarettes on the nightstand. He lit one and swirls of smoke spiraled upward to form patterns against the ornate gold-leafed ceiling. Taking another long drag, he passed it over to Chandra.

The satin sheets were damp against Chandra's naked skin. Franco got an A-plus for stamina, she admitted, but definitely not finesse. They'd been going at it for hours and her body ached. She was sore in places she didn't think it was possible to be sore. Franco's hands once more circled her breasts, cupping, teasing, laving the nipples with his tongue.

The man was a sex machine, virtually unstoppable, but not entirely in tune with a woman's body. She'd become an expert at faking dozens of orgasms. The trick was to get loud, pant out his name, grow breathless, and writhe under him. She was good at it. The best.

It hadn't been like this with Beau. With Beau she hadn't needed to use her imagination. She'd simply gone with the flow, given in to her feelings. Her orgasms had come in waves, been multiple. No faking needed. She supposed a woman couldn't have everything. Franco was beautiful but so was Beau. But Beau had lost the use of his legs and his sex drive had diminished rapidly. She'd wondered if something physical was wrong but hadn't been brave enough to ask him. Vibrators worked in a pinch but weren't exactly what she had in mind using for the rest of her life. She wanted a warm vibrant body on top of her, or underneath her for that matter.

The cigarette was stubbed out as Franco's hands settled more firmly on her breasts, squeezing gently. Chandra responded with what she thought was a sexy moan. Franco's hand moved lower, settling between her thighs, testing the moisture. His thumb plunged inside. Chandra winced. It circled, probed, tested. Chandra moaned.

She squeezed her eyes shut, summoning a vision. Beau's face floated before her. She could smell the musk of his skin, see his perfectly shaved dome, the slant of his cheekbones, the gray of his eyes. That devastating smile taunted her. She wanted to eat him up, wanted to take that gold earring between thumb and forefinger and give it a twirl. She really did miss her Beau-Beau. Missed the touch of his hands. Missed feeling him inside her. Missed him bringing her to the big *O*.

Chandra's body grew flushed. Sensations took over. She concentrated, thinking about Beau. His gentleness. His beauty. The timbre of his voice. It worked and the feelings grew in intensity.

"Yes, yes," she gasped, covering Franco's hand, pressing his thumb into her more firmly. "Oh, yes. God, yes." She was almost there.

The world exploded in various shades of rainbow.

Her body rocketed and surged, then found release. She cried out Beau's name.

The silence above her was so intense it was palpable. Had Franco heard? She couldn't afford ticking him off. She opened an eye; he was peering at her intently, adoringly.

"That was a good one, no?" he asked.

"The best." Chandra sighed contentedly. All the credit went to Beau.

She had only a few days left in Milan but Franco still hadn't mentioned anything about making their arrangement permanent. He hadn't even proposed they live together. She'd already extended her stay an additional ten days and Bellissima had footed the bill. Now she was scheduled to go back to the States and needed some sign of his commitment. Needed to know how to proceed.

He obviously needed persuading. Chandra's hand tightened around the base of Franco's shaft, squeezing gently. The other cupped the soft flesh below, applying gentle pressure.

He gasped and positioned her squarely atop of him. Under his permanent tan, his face was mottled. He was needy with want. Time to press her advantage.

"Honey, let's make love again."

"Ah, bella, we speak the same language."

Franco entered her swiftly. Chandra winced.

He had a lot to learn about a woman's body. No wonder she missed Beau. She would call him again. It didn't hurt to keep Beau as a backup if things didn't work out the way she wanted. She'd heard he was doing well. What if he managed to walk again? And ski? What if tomorrow he returned to being America's golden boy? Best not to burn all her bridges. Better not to burn them with Beau.

* * *

The van screeched to a halt in front of the doctor's office where Beau waited. Kelly stuck her blond head out of the open window and yelled at the top of her lungs, "Am I late?"

"You are," he said, quickly wheeling himself down the ramp. "You were supposed to be here half an hour ago."

"Sorry."

Kelly waited until he was comfortably settled in the back of the van before asking, "How did it go?"

"Dr. Weinstein says I'm making good progress. Better than he thought."

His sister's golden smile beamed back at him. "That's awesome. Somehow I've never imagined you not being able to ski again."

Beau gulped. It was a fate he now refused to consider. Even today, his doctor had been optimistic, hopeful that he might recover fully. He'd assured Beau the tingling in his legs was a good sign, meaning he was slowly regaining feeling. Continued therapy, he'd said, was the key to building confidence and muscles. Dr. Weinstein had felt there was a strong possibility that in the next week or so, Beau would be able to stand, maybe even take a few steps. The question was, would he ski again?

"Where to?" Kelly called, pulling out onto the crowded street.

"Hill Of Dreams. I promised to stop by."

"Oh. Sure you're up to it?"

"I'm up to it."

Beau had promised Reggie he would drop by on his very first day of volunteering. He hadn't told Mohammed he was coming and figured he'd surprise him.

Minutes later, Kelly came to a stop in front of the low brick building.

"We're here," she announced. "When would you like me to come back?"

"How about seven? That gives me a full three hours."

"Good, gives me time to run some errands. I'll wait until you're in."

A warm glow suffusing his insides, Beau guided his wheelchair up the ramp. To think he might walk. Oh, Lord, he might walk again. He wanted to keep the news to himself, allow it to germinate and grow seed, until he convinced himself the possibility was real. He would work on standing on his own, maybe even try taking a few tentative steps. He wanted to surprise Shayna the next time he saw her.

He had some difficulty opening the front door and finally resorted to banging the brass knocker.

Kelly honked at him. "Want me to get that?"

"No. Someone will let me in in a minute. At least they better," Beau muttered.

The door was thrown open and Mohammed faced him.

"Hey, man, what are you doing here? We didn't expect you." He clapped a hand on Beau's back.

"Thought I would surprise you. Is there a reason you're blocking the doorway?"

With a toot of the horn, Kelly was off and Mohammed moved aside.

Upon entering, he felt the frenzy in the air. Lots of negative energy swirling. "Tell me what's going on," he demanded.

Mohammed bit down on his lower lip sheepishly. "We had a new guy come in today. The man went crazy moments after he arrived. He began shouting obscenities, tearing the place up. It took at least four men to restrain him."

"Where is he now?"

"I had to call the hospital. They sent an ambulance. He was sedated and taken away in a straitjacket."

"Sounds like you had your hands full."

Raised voices came from down the hallway. A television blasted in some unseen place. Groups of men held animated conversation, the insane man still the topic. "I see we're still feeling the effects of this unstable person," Beau said, rolling his eyes in the direction of the men.

"Yeah, they're all still talking. It was scary for a while."

Beau looked around checking for Reggie. He was nowhere to be seen. "Where's Reggie DaCosta?" he asked. "Isn't he supposed to be here?"

"Out back, maybe, playing basketball with the men. I still don't like the idea of his being here, Beau."

"Why not?"

"The boy's not especially likable and he's involved in a high-profile case."

"We've harbored criminals before."

Mohammed flinched and Beau realized his dig had hit home. There'd been at least two cases that he knew of where there'd been warrants out for the arrest of a man who was a regular. He began wheeling himself up the hallway. "I might as well go check out the place. I promised the kid I'd be here for moral support."

Beau first stopped in the kitchen, where an enthusiastic Penny greeted him. He was encouraged to stay for dinner.

"I'm making your favorite, meat loaf," Penny said, "We'd love to have you."

"It's tempting, Penny," Beau said, thanking her. The more he thought about it, the more he realized that it would be a good opportunity to chat with Reggie and get to know him better. It would be interesting to see how the boy acted when he wasn't under the supervision of his sister. Maybe the teenager would relax and Beau could pump him for information about his sister. He was still angry at Shayna. Actually more hurt than angry. Why hadn't she thought enough of him to tell him who she really was?

His next stop was the recreation room. A television blasted in the middle of the room, and several men huddled in front of it. They sat staring at the screen with vacant eyes. High-pitched, angry voices greeted him as he entered. The conversation centered on the insane man violating their sanctuary and destroying their feelings of safety.

Apparently he'd attempted to break the very same TV they all sat around. That hadn't gone over well. Even now, evidence of his anger remained visible. Ping-Pong paddles were broken and tossed on the floor. Pool cues lay bent and discarded. There was even a dent in one wall where he'd hurled a man who'd tried to stop him.

"The guy went nuts, Mr. Hill," a graying man Beau recognized said.

"Beau."

"I mean insane. We need to get us security."

Beau had thought about getting security before, but had been reluctant to do so. He knew he took chances but he'd felt a screening process and metal detector out front sent a message that wasn't particularly welcoming. Hill Of Dreams was about taking chances, giving opportunities to people who no longer had dreams, and turning them into productive, contributing members of society.

His underdogs needed a place where they could come and go as they liked, where they were able to speak freely. There had to be an alternative. He'd have to think about it. He surveyed the damage, minor as it was, and realized how lucky they'd been. It would have been a totally different story had someone gotten seriously hurt. Lucky for them the man hadn't had a weapon.

On television a newscaster's solemn voice announced the five o'clock news. Beau paid scant attention to it until one of the men shouted excitedly.

"Mr. Hill, ain't that your father?"

"The name's Beau," he responded automatically.

Sure enough, a picture of his dad filled the screen. Beau scowled at the television, trying to pick up what was going on. His dad was out of town. This must be an old tape. Then Reggie's face flashed across the screen along with several other teenagers. The announcer dredged up the old story, adding his own editorial about unconscionable teenagers with penchants for trouble. So much for impartiality.

"That's exactly what I'm talking about," Mohammed muttered behind him. "We have our own problems here and you just added to them."

"Give it a rest, Mohammed," Beau hissed. "It's not like you're a saint."

Mohammed muttered something Beau preferred to ignore.

A strange woman's face flickered across the screen. She was introduced as the victim, and she went on and on about being beaten up and stuffed in a closet and how her place had been ransacked. The reporter kept mentioning the upcoming trial and said that Reggie DaCosta's attorney had insisted the boys were at a McDonald's at the time of the alleged vandalism and beating. "So far no witnesses that we are aware of have come forward," he ended.

"Is that so?" A voice behind Beau said. "I seen those boys. I seen them at McDonald's."

Beau turned to see the same graying man who had spoken up earlier. The one who'd said the destructive man went nuts. His eyes were fastened firmly on the television.

Beau looked at him sharply. "When?"

"The night that reporter says they beat up that old lady. Them boys came running out of a Saturn. I never seen anybody order so much food. They sat in the back stuffing it down before taking off."

"What were you doing in McDonald's?" Beau asked.

The man shrugged his shoulders. "I was cold. The building was warm and I had just scored a twenty working at the salvage place. I sat in the back sipping on coffee and eating one ah dem Big Macs."

"What time was that? I'm sorry I didn't catch your name."

"Ebenezer."

Beau knew that it must sound as if he was interrogating the man, but not everyone who came to Hill Of Dreams was up-front or honest. Before he went running off to tell Shayna the news, he wanted to be sure this wasn't some wacko with a cooked-up story.

Ebenezer scrunched up his nose, thinking. "Let's see, it must have been after eleven. The guy sitting next to me had his radio on so we could hear the evening news."

"Would you recognize any of the kids if you saw them again?" Beau asked.

"Sure thing. They sat for a while and they was noisy. The guy next to me had to ask them to shut up so that we could hear the radio."

"One of those kids is working here," Beau said matter-of-factly. "He's in a heap of trouble, so anything you remember will be much appreciated." Beau held out his hand.

Ebenezer shook it vigorously.

Through it all Mohammed had remained quiet. "Now shall I go find Reggie?" he asked quietly.

"Please. I'd like to have dinner with him in the private dining room. It would be interesting to hear what his impressions are so far. Can you join us?"

"Sorry. I'll have to pass. I need to run an errand and dinner's about the only time I have."

Beau continued to talk to Ebenezer as Mohammed took off.

Ten minutes later Mohammed returned with a sweating Reggie.

"Looks like you've been getting quite the workout," Beau greeted. "Having fun?"

"Yeah, man. It's been awesome." Reggie's wide grin flashed, and he high-fived Beau. It was the first time Beau had ever seen him this loose or animated. "My team kicked butt," the teenager announced, his voice impassioned with adrenaline.

"So you're enjoying yourself?"

"Oh, yeah. I thought it would be all work."

Beau winked. "Would I do that to you?" He beckoned to Ebenezer, who stood off to the side. "This is the kid I was talking about."

Ebenezer took his time assessing Reggie. "Yup, that's one of them, all right."

"I'm one of them? What's going on?"

Beau decided he'd better explain. He told Reggie that Ebenezer had been in McDonald's the night of the crime and thought he'd seen him.

"See, and nobody believed me," Reggie grumbled.

"Shayna did. How about you and I have dinner now?

You can tell me about that night and talk to me about your sister."

"So that's it." The old Reggie had surfaced. "You're using me to get close to my sister. Why not just call her and talk to her about whatever's on your mind?"

"That's always an option. Right now you and I are going to chill out. We're having some of that great meat loaf Penny cooked and we can shoot the breeze or remain quiet. It's up to you."

He turned his attention on Ebenezer again. "Call me if you remember anything else. You've got the number here. Mohammed can get in touch with me at a moment's notice."

"Will do." Ebenezer touched his head in mock salute.

Beau, beckoning Reggie to follow, wheeled himself out.

Chapter Seventeen

"How's Beau Hill doing?" Mary Jane Coppola asked, sipping her wine and eyeing the crowded LoDo sidewalk. Several men in business suits strolled by casting furtive glances at the female patrons seated under sidewalk umbrellas. "I've got to start hanging out down here more often." She ogled an attractive man in an expensive-looking trench coat, smiling when he looked her way.

"Beau's making progress," Shayna said carefully. "Right now he's not too happy with me, though."

"Why's that?"

Shayna told her how Beau had found out about her past. How she'd been Little Shay, a onetime Olympic hopeful.

"You've got to be kidding," Mary Jane said. "You mean I'm working with someone famous?"

"I used to be famous," Shayna corrected.

It felt good not to have to rush home and get dinner

started. It was Reggie's first evening at Hill Of Dreams, and Shayna and Mary Jane were finally having that promised drink. Shayna was enjoying Mary Jane's tart sense of humor and was incredibly relaxed. The cute sidewalk café lent itself to people watching, her favorite pastime.

"Do you truly believe Beau will walk again?" Mary Jane asked, downing her wine, her Kewpie-doll face carefully regarding Shayna's.

Shayna chose her words carefully. "I think he might, if he wants to badly enough. Like almost anything else in life, desire is a powerful factor. Beau doesn't have a spinal injury. His initial state of mind is what's held up his progress."

Mary Jane selected a chip from the basket in front of them. "You sound like you've gotten to know him well. How well?"

Shayna felt her cheeks heat up. The mere mention of Beau's name had that effect on her. She wasn't about to share that with Mary Jane. "When you work with a person, you get to know them fairly well."

Mary Jane's eyes twinkled knowingly. "I think it's more than that. You like Beau Hill more than you're willing to admit."

"And your point being?"

Mary Jane crunched loudly on her chip. "There's a lot to like about Beau. Admittedly he was a bear when he was first admitted to Denver Rehab, but there was always a certain charm under that gruff exterior. Several of the nurses saw it."

"Hmmmmm. That's why several of them quit or asked to be transferred."

"Not me." Mary Jane giggled even as the cell phone in Shayna's purse rang. The noise startled them.

Shayna flipped it open and depressed the yes button. "Hello."

"Shayna?" a male voice inquired.

Shayna's heart stopped. Reggie so seldom called her cell phone. Was he in trouble?

"I'm here," she answered, clamping the phone more firmly to her ear. She rose, walking a little way down the sidewalk. "What's going on?"

"I have good news, Shayna. The best." Reggie sounded as if he were hyperventilating.

"What's this about?"

"I found someone, Shayna. Someone who saw me. I thought you might want to call Colin."

Dare she hope? "And tell him what?" Shayna asked, carefully.

"Tell him that we found ourselves another witness. Someone who saw me and the guys at the McDonald's. I'll put Beau on and he can tell you all about it."

Shayna's heart pounded. Beau had been angry with her. They hadn't spoken since the evening of his barbecue when Alia had so loudly announced her past identity. Sure they'd managed to be civil to each other, even made it through the meal, but she'd sensed his disappointment in her and knew that she'd lost his trust.

"How are you, Shayna?" Beau's rich, deep voice came at her, making the goose bumps pop out. Shayna's stomach went into instant revolt. She should never have had that second glass of wine.

"Is what Reggie's telling me true?" she asked without preamble.

"Yes. It's a really small world. One of the guys saw Reggie on TV tonight. He recognized him from the McDonald's."

Beau went on to explain about Ebenezer providing

the details about how it had come about. Shayna's excitement built. "Is this guy reputable?" she asked.

"All I know is that he's been coming to the center for a while. Mohammed says he's usually fairly neat and doesn't appear to be under the influence of a substance."

"If I call Colin he's going to want to know how he can reach Ebenezer," Shayna said.

"Who's Colin?" Beau asked, his tone possessive.

"Reggie's attorney."

"That might pose a problem. These men usually aren't forthcoming about addresses and phone numbers. Some have been in trouble with the law previously. Makes them skittish. Why doesn't Colin try to contact Ebenezer here? Meanwhile I'll try to pin him down, establish a time and day when he'll be back. If Colin can come to Hill Of Dreams and meet Ebenezer, so much the better."

"I like that idea. You have therapy scheduled for Wednesday, see you then."

A car pulled up at the curb next to her. High-pitched voices shrieked excitedly as four women dressed to the nines alighted. Too-tight clothing and strongly scented perfume signaled an interesting evening ahead.

"Where are you?" Beau asked sharply.

"In LoDo."

"What are you doing there?"

"Am I being interrogated?" Shayna asked lightly.

"Sorry."

She chuckled as the four women sashayed down the street, arm in arm, butts twitching.

"Sounds like you're having a good time."

"I am. Actually I'm having a drink with Mary Jane Coppola."

"I didn't know you two were friends," Beau said. "Be

sure to say hi to Immaculata for me. Tell her I miss her."

"I will. See you on Wednesday then. Make sure Reggie goes straight home. He's got a nine o'clock curfew."

"All right, hon."

Shayna disconnected, thinking she wasn't his "hon." Not by a long shot.

Colin Johnson tapped the capped Mont Blanc pen against his polished wooden desk, contemplating out loud. "What if this guy Ebenezer, well meaning as he might be, isn't credible?"

"We'll deal with it then." The tapping noise was grating on Shayna's already wired nerves. "You're prepping me that this may be a waste of time. We found ourselves another witness, and just because he's a vagrant, it doesn't mean he's not telling the truth."

Shayna's voice wobbled in her frustration. She tried desperately to hold back tears. Ebenezer had represented hope.

"Tell that to a jury. The prosecution will most definitely run a background check on him. We should too. We need to remain one step ahead of them. We want no surprises."

"But I spoke to Ebenezer myself," Shayna cried, her voice heavy with conviction. "He was lucid, seemed honest. He was positive that it was Reggie and his friends he saw. He remembers the Saturn pulling into the lot. Remembers the clothes the boys wore. The loud rap music coming from the car. How could he make all that up?"

"This case got a lot of media coverage," Colin reminded her, gulping his already cold coffee. "I'll get our PI to check him out."

Shayna's own coffee remained untouched. Just their luck to have found a witness that might be discredited. They still had another, she remembered. She couldn't lose hope.

Colin scribbled notes and spoke out loud. "If Ebenezer's description of the boys' arrival is accurate, there had to be others that saw them."

"But will they come forward?" She knew most people didn't like getting involved especially when their anonymity might be at risk. She voiced another thought out loud. "Is it possible that Ebenezer knows the name of the man with the radio? They were both listening to the evening news. They must have had conversation, maybe even exchanged names."

"That's an interesting thought. I'll have to pursue that."

Colin's Mont Blanc beat another rapid tattoo against his desk. Shayna wanted to strangle him. The noise made her jumpier than ever. The trial was less than two weeks away. Her parents would be coming in from Seattle for it and the outcome was uncertain.

Colin smiled at her, affection and caring clear in his eyes. "I'm speaking with Ebenezer tomorrow. I'll see what more I can find out," he said. "Hang in there, will you?"

Shayna knew she would have to deal with Colin at some point. Their heart-to-heart would have to wait until after the trial. "I'm coping as best as I can," she said. "I can't wait for this thing to be over with. I want Reggie's name cleared. I want him sent off to college. I want to go on with my life."

Emotions overcame her. She hid her head in her hands, shoulders silently shaking. It was too much. The pressure of having a brother to care for, one in danger of being incarcerated for a crime he didn't commit.

Her unexplainable feelings for Beau, and now this man seated across from her with such hope in his eyes. Everyone wanted a piece of her, it seemed. She was only one person and right now she didn't feel very strong.

"Shayna," Colin said, his hand squeezing her shoulder, "it'll work out. I'll do everything in my power to get Reggie off. We could consider plea bargaining if you'd like."

"Sounds like you've given up on Reggie. He's innocent, you know. He's stuck to his story from the very beginning, he'd never agree to that."

"Okay. Just thought I'd mention it. Thought it might be easier on you. We'll check out Ebenezer's background. We'll get the name of his friend. Maybe he can provide us with names of others patronizing the fast food joint. These regulars usually know one another."

Shayna had stopped crying. She brushed a hand across her eyes and accepted the tissue Colin handed her. "Want to go out and get a drink?" he asked.

"Thanks, but I have to get home. I've got an early day tomorrow."

"If you're at loose ends later this week, give me a call."

"I'll do that," Shayna said, rising. "Thank you for your support. Your dedication."

"Thank you for allowing me to get to know you."

Shayna avoided his eyes. She'd meant what she said. He'd been wonderful so far, committing a lot of his time. She was certain Reggie wasn't the only person he represented.

Colin took her hands between his large ones and forced her to look at him. He regarded her with such fondness it made her uncomfortable. "I really would like to get to know you better," he stated. "But I am a patient man and I'm willing to wait until after the trial."

What did one say to that? "Thank you, Colin," was the only thing that came to mind.

Still holding her hand, Colin escorted her out to the parking lot.

On the other side of town, Beau's agent, David, was making his own phone calls. But everyone he was able to reach claimed to know nothing about Beau's equipment. That wasn't entirely surprising given that it had been months since the accident. He'd started off calling Beau's coach and had ended up leaving a message.

Trying to remember all of the details, he replayed the day of the accident. What could he have missed? It had started out so hopeful. His star, the person he had nurtured, was a surety to bring home gold. He'd had such big plans for Beau.

The entire ski team had been psyched, confident that day. Their practice run earlier that morning had gone well and they'd been elated. In high spirits they'd gone to breakfast. At least that's what he'd been told.

He'd heard the scuttlebutt about Peter Turner seeing a man hanging around the equipment. The guy had allegedly taken off when Peter had called out to him. He'd assumed it was a fan. It wouldn't hurt giving Peter a call. They'd only spoken briefly at Beau's.

Everything had happened so quickly that day. Beau's fall, his being rushed by helicopter to a hospital. David had taken a commercial flight and it had been days before Beau was up to having visitors. The team had been left to pack up Beau's personal effects. David had automatically assumed Beau's skis and boots were among them. But they had not arrived in Denver with his other stuff and he'd concluded in the rush to get Beau medical attention they'd been abandoned.

David dug deep in his pants pockets and found the number Peter had given him at Beau's house. He punched in the digits and counted the amount of rings. Four. Five. Six. He was about to hang up when a woman answered.

"Hello."

He identified himself. "This is David Mandel. I'm calling for Peter."

"One second, please."

After a lot of rustling, Peter was put on. "Hi, David," he greeted. "What's up?"

"Sorry to bother you. I've been calling around trying to find out who might know something about Beau's equipment. I thought you might recall who packed Beau's things after the accident."

"It was a joint effort," Peter said, sounding as if he wasn't totally awake. "Everyone pitched in. I packed his clothing. Joshua helped gather his toiletries, and another guy was put in charge of his equipment. Beau had brought several pairs of boots and skis, like we all did."

"Who was the person in charge of gathering Beau's equipment?" David asked.

"I don't remember. I do know that most of the heavy stuff was supposed to be sent UPS ground."

"Honey," the woman called in the background. "Come back to bed."

"You've got to go," David said. "Please call if you remember anything else, like this person's name."

"Will do," Peter answered, abruptly hanging up.

David wondered why he felt so uneasy about the conversation. Peter was the one who'd gone out of his way to get in touch with Beau. He'd alluded that Beau's accident wasn't an accident at all. According to Beau their discussion had been aborted. Yet it seemed strange that Peter had had such a clear memory of everyone's responsibilities but couldn't remember who was in charge of packing Beau's equipment. Maybe this mystery man seen snooping around the equipment wasn't a mystery man at all. Maybe he was someone that both Peter and Beau knew. Something didn't smell right.

David picked up the phone and punched in more numbers. He needed to remind Beau of the commercial shoot later that week. It was to his advantage to film. To show the world that he was alive and well. Deep in his heart David had always believed Beau would ski again. Beau was a fighter. He had courage.

Chapter Eighteen

Colin faced Ebenezer Williams across Mohammed's crowded desk. He assessed the older man carefully. While he appeared down on his luck he was neatly if inexpensively dressed. Ebenezer's graying hair had been carefully brushed to order and there were no unpleasant odors emanating from him. So far he had answered all of Colin's questions carefully, and coherently. He appeared lucid and together. Still, Colin could not risk unpleasant surprises. He would have the private eye run a background check on Ebenezer.

"So how long have you been going to this particular McDonald's?" Colin asked.

There was no one to overhear them. Mohammed had been kind enough to allow them use of his private office. Having a closed door had helped eliminate distractions. Colin had engaged in primarily small talk hoping to make Ebenezer comfortable.

The older man ticked the years off on gnarled fingers.

"Let's see. Used to be a laundromat on that corner up until 1992. Then the McDonald's replaced it. When it was new and shiny folks like me wasn't welcomed inside. I started coming in 1996. There were only a couple of us then. We'd drift in out of the cold, buy a coffee, and catch up on the goings-on in the community. Word soon spread if you bought something and didn't bother no one, management wouldn't bother you. Then they started giving us food, the stuff they would normally throw away, and more and more of us started coming in."

"You must live close by?" Colin commented, peering at Ebenezer over his spectacles.

"Not too far away. Walking distance."

"That's good. The neighborhood's fairly safe then?"

"It's had its share of crime. Happens when people don't have no money. Know what I mean?"

Colin nodded and watched Ebenezer use the cuff of his sleeve to wipe his nose. Colin passed him a tissue. He did know what Ebenezer meant. He'd grown up in a poor neighborhood. The kind where parents scrimped and saved to send their kids off to school, hoping that they would have a better life. Some grabbed the brass ring and went for it, others succumbed to a life of crime, hoping to make a fast buck.

Colin persisted. "This guy you were sitting next to, the one with the radio, how long have you known him?"

"You mean Bert? Let's see." Ebenezer began ticking the years off on his fingers again. "He started coming to McDonald's in 1997 after his wife left him."

"So you've known him for quite some time then?"

"Yes. We listen to the news. Talk a little politics. Discuss what's going on in the world."

"Does Bert have a last name?" Colin asked, scribbling on a notepad.

"What you doing?" Ebenezer regarded him with rheumy eyes. He'd become uneasy.

"Taking notes so I can remember. I'm representing a teenager who's in danger of being tried as an adult. That boy didn't commit any crime and I'm trying to keep him out of jail. I need your help, Ebenezer. Help me to help Reggie."

"He the boy I seen around? He seems pleasant enough."

Colin paused in the middle of his writing, thinking how he could best reach Ebenezer and drive home the importance of his testimony. "Boys like Reggie are our future, Eb. They're the only hope we have. So many of our young men are in jail or barely eking out a living. That's why I need you and Bert's help."

Ebenezer nodded his woolly head sagely. "I hear that. I'll talk to Bert."

"And Bert's last name is?"

"Templeton," Ebenezer finished after a pause.

Colin scribbled the name down. After he was through he cleared his throat and looked at the older man full in his face.

"Ebenezer, what if I need you to testify, would you be willing to do so? Have you ever been arrested? Any history of mental illness? Anything I should know about?"

Ebenezer hissed out a breath. "I used to like my drink but I stopped."

Great. His star witness was a drunk.

The older man elaborated. "I stopped drinking in 1995 after I lost my house. I promised my wife on her deathbed I would. And I've been good ever since. My children were gone. It was time I got my act together."

From the glazed look in Ebenezer's eyes it appeared he'd drifted back in time. While Colin felt bad for him he needed to keep him focused.

"I'll have to have a professional check out your background. I can't risk surprises."

"What about Bert? Are you going to check out his background too?"

"Absolutely. I'll need to speak with Bert. Can you arrange it?"

"Let me talk to him first. Tell him you're all right. If he finds out you're a lawyer he'll get scared. What's in it for us?" Ebenezer asked slyly.

Colin grinned back. "A good steak dinner."

"Porterhouse. And a good peach cobbler for dessert?"

"You got it." The men shook hands. Colin handed over his card. "You and Bert can reach me at this number anytime."

"We'll be in touch. You wouldn't back down on our porterhouse?"

Colin winked. "Hey, I'm a man of my word."

"So are we," the older man said, shuffling off. "We's got our rep to maintain."

"Hey," Shayna said to Beau, "You've been working on your exercises at home. It's noticeable."

He was flexing and kicking out his legs as if his life depended on it. He was still upset with her. Upset that she hadn't trusted him enough to tell him about her past. He'd gotten over her omitting to tell him about Reggie, but this recent revelation now had him wondering what other secrets would surface.

"How can you tell I've been practicing?" Beau asked, sticking to a topic that was safe. Heavy weights were still strapped to his ankles and he kept moving his legs back and forth as she had instructed.

"You're more coordinated, for one. Your muscles appear stronger."

"And that's a good thing?"

"Absolutely."

He was saving his surprise for last. He had indeed been working at home. Fiercely. Furiously. He'd been pushing himself to the limit. Kelly had on more than one occasion been forced to rescue him when he'd gone toppling. Still he'd persisted. His sister had finally talked him out of hiring an aide. She'd extended her stay by several weeks when her husband announced he was off to Tokyo on a business trip.

"So how come you never told me you were Little Shay?" Beau puffed, changing his mind, and deciding to address the issue. He flexed his legs, groaning at the effort.

"It wasn't relevant."

"Maybe to you it wasn't, but it sure as hell would have helped me understand where you were coming from. Why you took such an interest in me. You just kept pounding away, telling me I needed to get into the right mental shape. You must have had a difficult adjustment going from exalted athlete to plebeian. You were every bit as famous as me."

"True. But I tried not to get a big head. My parents wouldn't let me. They reminded me on every occasion my talents were God given and should never be taken for granted. When I fell I was humiliated. I felt I had failed them, failed the world, failed myself. They were the ones that reminded me that Shay DaCosta still existed. That once I healed I could still make a contribution.

"They gave me inspirational books to read. Made me pray. They reminded me how restricted my life had been as an athlete. All of it was true. I did love my sport but I'd been confined, unable to live a normal life. I never knew if people liked me for the person I was, or because of my celebrity status. I'd been Little Shay for so long it took me a while to find myself."

"You are remarkably well adjusted," Beau conceded, watching Shayna bend to increase the weight on his ankles. "Are you happy with your life now, Shayna?"

"For the most part I am. I love what I do."

She looked up and flashed him a smile that made his heart flip-flop. Shayna was a truly remarkable person, he thought. She'd dealt with her fall from celebrity status and started a new career. Why couldn't he? She was raising a troublesome teenage brother on her own. How different she was from his self-centered ex. It was silly of him to stay mad at her.

Beau couldn't stop himself from bending over and running his fingers through the shiny curls that clung so closely to her scalp.

She went deadly still. "Beau, don't."

"Why not?"

"Because. . ."

Those liquid eyes beckoned him. The warmth of her scalp under his fingers triggered a need in him.

"Because we're patient and therapist?"

"Something like that," Shayna finally got out.

Beau pushed out of his chair and, wobbling slightly, stood on his feet. Shayna reached out, grasping him at the waist, steadying him.

"Beau, you're not ready."

"Says who?" He straightened, all six feet two inches of him towering over her. "Come closer," he ordered.

Wonder and amazement in her eyes, she did. Beau was suddenly conscious of the clean fresh smell of her, of the fact that they were alone in this room, of the very strong physical attraction that they couldn't turn off.

He wanted to touch her, needed to hold her in his arms. Despite the fact that he was beginning to tire, he reminded himself of what it was all about. Mind over matter. The desire to win.

Beau embraced her, burying his face in the back of her neck, inhaling Shayna's unique smell.

"Beau," she said, gasping his name. "This isn't a good idea."

He kissed her, capturing her tongue between her teeth, sucking on the tip, teasing her mercilessly. His legs were really hurting now, all the long unused muscles beginning to ache. Still not breaking the kiss he sank onto his chair, bringing her down with him. Shayna made him feel as if anything was possible, as if he could hold on to her forever. She was what he needed to feel complete.

One of Beau's hands slipped under her billowing shirt to find her lace-covered bra and delve inside. His thumb circled, explored, and circled again, teasing a nipple into a turgid peak. She gasped. Her breathing now came in erratic little bursts. Beau's hand worked its way under her bra, finding soft flesh. His fingers closed around a nub. Oh, God, it had been so long since he'd made love. He wanted to feel himself inside her. Hold her even closer to him. Smell that unique scent that made her his.

"Beau," Shayna protested even as his erection pressed against her bottom. "Beau, we have to stop."

It felt as if she'd doused him in cold water. He didn't want to stop. He wanted to hold her forever. Make her part of the new life he intended to live. He was able to stand now, and in time he would walk and eventually ski. By God, it would feel good to be out on the slopes again. That feeling of exhilaration could never be reproduced.

"Shayna, I love you," he said impulsively.

"You couldn't possibly love me," she argued, shooting to her feet.

"I do."

He didn't like being rejected. Telling her he loved her hadn't come easily but the sentiment was nevertheless real.

She faced him. "Are you that fickle? A few months ago you were in love with Chandra, ready to marry her."

"I hadn't met you. Now I know for certain my relationship with Chandra wasn't about love."

Shayna fisted her hands on her hips. "Shame on you. You were going to marry a woman you didn't love."

"I said I loved Chandra. I didn't say I was in love with her. There is a difference, you know."

"But you were willing to settle?"

"Why not? Most of the world doesn't even have love."

"I'm your therapist, Beau," Shayna ground out. "You're confusing gratitude for love."

"Damn it, woman, I know the difference. Deny it all you want, you feel the same way about me. You're just determined to fight it."

How dare she say he wasn't in love with her when his heart was filled to overflowing with this aching need? This all-consuming feeling of completeness that started in his head, spread throughout his body, and ended in his toes. He loved Shayna with a passion that burned brightly. That hurt. Maybe it had something to do with her never being awed by him. She'd seen him at his worst and had stood up to him, challenged his capabilities, and made him want to live again. He was grateful to Shayna for many things, but he did know the difference between gratitude and love.

Chapter Nineteen

In Beau's mountain home the phone rang for what seemed the hundredth time. Kelly was sick and tired of racing to pick up, only to be greeted by a rude dial tone in her ear. The caller was a persistent bugger and a rude one at that.

When the phone rang again, Kelly sighed, and took her time getting it. She was tempted to let the answering machine pick up, but what if it was Kazoo calling from Tokyo? What if he had a faulty overseas connection? She missed her husband. Buoyed by the possibility of him being on the other end of the line, she picked up her pace, raced to get the receiver, and breathlessly answered.

"Hello."

"What took you so long?" a woman snapped.

"Who is this?" Kelly countered.

"What does my identity matter? I'm looking for Beau."

"He's not here."

"Where can I reach him? On his cellular phone?"

"I don't know."

"What do you mean you don't know?" the woman ranted. "This is Chandra Leon. Why are you answering Beau's phone anyway?"

"Chandra? Do I know a Chandra?" Kelly knew her purposeful denseness would irk the heck out of her brother's ex.

"I don't need to explain myself to domestics," Chandra snapped. "I'll just call Beau on his cell phone."

"Do that. Incidentally, I'm not a domestic. I live here."

Keep Chandra guessing. Let her believe Beau had moved her in. No wonder her normally tolerant mother disliked this woman. Beau had done a good thing by losing Chandra Leon.

Chandra's crude expletive made Kelly wince. She cut off the model's rantings by hanging up and returned to the couch where she'd been sprawled. No need to mention to Beau that Chandra Leon had called. It would serve no purpose.

When Beau's cell phone rang, Shayna was grateful for the reprieve. She needed time to process what Beau had just said. His confessions of love had her head in a whirl. Instinctively she wanted to run away from the emotions that churned.

Beau groped for the phone at his waistband and came up empty. "What the hell," he said, scanning the floor where the ringing seemed to be coming from.

"There it is," Shayna said, spotting the cell phone at his feet. It must have fallen when he'd embraced her. She bent down, retrieved it, and handed it to him.

"Hello," Beau growled, his voice impatient by the interruption, his gaze still on Shayna's face. After a while his expression underwent a lightning change, anger, outrage, and caution all vying for dominance. He listened intently and finally got a word in.

"What woman at my house?"

The person on the other end must have gone on and on.

"Could be Kelly," Beau said. "But why am I even giving you an explanation?"

Shayna didn't even try to hide the fact that she openly listened.

"Now's not a good time to talk. I'm in the middle of an appointment. When will you be back?" Beau asked.

His clenched jaw meant that every one of his buttons had been pushed.

"What are you not understanding?" he snapped. "Your actions have clearly demonstrated our relationship meant nothing to you."

Must be Chandra on the other end. What rotten timing. The model obviously had no intention of just walking away from Beau. Well, guess what? Shayna wasn't walking away from him either. To heck with waiting until after therapy was over to see where this would go. She too had feelings for Beau and she needed to explore them.

A smart woman would most likely run away from this mess. Chandra would be a formidable opponent, especially when she discovered that Beau was involved with his physical therapist. And though Beau claimed not to be in love with Chandra they'd had a codependent relationship that was difficult to break.

Mumbling something less than complimentary, Beau

depressed the button on his phone, successfully disconnecting the call.

Shayna had just enough time to slip on her professional mask and say, "Can we resume our business?"

Beau reached for her and began to nip at her neck. "With pleasure. No one kisses better than you. No one even comes close."

Shayna batted his hands away. How could he change gears so quickly when her emotions still churned? "We've got fifteen minutes left of therapy. Let's make it count," she said, hoping that her voice didn't shake.

"I had planned on making it count. Is there a problem?" Beau said coolly.

He acted as if his ex hadn't just called. That Shayna didn't have a reason to feel insecure or jealous. She was too old for this.

"The problem is," Shayna said, her eyes challenging him to object, "two seconds ago you were telling me you loved me."

"That hasn't changed."

"It will when Chandra comes back into the picture."

"We're no longer involved," Beau said with such finality that even she was beginning to believe him. He reached for her again.

This time she let him wrap an arm around her waist. "I'll never be satisfied playing second fiddle and I have no intention of working around her."

Beau's gray eyes twinkled. "Understood. Does that mean we're an item?"

Shayna's stomach flip-flopped. What an old-fashioned word. It was an expression her mother might use. She seriously wondered if she could put her heart on the line again and give Beau access.

"Item isn't exactly what I would call us," Shayna joked. "Let's see how it goes."

When Beau leaned over to kiss her, Chandra was forgotten. At least for now.

The commercial shoot had gone amazingly well. The scene did not require Beau to do much more than raise a cup of steaming coffee to his lips while staring lovingly into an actress's eyes.

"You get my vote," the cute dark-skinned actress said, balancing a cup of coffee, while reaching for the gold medal hanging on a ribbon around Beau's neck.

He leaned in closer, closed his eyes, and sipped from her cup. "My vote goes to Olympic Gold. Nothing tastes better."

"I beg to disagree." The actress winked at the camera. Sotto voce, she said, "He's better." She set down her cup and held the coffee jar high, label forward. "Why don't you put it to the test? Drink Olympic Gold."

"That's a wrap," the director, a ponytailed man of indeterminate age, shouted.

David waited with Beau's wheelchair. "Great job," he said. "You're a natural. You might want to take up acting."

"I don't think so."

Beau managed the few stilted steps with some assistance from the camera crew. Every agonizing step gave him hope that one day he would again walk without assistance. Winded, he sank gratefully into the wheelchair David held out for him.

"Ready to head home, Beau?"

"You said it."

The script writer had had to change the lines a bit to accommodate his defeat. But at least the coffee company hadn't tried to weasel out of the commercial as so many had. Even Olympic Gold's company representative had perked up immensely when she realized he wasn't totally immobile. She'd even mumbled something about shooting another commercial after seeing how this one went.

Inside the van, David commented, "Would Towanda be the obvious person to sign a UPS slip if a delivery came to your house?"

"It's possible. What's up?"

David shifted gears and took off. Beau sat in the passenger seat, his wheelchair relegated to the back. He waited patiently for David to answer.

"Peter Turner says your personal items were sent ground UPS. Let's chat with Towanda when we get home, maybe she can tell us where your things are stowed. Needless to say, Peter's since forgotten who was responsible for sending them."

"Selective memory, you think?"

"That's what I'm thinking."

David steered the van up the steep mountain road, carefully navigating the hairpin bends and treacherous curves. They parked in the circular driveway.

Once they were inside the house, he said, "Would UPS have dumped several boxes on your doorstep without getting a signature?"

"Hmmmm. I don't know. But I would think that most of the boxes would have been itemized or had the contents listed."

"You're right."

"Anybody home?" Beau called, "Kelly, Towanda, where are you?"

The house had been deadly quiet since they arrived. But since it wasn't exactly small, its occupants could be anywhere, including out back. Beau depressed the intercom button. "Hey, Kell, Towanda. Where are you?"

"I'm here, Mr. Beau," Towanda said, racing in, looking guilty.

"Where's Kelly?"

"She went out. Says she had errands to run. By the way, Ms. Leon has called you several times. I wrote down the messages."

Beau groaned. Lucky for him he'd had his cell phone off. He'd figured it made good sense not to be disturbed during the commercial shoot.

"Do you remember getting any packages for me?" Beau asked.

Towanda screwed up her face. "Not recently."

"What about a UPS delivery a few months back?" David interjected.

"I think I remember something."

"Think, Towanda, think," Beau urged.

"If there were several cartons, I would have had Harry put them in the utility room."

Harry was his handyman. He and Towanda were friends.

"It would have been lots of boxes. My ski gear, bulky sweaters, that sort of thing. The stuff I took to Salt Lake City with me."

"Oh, those boxes. They're in the utility room. I didn't want to touch them until you got home."

"All right, let's go check them out. Lead the way," David ordered.

The threesome headed down a long corridor and after several twists and turns came to a closed door. Towanda removed a set of keys and selected one. The open room revealed floor-to-ceiling cartons. Just the sheer number of boxes was overwhelming.

"What's all this?" Beau asked.

"Mostly Christmas decorations. Items we never unpacked when you moved from the town house."

"And the UPS boxes?" David asked.

Towanda shrugged. "Somewhere in that pile."

It would be a daunting challenge to search through the maze of stacked cartons.

"Maybe Harry can help us," Beau suggested. "You did say he helped you put them away."

"Good idea, let me call Harry."

She turned and left the room. They both followed.

In the kitchen, Towanda tried reaching Harry. "He's not home," she said, the receiver pressed to her ear.

"Leave him a message," Beau prompted.

"Call me when you find something out," David said, preparing to head off.

"Absolutely. Meanwhile I'll be phoning Josh Vanderhorn to see if his memory's better than Turner's."

"Good luck. You almost get the feeling there's a huge cover-up."

"I'm beginning to think there is," Beau said. "And I'm determined to get to the bottom of it."

"Me too," David said. "If we confirm you've been sabotaged, there will be hell to pay."

"You know it."

It wasn't until the following day that Harry surfaced.

"Hey, boss," he said, sauntering out to the patio, Towanda falling into step beside him. "Heard you had some questions for me."

"There were some UPS boxes Towanda mentioned you helped put away."

"Yeah, there were several, all various shapes and sizes. I stacked them in the empty stall in the stables."

"Can you bring them up to the house right away?"

"You got it, boss."

"Beau."

No matter how many times he'd told Towanda and Harry to call him Beau, it didn't seem to matter. He supposed calling him mister or boss was their way of showing respect.

After Harry and Towanda left, Beau got on his cell phone and called David. He hadn't been able to reach Josh Vanderhorn, who was supposedly in Cancun.

"I'll be right over," his agent said.

Beau was grateful that he would be by to provide support. Who knew how he would feel when Harry unpacked those boxes? It could be a traumatic experience and a very painful reminder of what he did not achieve.

Suddenly Beau wanted Shayna there with him as well. He picked up the phone and punched out her number. It was risky letting her see the vulnerable side of him, the side he kept hidden from the rest of the world, but he needed her strength and having her there would make things easier.

She answered on the second ring.

"Hi," she said, her voice breathy. "I was hoping you'd call."

"I'm thrilled at the enthusiastic welcome."

She chuckled. "Beau. I was expecting my mom."

"That explains the greeting. What are you doing right now?"

"I've been out jogging. I'm about to jump into the shower."

"Stop by when you're through. David's on his way over and I could use the moral support. We're about to open the boxes with the stuff forwarded from Salt Lake City."

"Sure you want to do this, Beau?"

"Yep, I'm sure."

"Okay. I'll be right over."

Mission accomplished, he hung up the phone. Shayna was coming over. He was in a much better mood now that he knew she would be there by his side.

Chapter Twenty

Shayna was in and out of the shower in record time. She dressed quickly and stuck her head in the refrigerator, scoping out the possibilities. Reggie was volunteering at the center and would most likely eat there, but there was plenty of leftover chicken and macaroni salad if he didn't. She managed a quick nibble.

After driving like an insane person up the twisted mountain roads, she parked in the driveway behind David's red Jaguar. Beau met her at the door, greeting her with a kiss. She followed him into the den, where David and a strange man sat surrounded by boxes. Shayna tapped the decorative vases holding Salt and Pepper.

"Hey, kids. Looks like you're doing well," she said to the fish, who swam lazily back and forth.

"You look even better," David responded, hugging her. "Elegant and lovely as always."

Shayna thanked him.

"Hey, that's my line," Beau interrupted, a gleam in his eye. He inspected her beige leggings and oversize man's shirt closely. Shayna blushed under such intense scrutiny. She felt as if she were being x-rayed, as if he were peeling off layer after layer, visualizing her naked body beneath.

David held on to both hands and kissed her cheek. "Thanks for coming over given such short notice." He introduced her to Harry, then gestured to the boxes. "We were just about to begin."

Beau addressed them both. "Would you like something to eat? Drink?"

"Not right now. Maybe later," David said.

The strapping man named Harry began opening boxes. Out of them came an assortment of sweaters, goggles, pants, and personal effects. But no skis and certainly no boots.

"Shall we try that one?" David pointed to an oversize box.

"Sure."

It yielded a CD player, several CDs, more clothing, still no skis and boots. They opened another three boxes with similar results. Eventually a smaller carton yielded several pairs of boots and a long rectangular box held Beau's poles.

"Well," David announced, "we've got boots and we've got poles."

Beau, aided by a walker, shuffled toward the items on the floor. "Not the ones I used that day."

"Beau," Shayna exclaimed, round-eyed with awe. "Why didn't you tell me you'd graduated to a walker?"

He winked at her. "I wanted it to be a surprise. I can even manage with a cane, but not for long periods. I tire easily."

"This is wonderful," she cried, hugging him carefully

so as not to send him toppling. She kissed him squarely on the lips. "Seeing you up and out of that chair has made my day."

"And having you here with me has made mine."

David cleared his throat behind them as they hugged again.

"Okay, you lovebirds, I have to leave. I'm having dinner with Alia and she doesn't like to be kept waiting." He began to walk away, then turned back. "I spoke with Miles Williams earlier."

"Miles? How is my old teammate?" Beau asked.

"Holding his own. Incidentally he tells a very different story from Peter and Josh. He says they both volunteered to pack your stuff. He remembers one of them having your skis."

"Did he say which one?"

"Nope. I tried probing but he clammed up. Call him. He might be more forthcoming with you."

"I'll do that," Beau said, waving him off.

"Are we finished in here, boss?" Harry asked.

"Yes, thank you. You can go."

Left alone, Beau sat on the couch next to Shayna. He took her hand and pressed her palm to his lips. "Thanks for coming. It meant a lot to me that you're here. Reggie's trial's next week, isn't it?"

"Yes, and I'm really nervous. Actually I'm scared. God, Beau, if my brother gets locked up for a crime he didn't commit, it will kill my parents. It'll probably kill me."

Beau kissed her temple. "Let me see what I can do. I'll talk to my dad. Maybe he and Reggie's attorney can work something out. I'm certain your brother didn't do it. I've gotten to know him these last couple of weeks. He's a good kid. Comes across as tough, but under that hardened exterior is a vulnerable boy with incredible hopes and dreams. Did you know he wants to be a psychologist?"

"Actually I didn't. I've been pushing him to register for college. His grades aren't that good because he slacked off."

Beau threaded his fingers through hers. "I helped him fill out an application for community college last week. Let's hope he's able to go."

Shayna's eyes misted. "That's wonderful. See, you're a good influence on him." She kissed him again.

Beau returned her kiss with urgency and need. He slipped her his tongue and it was a long time before they spoke again.

"If you keep this up, you know where this will end," he admonished, coming up for breath. Then suddenly he changed the conversation. "You think my dad knows about Ebenezer? If that man and his friend Bert saw those kids in McDonald's, Reggie and his buddies should go scot-free."

"I pray they did see them. I hate having you speak to your dad though." She held up a hand, stilling his protest. "Your father's going to want to know why you're interested. What are you going to tell him?"

"That Reggie's a good kid. That he volunteers at Hill Of Dreams."

"I still feel guilty. Like I'm using you."

"Shayna, you must know by now I would do anything for you."

The sincerity in his voice made her uneasy. He'd said he loved her before, but she was still up in the air about where it would go. And yes indeed, she did feel guilty and manipulative.

"I don't want you jeopardizing your relationship with your father," she insisted.

"Dad's tough but fair."

When he kissed her again, Reggie and his problems ceased to exist. "It'll all work out. You'll see," Beau said. "Hungry?"

"No. I raided the refrigerator before coming over." She pointed to the boxes. "What'll we do about these?"

"Harry will take care of them tomorrow."

Shayna liked the way Beau's hand felt in hers. As though they belonged together. "I can't believe your boots and skis are still missing," she said. "Why would Peter and Joshua have a convenient lapse of memory?"

"Why indeed? I'll call Miles Williams tomorrow, see what he has to say. Then I'll try reaching Peter and Josh. Hey, enough about them. Let's talk about us."

This growing attraction probably needed to be discussed. But putting it into words made it seem real. By kissing him she'd already violated their patient-client relationship. Beau was still very much her patient.

"Look, I hadn't planned on feeling this way about you," he said, cutting to the chase. "I love you, Shayna. Is the feeling mutual?"

How could she lie when his thumb skimmed her cheek and just sitting next to him made her insides quiver? How could he sound so serious, so sure about his feelings, when she vacillated back and forth? She was afraid. Petrified. She'd had her heart broken before, and it was a painful experience. Michael, whom she had loved and trusted, had humiliated her, cheated on her, left her for another woman. Her ego couldn't take that kind of beating again, nor could her heart.

Beau's fingers outlined her lips. "What are your thoughts, Shayna?"

Thoughts?

"Beau," Shayna began hesitantly. "You've had a bad accident, you've been forced to live a different lifestyle. You're just coming out of an intense relationship. You need time. This is all happening too fast. Let's talk again after you're completely mended. After Reggie's situation is resolved and you aren't my patient.''

"My feelings won't change." Beau's slender fingers stroked the hollow of her neck where the buttons of her shirt opened.

She couldn't think clearly, not with him touching her. Not when his clean, fresh cologne tickled her nostrils. Not when he was so near. "This is madness, Beau. We can't do this.''

"Do what?" He pressed his advantage, leaning over to trail his hands across her breast and kissed her again. "We're consenting adults, Shayna. We're single and free to do as we like. Who's to stop us from spending time together, getting to know each other.''

There was plenty to stop them. Good sense, for one, plus the fact that his father was prosecuting her brother. Not to mention the patient-therapist thing. She'd left Beau's world behind a long time ago and didn't know if she could deal with the type of adulation athletes like him received from the public. The invasion of her privacy, having always to maintain a public persona, was all too much. She'd been there, done that.

She already knew what would happen when it became common knowledge Beau was on the mend. The press and public would be all over him again. Females would come out of the woodwork, not to mention Chandra would be there to stake her claim. She was already trying to edge her way back. Too many concessions would be required on Shayna's part. She'd be forced to look the other way, put up with nonsense. That went against her very nature.

While she contemplated, Beau managed to work a button of her shirt free. He pressed his nose into her cleavage. "God, you smell heavenly.''

"Stop," she ordered, slapping his hand away. He pressed a kiss against her neck, and his fingers worked another button. His hands dove into the open space to claim her lace-covered breasts.

"You've got the most perfectly shaped pair," he said, his fingertips circling her nipples.

Jolting sparks of electricity raced through her body. Her mouth went dry as reason took a backseat to sensation. She should stop him now before it went too far. Before things got further out of control.

Beau's fingers dipped below the fabric of her bra. She pulsed in places she hadn't pulsed before. Oh, God, what was she to do? His hands fondling her bare breasts were hot. Palms rough. When he circled her nipples it elicited a groan. Another wet kiss was planted on her mouth. She parted her lips, letting his tongue slip inside. It danced, dipped, teased, tempted, and tantalized. She was a mass of pure feeling. Unbuttoning some of the buttons on his shirt, she ran her fingers through his thick chest hair, reached for his belt, and unbuckled it.

Beau's hungry tongue probed her mouth. Delightful sensations ricocheted through her body, and she kissed him back with an enthusiasm never displayed before. His fingers plucked at her nipples, circled, squeezed, molded. The kiss was broken only when he drew a nipple into his mouth and laved it with his tongue. His hand worked magic on the other one.

"Oh, God!"

Was that her voice she heard? It sounded hoarse, needy, out of control. Was that her pressing up against him, gyrating with such wild abandon?

"Time to move things to the bedroom," Beau said, his own voice rough.

"No. Not a good idea. What if Kelly comes home?"

"What if she does? This is my home. We're consenting adults."

She'd forgotten about Kelly. Forgotten about everything except the way he made her feel. Still, going with him to his bedroom meant that she'd made a commitment to move this relationship along. She couldn't deny that she wanted to make love to Beau. But once that line was crossed there'd be no turning back. And her conscience stood in the way.

Beau was already up, leaning heavily on an ornate walking stick. He held out a hand to her.

"Wouldn't you be better off in your chair?" she asked.

"I'm not about to roll out of a wheelchair and make love to you," he growled. "I'm walking up that hall."

She could tell every step required effort. She held his hand, hoping to bear some of his weight. Slowly they treaded down the hallway.

Beau's bedroom had been made wheelchair accessible and held minimal furniture. The idea being that Beau would not have to navigate around unnecessary obstacles. It was sand colored and had vaulted wooden ceilings. A giant bed with an elaborate wrought iron headboard and plush rust comforter dominated. Two nightstands were positioned next to it. A Queen Anne chair sat in close proximity to the bed, and an armoire holding a television set, VCR, and CD player, with assorted videos, had its doors wide open.

"Close the bedroom door," Beau ordered, plunking himself down on the bed and gulping deep breaths of air.

Shayna poured water from the pitcher on top of the nightstand and presented Beau with a glass.

He took a long sip and continued barking orders. "Light those candles, will you?"

Shayna lit them and they emitted the subtle scent of vanilla.

"Now pick out a CD. We need music."

"Aye, aye, sir."

"Sorry," he said, sounding sheepish. "Guess I better tone it down."

"Good idea." She tried not to smile. Beau's personality was to take the lead. Control. She selected the sultry sounds of Toni Braxton and turned back to him. "Is this okay with you?"

"Perfect."

The only thing missing was wine. But who needed it when she was already heady with desire? Desire for the man seated on the bed looking at her with such pent-up passion in his eyes.

Returning to Beau's side, she took his face between her palms. "You are sweet. Let's take it nice and slow. Foreplay is a big thing with me." Nothing like being assertive.

"With me too," he said, exhaling a breath slowly in her ear.

Shayna kissed him with all the love she'd held in these last few months. Soon she was lost in the feel of him, conscious only of the candle's smoky vanilla scent. Beau's hands were on her body, molding the flesh. She worked the remaining buttons of his shirt open and spread her fingers, letting them tangle in his chest hairs. She nuzzled her nose against his chest, found an already taut nipple, and tugged at it.

"Easy. No teeth."

But even as he said that he grew hard under her. Time to turn the heat up a bit.

Shayna caressed the spot where Beau's pants had tented. He gasped, and his hands moved lower, slipping under the elastic waist of her tights, to cup her buttocks. Together they fell backward on the bed.

Beau tugged at her tights, sliding them down past her ankles. Shayna kicked off her cotton leggings and heard his sharp intake of breath as her red lace panties were revealed. She tugged at his zipper and was surprised to find that he wore black briefs.

"Let's get you out of these," she said, sliding his pants down muscular legs and peeling off his shirt.

He was beautiful to look at. All Hershey skin and toned physique. His shoulders were wide, his waist tapered. Those black briefs held a definite promise of fulfillment. The remaining buttons of her shirt were ripped open, the fabric pushed aside. With a deft movement he unfastened her bra and her breasts spilled out into his hands.

She heard him gasp even as his mouth paid homage to her nipples and his hands kneaded the surrounding cushioning. Shayna responded to his touch with an abandon she did not know she possessed. She needed him to touch her all over, make her feel good. She squirmed against him. Beau's hands moved lower, circling her belly button, playing with the gold stud imbedded there. He found the elastic of her panties.

"Take them off," he whispered in a strained voice.

"No, you take them off."

"So we're going to play that game, are we?" He snapped the elastic band playfully.

"Ouch. No, we're going to play this game." Shayna clasped him through the black material of his briefs, reached inside, circled his shaft, and squeezed gently.

"Ah, baby, that feels good."

"This will feel even better," Shayna said, peeling his underwear aside and bending to give his member attention.

"Oh, God, it does. It does."

The scent of the potent candle filled the air. Toni's sex-laced voice added to the hypnotic feeling, wrapping itself around them, providing a warm cocoon, a safe haven. Even wine could not produce the heightened effect of this totally sensual experience. Shayna's core throbbed. Her heart pounded. The roaring in her ears threatened to drown out Toni. She was hotter than hot. If the fire wasn't put out soon she'd spontaneously combust.

Beau gently nudged her onto her back. His tongue trailed her stomach, played with the stud again, then settled in her belly button briefly, before moving down. His fingers stroked her inner thighs, and she clamped them shut, successfully trapping his hand in the moist, warm heat of her. Beau inserted a finger, and slowly rotated, finding the nub. Satisfied by her outcry, he inserted another.

The heat moved up a notch. Her body burned, aching for fulfillment. The ultimate release that only he could give her. She writhed beneath him, claimed his free hand, and gave him direction.

But even the touch of his hand did little to satisfy this all-consuming need to have him in her. She was beyond caring about obstacles that stood in their way. Everything would have to work itself out, somehow. Beau was well on his way to a complete recovery. He could find himself another therapist. In fact, she would recommend one. That would leave them free to embark on a relationship.

Beau stopped his ministrations to kick off the briefs trapped at his ankles. He returned to kiss her in places that had never been kissed before. To bury his nose in her mound, and drink deeply of her. Shayna wrapped her thighs more firmly around his broad back, urging him on.

When he surfaced to catch his breath, he kissed her mouth. "Are you ready, hon?"

Unable to speak, she nodded. Beau reached onto the nightstand, found a condom, and slid one on. Propping himself up on his elbows, he used his knees to force her legs apart, positioning himself for entry. White heat engulfed her as his hot breath warmed her face.

Toni Braxton's voice dipped and soared in the background and the scented candle filled the air. Toni now encouraged them to give it all up for love. Slowly Beau inched inside Shayna, letting the rhythm build. He was driving her wild with his careful invasion, his methodical entry and retreat. She clutched the bedclothes and tried not to scream, but one ripped forth.

"God, Beau," she said, stuffing a curled fist in her mouth.

Every entrance and exit brought with it another compliment.

"I love the touch of your skin, baby," Beau whispered. "The feel of me inside you. The scent that makes you you. I love you. Say it, baby, say it."

"I love you, Beau."

"Again."

In, out. In again. He pounded away, demanding what she wasn't sure she ready to give.

"I love you, Beau." Was that her voice?

She'd never have guessed he could be so loving. So good at making love. Beau called out her name.

"Shayna."

She matched him move for move, oblivious to anything except his body wrapped around her and the driving heat that kept building. The muscles around her vagina clenched, trembled, and spasmed. Shayna exploded in a white ball of fire, choking out one final endearment.

"I love you, Beau."

"And I love you."

Somewhere in the background a phone rang. An answering machine eventually picked up. The requisite greeting came and went, followed by the usual beep. A woman's voice came over loud and clear.

"Beau-Beau, I'm back. Missed you like crazy, baby. Ice the champagne. Get out the caviar. I'm coming over."

"Better get dressed," Beau ordered, breaking their connection abruptly. "She's still got my key."

Reality had returned rudely in the form of Chandra.

Chapter Twenty-one

Chandra's call couldn't come at a worse time, not when he'd just gotten through to Shayna and convinced her he loved her. She'd told him she loved him too. By expressing that sentiment she'd granted him a very special gift. He felt as if anything was possible now, that soon he might even ski.

Beau bolted upright, that abrupt action successfully dislodging Shayna, who was still in a just-been-loved coma.

"Get dressed," he repeated, dousing cold water on her.

He was already scrambling for the clothing he'd tossed on the floor, and flung items he thought were hers at her. Beau found his pants, struggled into them, sans underwear, and helped her button her shirt. Shayna still hadn't uttered a word.

"I'm sorry, babe," Beau said. "Let me get rid of her."

She eyed him warily, words finally coming. "Don't do it on my account, I'm leaving."

"What? Hey, what did I do to upset you? Why are you blaming me?" He found his shirt and buttoned it.

"I'm blaming me. I should never have allowed this to happen. Didn't you tell me you and Chandra were over?"

"We are," he said, kissing the back of her neck.

She jerked away from him. "Don't touch me."

Shayna's voice was cold and unyielding. Ice.

"How was I to know she would take it upon herself to come over uninvited?" Beau argued.

Shayna faced him, looking ready to spit. "The woman has your key," she enunciated. "That implies she's welcome here anytime. Men don't give women keys unless they're important to them."

"At one point she was," Beau admitted. "But she no longer is. I just didn't have time to get the key back."

"I don't believe this." Shayna shook her head and turned away. "Is there another way to get out of here?"

The sound of the front door slamming got both of their attentions.

"Shit," Beau repeated. "Shit." It was the only word that seemed fitting for the pickle he'd gotten himself in.

"Yes, there's another way out." He grabbed Shayna's shoulders and steered her toward the French door at the rear of the bedroom. "Cross the patio and you'll come out at the back of the house. I'll call you later." He tried a quick kiss, but she glared at him, tensing as if he repulsed her.

"Don't bother."

Shoeless, she took off.

Footsteps headed his way. Too late Beau realized that Shayna had left her bra and panties on the floor. He picked up both garments and stuffed them in his pants pocket.

The pounding began on his door.

"Beau. Open up."

"What do you want?"

"Beau, it's Kelly. Is everything okay?"

His sister, thank God. The fight went out of him. Beau yanked open the door and faced Kelly. He could tell by the surprised yet slightly amused look on her face that she knew what had just happened.

"Uh," she said. "Uh, do I need to give you time to get decent?" Her eyes roamed the vicinity of his slacks. "Yes, I see I do."

Beau looked down and realized his fly was still open. He yanked his zipper up.

"Sorry. What was it you wanted?"

Kelly kept a poker face. "I think you've got a red flag trailing from your pocket."

It took him a while to comprehend. He pulled Shayna's underwear from his pocket and sent both items sailing across the room.

"Come in," he said, yanking the door wide. "I could use some advice. I screwed up this time really bad."

"Where's Shayna? Her car's out front," Kelly said as she walked into the room, eyeing the rumpled sheets, and the candles still burning. She wrinkled her nose. "Smells like sex."

Beau thought it best to ignore the comment. He gingerly made his way to the window, opening it. A gust of fresh air blew in, stirring the curtains.

"Better?"

"It'll take a while."

Kelly sat on the Queen Anne chair, staring at him. "Okay, bro, fess up. Where's she stashed? Closet? Bathroom? Under the bed?"

"Neither. She's gone, through the back door." He knew he sounded woeful.

"Your, uh . . . prowess scared her off? Or was it your dimensions?" Kelly chuckled.

"It's not funny. This is serious, Kell."

His sister's expression changed from playful to stern. "Okay, let me see if I understand this. You had your therapist here?"

"That's correct."

"You banged her."

"Made love to her, Kell."

"Okay, you made love to her." She frowned at him. "So why do you need me?"

"Because now I've pissed her off."

"You're not making sense. You banged . . . no, made love to her. She walked out on you. You've lost your touch, little brother."

Exasperated, Beau yelled, "Listen to me. Shayna left because Chandra's on her way over."

Kelly blew air through pursed lips and squinted her eyes. "Why is that hootchie mama coming over? I thought she was in Europe." Comprehension seemed to dawn. "You two-timing bastard, you expect me to bail you out?"

"No. No. It's over with Chandra, Kell. I love Shayna, but Chandra still has my house key."

Kelly stood up abruptly. "So she's invited herself over. Pretty dumb not to get your key back. Sounds like your sorry butt's going to have to do lots of explaining to get out of this one."

"I need advice," Beau pleaded.

"Grovel." Kelly tossed her blond ponytail and headed out, flashing him a smile over her shoulder. "You got yourself in this mess, now get yourself out."

"Big help you are," Beau muttered to her back.

The front door banged open and a woman's voice called, "Beau-Beau, I'm here. Hot, ready, and waiting. Here goes my top." A rustling sound followed.

Kelly turned back to him, rolling her eyes. "Baby's back, all right. Boy, do you know how to pick them." She danced off.

Chandra's raised voice got Beau's attention. She must have encountered Kelly. The two had never met.

"Who are you?" she demanded.

"I could ask the same," his sister said. "Any reason you're standing in my living room half naked?"

Beau ran a hand across his shaved dome. Better get out there before the two killed each other. He tucked his shirt in his pants, made sure his fly was closed, and grabbed his cane. No wheelchair tonight, he needed to make a dignified entry.

Beau walked onto a scene that had potential for violence. He hovered at the entrance as his sister faced his ex-girlfriend, fire flashing from her eyes.

Chandra had put on her shirt but hadn't buttoned it. Her breasts hung brazenly through the opening.

"You still haven't answered," Kelly demanded. "Why would you just barge into someone's home?"

"In case you missed it, I have a key." Chandra dangled the key in front of his sister's face. "You're Beau's latest?" She wrinkled her nose. "Can't account for taste. Move aside, please."

Kelly planted her feet firmly and refused to budge. "Where do you think you're going?"

"To find Beau."

"You're no longer a part of his life."

Chandra was close to erupting. Her breasts jiggled freely as she placed fisted hands on her hips. How had he ever thought himself in love with her?

There was charged silence as the women sized each

other up. Time to intervene. Beau hobbled in, making his presence known. "Time out, ladies."

"Beau," Chandra said, flying at him, completely unconscious of her exposed chocolate-tipped lobes. She rubbed her breasts against him and began kissing his face.

"Oh, Beau-Beau, you're walking again, not perfectly, but you're walking. Tell that woman she needs to go. That she means nothing to you."

The humor of the situation suddenly struck him. His lips quivered. "Kelly and I go back a long way. We live together."

Chandra poked out her bottom lip. "You love me, Beau-Beau. Love these." She cupped her breasts, offering them to him.

"Pathetic," Kelly muttered. "The poor thing has to use sex."

"Button up, Chandra," Beau ordered.

"You're embarrassing Beau," Kelly said, linking an arm through his.

"You're living with a cripple?" Chandra shouted, tears falling freely now.

"My cripple is virile and satisfies me," Kelly said smugly. "Weren't you the one who arrived hot, ready, and waiting?"

Beau burst out laughing.

"Shut up," Chandra shouted, throwing Beau a murderous glance. "I don't need this."

"Then you'll leave?" Kelly said.

Beau saw the too-short skirt, the open blouse, the distended nipples, as if for the first time. Kelly was right. Pretty pathetic. How had he ever hooked up with Chandra? She'd manipulated him with sex, confused him with her intentions. He'd fallen for her act, hook, line, and sinker. The joke was on him.

"You had a very public affair with an Italian gigolo," he said. "Now you're expecting me to take you back."

"Franco was a PR ploy," Chandra pleaded. "My agent thought it would bring me press."

"And it did," Beau finished. "It also woke me up."

"I'm not done with you," Chandra fumed, flouncing off.

"You're forgetting something," Kelly called after her. "We need our key."

The key was flung at them unceremoniously. Beau was forced to duck to avoid getting hit in the head.

"You've got lousy taste in women," Kelly whispered.

The comedic aspects of the scene kicking in as the door slammed behind Chandra, they howled.

"Oh, Beau," Kelly said when she was able. "How could you have gotten involved with that woman?"

Beau wiped away tears. "I should have been declared temporarily insane."

Time to put this chapter of his life behind him, finally. Every effort now had to be focused on winning Shayna back. It would be a difficult task but he was up to it.

A week went by with no word from Shayna. Beau had tried calling numerous times and had left messages on her answering machine but there'd been no return call. He'd even spent time at Hill Of Dreams, hoping that Reggie would plead his cause, but the teenager remained adamant about not getting involved.

"You don't know what Shayna's like when she's pissed off," Reggie informed him. "Nothing I say is going to make a difference. You better figure out some way of winning her back."

"How can I do that when she doesn't seem to want to talk to me?"

Reggie had tugged on the bill of his cap. "Better come up with something, man, and quick. I got my own problems to think about."

Beau supposed Reggie did, with only a week or so left to his trial.

If anyone should be angry it should be he. Beau had shown up for physical therapy a few days ago to find another therapist assigned to work with him. The new person had introduced herself, mumbling something about Shayna calling in sick, and her being called in at the last moment.

Beau stepped gingerly, relying on his cane to provide maximum support. With some difficulty he managed the few steps leading up to his father's law offices. Since the day was warm, almost sticky, the ride over had taken place with the top down. He'd worn a collarless shirt, rolling up the sleeves. Now the Saab convertible was parked in a space out front, and he was here minus a chauffeur, driving against his doctor's orders.

"Hey," a familiar-looking paralegal greeted. "It's been a while since you've been around. Good to see you up and walking." She tossed a headful of braids his way. "Feeling better?"

"Much. Is my dad in?"

"I think so. You know Flossie, his foo-dog, watches over him."

Flossie, his dad's secretary, had been with him as long as Beau could remember. She was sixty if she was a day, plump, and very capable. Physically she looked like Mrs. Claus.

Beau headed in the direction of his dad's office.

"Ring me if you're ever at loose ends," the paralegal called after him.

Beau flashed her his signature smile and continued on.

Flossie presided in a comfortable outer office. She placed tentative fingers on the keyboard and painstakingly typed out a message. It was obvious she hadn't mastered the mechanics of a computer.

Beau cleared his throat.

"Just a moment," Flossie said, one finger in the air. She plonked each key laboriously while scowling at her monitor.

"Are you here to see Mr. Anderson?"

"Yes, and you."

The answer got her attention. She looked up, a wide smile creasing her Mrs. Claus face. "Beau, you're a sight for sore eyes. Is your dad expecting you?"

He was enfolded in her lilac embrace, pressed against her more than ample chest. It was déjà vu all over again. Memories of his maternal grandmother surfaced. She'd died several years back, but had worn the same scent.

"What kind of day is Dad having?" Beau asked. He'd called earlier that week and been assured it wasn't particularly busy, but things might have changed.

Flossie thumbed through her appointment book, oblivious to the fact a calendar existed in her computer.

"You're in luck. Ed's free for lunch." She beamed at Beau. "Take him to that nice place around the corner. All the young people go there. Shall I tell him you're here?"

"Please."

Beau waited on one of the plush couches while Flossie waddled away. The office had been redecorated since his last visit and it was more aesthetically pleasing to the eye. It was now all cream wallpaper, polished mahogany tables, and leather couches. Bound books were neatly lined up on floor-to-ceiling shelves, and potted bamboo plants added a touch of the exotic to the setting. The paintings on the walls were one of a kind and expensive.

When Beau thought Flossie had disappeared forever, his father appeared in her place. Ed's glasses were balanced high on his shining dome as he pretended to scowl at Beau.

"You need to keep busy," he said.

"I am. I'm very involved with the center."

Ed's gaze lingered on the tiny gold hoop in his son's ear. It had remained a bone of contention between them though neither broached the subject anymore. He closed the space between them and embraced his son.

Beau hugged him back. "I'm buying lunch," he announced. "Get your jacket, we need to talk."

"Sounds serious. You in trouble, son?"

"No, those days are behind me. We're going to this little place right down the street."

Ed's jowls shook. "You did say you were buying?"

"Absolutely."

"Fine. I'll wrap up what I was doing and be back here in a flash."

Prepared for a long wait, Beau crossed one denim-clad leg over the other. He'd worn his boots, and the combination of snakeskin, gold earring, and shaved dome would be too much for his normally conservative father. Lunch promised to be interesting.

He loved his dad but they were as different as two folks could be. Physically and mentally. As a child Ed had tried his best to turn him into junior white bread. Beau had resisted and there'd been frequent tussles.

Beau had grown up wheat and was going to stay wheat. He clung to his roots, needing to remember where he came from. It hadn't always been easy being black in an all-white family, but he'd maintained his friends, and frequent visits back to the old neighborhood had kept him real.

It wasn't as if he didn't adore his adopted family. Kelly with her debutante looks, and whiter-than-white smile. Victoria, who looked as if she could give Debbie Reynolds a run for her money, and Ed, with his scowling demeanor and sometimes righteous air. Even his brother Jason, who looked as if he'd stepped off the cover of *Success Magazine,* had been good to him. The Anderson family had embraced him as if he were their own, giving a poor hurting boy some very fine memories.

Chapter Twenty-two

Beau and his dad walked the short distance to the restaurant, Beau taking halting steps beside his father.

"How are those legs holding up?" Ed asked, his concern disguised behind his usual scowl.

"As good as can be expected."

All around him were breathtaking views. Scenery he'd never appreciated before.

Ever since his recovery, Beau had been acutely aware of what a treasure this part of the country was. He had renewed appreciation for being outdoors. For so long he'd taken all of this wide-open space and invigorating air for granted. He'd gotten used to the majestic mountains that towered above, bathed in their pinkish blue hue, snowcapped in winter, a lush green as summer approached.

Feelings of nostalgia washed over Beau. What he wouldn't give to be up there, conquering those faraway slopes. Skiing had been to him what breathing now was.

"Smells like summer's on its way," he commented, determined to put any thoughts of skiing behind him, at least for now.

"It's already here," Ed responded, using his usual economy of words. "Memorial Weekend is only a few days away."

A modern saloon loomed ahead of them, its sign shaped like a gigantic cowboy's hat. It read THE TROUGH.

Ed repeated the name on the black-and-white sign swinging out front. "Everyone's got a gimmick these days."

Inside, hay covered the floor and the smell of parched peanuts and brewed ale dominated. A perky brunette wearing an itsy-bitsy skirt, boots, and a jaunty neckerchief escorted them to a booth at the back of the room.

"Is this all right?" she asked, eyeing Beau as if he were on the menu. "Hey, aren't you Beau Hill?"

Beau nodded a greeting. It was starting again, recognition that he was somebody. He threw her a brilliant smile.

"Yes, you are," the hostess insisted loudly. "No one else can make a girl's heart throb like you can. No one has that smile. Everyone, Beau Hill's here," she shouted.

Thank God the lunch crowd didn't seem overly impressed. It was he who wanted to die. There were a few cursory looks and some whispered conversation, but most patrons returned to their meals. It might have something to do with the pugnacious look his dad threw them. Beau couldn't be sure.

Beau faced his dad. The two began a tentative but somewhat awkward conversation. This continued up until their entrees were served.

"Nice boots," Ed said sarcastically, scowling at Beau's gray snakeskin boots.

"I know you hate them, Dad."

"When are you going to grow yourself some hair?"

Beau ran a hand over his pate and said placidly, "When Michael Jordan does the same." Twirling his hoop earring for effect, he dared Ed to continue.

"All right, I give up," Ed said, a twinkle in his eye.

In an attempt to defy his wife's efforts to keep him on a diet, Ed began to devour most of the oversize portion of ribs set down before him.

"Okay, let's talk turkey, young man," he said, picking up the napkin again and dabbing at his lips. "You took me out to lunch for a reason, let's get to it."

Beau swallowed his burger in a quick gobble. The opening had presented itself at last. "I want to know what's happening with the Simpkins' case."

Ed squinted at him. "Why are you interested in my clients?"

Beau explained that Reggie DaCosta was volunteering at his center, adding, "He seems like a good kid."

"Yes, and he just happened to pick your center to volunteer at, never mind there are others in Denver. Don't you think it's a little late for him to try to gain respectability? His attorney's coaching him."

"That might be so. Reggie's sister is. . .was my physical therapist, Dad."

Beau had just received official notification that someone else would be taking over his therapy. The idea made him mad. He still hadn't been able to talk to Shayna.

"How long have you known they were related?" Ed cross-examined.

"Not until recently."

"And you're not suspicious of that woman's interest in you? Your mom tells me she's been over to your house numerous times." Ed scowled at Beau.

He continued peppering him with questions, which Beau tried his best to answer. He could only imagine how any witness must feel. Browbeaten.

Apparently running out of questions, his dad said, "Johnson, who represents the boy, dug up three witnesses." He nibbled on a rib. "None of them are credible. One's a vagrant, the other two are drunks." He harrumphed.

"Four witnesses," Beau corrected. "The most recent seemed to be on the ball."

"How come you know so much?"

"Shayna filled me in."

"Sounds like this Shayna is a lot more to you than a therapist?"

Beau snapped his mouth shut and watched his dad wipe his hands and mouth on the checkered napkin.

"I guess it's worth checking out this new development," Ed said. "I have to call Colin Johnson anyway. The trial's only days away and Mrs. Simpkins is waffling back and forth. She's worried she may have identified the wrong kids. She claims she doesn't see too well, and to use her words, one black boy looks like the other."

Beau bristled. "And because she's confused and obviously bigoted, she's willing to risk a young boy's reputation and ruin his life." He shook his head.

"That's most of the world for you," his father answered, standing abruptly. "I've got work to do. You did say you were picking up the check." He beckoned the skimpily clad waitress over. "My son's got it covered."

Beau removed his wallet and slapped down a credit card. Who knew how this would all turn out? He'd given it a try in terms of Reggie, and he hadn't given up on Shayna. Not speaking with her for a whole week had been agony. Now he was determined to find her, make amends, and move their relationship along. But first he needed to call Miles Williams.

Instead of returning home, Beau drove up the steep mountain road and parked his car on the side of the road. The fresh air always helped him think better, and he needed time to plan a strategy, and not just with Shayna. While he couldn't prove it yet, he was more and more convinced that someone had deliberately tried to sabotage him.

He took a deep breath, got out his cell phone, and dialed Miles's number. It rang forever. Eventually an out-of-breath man picked up. Beau didn't know Miles well enough to determine if it was he that had answered.

"I'm looking for Miles Williams," he said.

"That's me."

"Miles. This is Beau Hill."

There was a discernible pause on the other end, then, "How are you, man? I meant to visit you. But time has a way of getting away from you."

"Of course it does."

Maybe it was his imagination, but Miles sounded uncomfortable. Beau leaned over the railing staring down at the steep precipice that was mantled in varying shades of green. He let the silence build.

"It's good to hear from you, man," Miles said. "Was there something you wanted?"

"I'd like some information, for starters."

"I'll help if I can." Miles's voice sounded steadier. *How come he hadn't asked, information about what?*

"Is this a good time to talk?" Beau pressed.

"As good as any. With all the rumors flying, I guess you want to find out what happened that day. David must have told you what I said."

"Actually he told me what you didn't say."

"Where are you right now?" Miles asked.

"Driving around. Sorting out my life."

"Stop by tomorrow, say around two. We'll talk and I'll try my best to answer your questions."

After getting directions Beau hung up. He stood for a long time staring down into the endless greenness, strategizing a plan. Miles had initially been uncomfortable, almost wary, but he'd invited him to his home. He could easily have blown him off. Maybe he was suffering from a guilty conscience and needed to unload.

Tomorrow he'd let Miles do most of the talking. Right now he had one more stop to make; then he was off to see Shayna.

Across town, Shayna faced her parents in the tiny town house's kitchen. Kara and Vincent had flown in from Seattle the evening before and Reggie was volunteering at the center. He seemed to be spending more and more time there. So far he was putting in more time than the days he'd committed to.

Kara's fingers circled the cup of coffee she was sipping on. "I have to admit I'm worried about this case," she said. "Your brother hasn't had a very good track record."

"He does have a good attorney," Shayna offered. "Colin Johnson was a find. He's been nothing but wonderful."

"Single too," Vincent said astutely. "Bright and successful."

"Single is a good thing," Kara said, perking up. "You two get along?"

Shayna scrubbed at an imaginary spot on the kitchen counter. "Yes, we get along." She held her breath, waiting for the inevitable questions. Her mother had already voiced the concern that maybe she was too picky or simply afraid of getting involved. She feared that by the time Shayna got serious it might be too late to have kids.

Her mother surprised her by letting it go.

"We've got four witnesses," Vincent said, changing the subject. He looked to Shayna for confirmation.

She nodded.

Vincent was a medium-sized man, about five foot ten in his stockinged feet. Shayna had taken after her mother, who barely made it to five feet in heels.

"And this Bert person is our best shot?" he quizzed.

"Looks like it."

Her mother put her head down on the table and began to sob.

"What am I going to do if my baby boy gets put in jail," she said, sniffing.

"He's not going to jail," Vincent said stoically, placing comforting hands on her shoulders. "Johnson knows what he's doing and Reggie doesn't have a history of previous arrests. Juries take that type of thing into consideration."

Shayna certainly hoped that he was right. She stood awkwardly looking at her mother. What did you say when your parent was so obviously in distress? Words were not appropriate enough to comfort. The phone rang and Shayna's dad signaled that he would pick up.

He spoke into the mouthpiece briefly and held out the receiver.

"It's for you."

Shayna swore there were tears in his eyes. Her heart pounded and her mouth went dry. Oh, God, something must have happened to Reggie.

"Hello," she said tentatively, conscious of her father in the background conducting a whispered conversation with her mother.

"Hi," Colin said. "I'm glad I was able to catch the whole family at home."

"Has something happened?" The question popped out before she could stop it.

"Actually something has happened. You probably aren't ready for this."

Just break the news to me, Colin. Bad, good, or indifferent.

More than a beat or two went by.

"Shayna, Ed Anderson called."

"What did he want?" Her voice sounded strained. Nervous.

"It's good news, Shayna. Mrs. Simpkins has second thoughts. I know she identified Reggie in the initial lineup, but she's since had an attack of conscience. She's waffling now. She's not sure Reggie's the right person. She told Ed that the teenager who accosted her had a tattoo on his right bicep."

"Reggie doesn't have any tattoos. We wouldn't let him," Shayna said, her voice stronger.

"I know that."

"So what happens now?" Shayna asked.

"Ed says he's going to speak with the judge, tell him about Mrs. Simpkins's doubts. The fact that we have four witnesses may have helped change her mind. Bert Templeton is a credible witness. He'd down on his luck but has no history of mental instability or substance abuse. He was very clear on the time the kids came in and ordered their burgers and fries. He remembers their clothing in detail, and can describe each and every one of them. He even remembers what they were talking about."

"Thank God for Bert," Shayna said, rolling her eyes heavenward.

"I'll be sure to keep you posted then."

"Please."

"Maybe next week you and I will be having drinks and this whole episode will be a bad memory."

"I doubt that."

Colin hung up and Shayna rejoined her parents, who now stood, arms around each other. They broke their hold long enough to include her in their protective circle.

"Thank you, Lord," Kara said, tears flowing freely. "You're an almighty Lord. My baby boy's been saved."

"Thank you for listening to our prayers," Vincent added.

"It's not over yet," Shayna reminded them. "There's always the possibility the Simpkins woman could have another change of mind. Let's wait to get official notification before we go out and celebrate."

"That's probably smart. Still, I feel good about the way things are shaping up," Vincent said.

Shayna kept her fingers crossed behind her back. She smiled brightly at her parents, assuring them she had every confidence Reggie would go free and an apology extended. This break had come from the most unexpected source, the alleged victim herself. God did work in mysterious ways.

The front door opened and heavy boots thudded across the wooden floors. Reggie had brought home a herd of elephants, it seemed.

"Come into the kitchen, son," Vincent called.

"I have company," Reggie announced. "Shayna, Beau's here."

Beau, cane and all, made his presence known.

"Hi, Shayna."

She gaped at his western attire, the whole urban chic look. She'd never see Beau in boots, and snake, no less. His jeans hugged his slightly rounded butt and his muscular legs made her think of that night when he'd ridden her to the sky and back. All those months of sitting idle hadn't seemed to affect his muscle tone.

Shayna's eyes shifted to the hollow of his neck where the designer shirt lay open. His strong column of a neck beckoned. She resisted the temptation to run her fingers through the few escaping hairs, to lay her head against his chest, and breathe in his musky male scent. She was still mad at him. She wanted him gone.

"What are you doing here?" she asked brusquely. "I wasn't expecting you."

"Figured I'd surprise you." He turned to her parents, acknowledging them by saying, "Mr. and Mrs. DaCosta, I'm Beau Hill." Then he planted a kiss on Shayna's cheek. "What a way to greet your boyfriend."

"Boyfriend," her mother exclaimed. "Shayna, you never mentioned a boyfriend."

"Beau's pulling your leg," Shayna protested.

"I am not."

Why was he putting her in an awkward position? Now she would have a lot of explaining to do.

"Well, are you, or aren't you?" Vincent demanded, his scowl apparent. Shayna knew that look. It meant mess with my little girl and I'll rip your eyes out.

"Shayna's still not comfortable with it. We just started dating. She was my physical therapist before we fell in love," Beau said.

"Why didn't you tell me?" Kara implored. "You had me believing that you weren't interested in a man."

"There was nothing to tell. See, Beau, look what you've done." Shayna glared at him and thudded the heel of her hand against his strong bicep.

"Don't we have something to do?" Vincent asked, corralling his wife and son. "These two lovebirds need to talk."

They were gone before Shayna could stop them.

More than a little irritated, Shayna faced Beau. "The nerve of you to come stomping in telling my parents some bull, acting like nothing's happened."

"Something did happen," Beau said calmly. "We made wild, crazy love and told each other how much we cared."

She wanted to toss one of her china plates at him, watch that smug expression go crashing off his face. What did he think? That she'd so easily forgotten that his ex-girlfriend had walked in? She'd had a key. That in itself said something. Shayna had been the one forced to get dressed and who'd rushed out the back door minus underwear. When had she become the other woman?

"Do I look stupid?" Shayna challenged. "You con Reggie into bringing you home. You try to sweet-talk me."

"Sweet-talk you? That's impossible. You can't be sweet-talked."

"Amen."

Intentionally leaving his cane behind, Beau advanced, successfully backing her into a corner. Shayna was pressed up against the kitchen wall and trapped between his muscular arms. The scent of musk and man overpowered her.

"This isn't fair," she said weakly, even as his gray eyes pierced hers.

"Life isn't fair."

"This is harassment. I'll start screaming."

"Better start now."

"You owe me an explanation. An apology."

Shayna looked up at Beau's wide mouth, sculptured cheekbones, and gunmetal eyes. There was no man more beautiful in the whole world.

"First of all," Beau said, "Chandra and I are over with.

There's not a snowball's chance in hell of us getting back together."

He silenced her by placing a finger to her lips. "I don't love her. I love you."

"Then why was she there?"

"To see if she could rekindle a flame that was already dead."

"And did she?" Shayna asked, knowing that if he answered in the affirmative it would break her heart.

Beau reached into his pocket and dangled a tiny metal object at her. "I've got my key back."

"She could have made a copy." She wanted to believe Beau. Believe he'd ended his relationship with the model. He'd never lied before. If anything it was she who'd lied by omitting to tell him the full story.

"I want you to have this," Beau said, pressing the key into her hands. "I'm changing my locks, but till then it's yours. You may come and go as you like. When the new locks are installed I'll give you another."

"I don't know what to say."

She couldn't stay mad at him, not when he'd confirmed he loved and trusted her by giving her his key.

"I really don't know what to say," Shayna repeated.

"Say nothing. Just kiss me."

And she did.

Chapter Twenty-three

Miles Williams lived in one of the many sprawling Denver suburbs. His house was small, but architecturally laid out to appear open and spacious. Inside was definitely a man's world, and workout equipment was plopped everywhere. Beau had to step over a pair of dumbbells and edge around a stationary bicycle to find a seat.

Miles greeted him at the door outfitted in athletic gear. He'd handed him a beer and disappeared into what Beau assumed was a bedroom.

"I'll be right back," he'd shouted.

The athlete still appeared jittery and uncomfortable. Beau wondered whether his disappearing act was simply a ploy to buy time and get himself together.

Miles reappeared when Beau was halfway through his beer. He had changed into jeans and a polo shirt, the short sleeves showing off his well-defined biceps.

"Sorry," he said, folding himself into a leather armchair and crossing one bulging thigh muscle over the other. "I've been working out for the last hour and needed to clean up." He chugged a mouthful of beer.

Letting the silence stretch out, Beau continued to sip on his brew. Miles had finished in the top fifteen in Vail. He had had an interesting skiing history and great things had at one time been predicted for him. But a series of injuries had laid him up, the most recent being when he'd shattered his femur and messed up his knee at the World Cup finals. Everyone had thought a comeback would be impossible, but Miles had shown them. After twenty-two months of rehabilitation he was back.

Beau looked at the man lounged across from him. He appeared the picture of health and vitality. He and Miles had never been particularly friendly, but the athlete had always appeared supportive if a little distant. *If Miles can do it, so can I,* he thought. *Look at that Lalive woman who raced with a broken back.*

At last Beau broke the uneasy silence. "I'm here because I'm trying to put some missing pieces together."

Miles's ice-blue eyes flickered but he didn't say a thing.

"I'm sure you know I've been out of commission for several months. It's a miracle that I'm even here on my own," Beau said.

At last a movement. Something. "Yeah, I heard. You weren't supposed to ever be able to walk again."

"Exactly. Now I'm hearing conflicting stories about what happened the day I was hurt. I've already spoken to Josh Vanderhorn and Peter Turner. Peter claims to have seen a man hanging around my ski gear. Josh claims Peter knows more than he's saying. But both men have memory loss when I asked who packed my skis and boots and sent them back. Any thoughts?"

Miles took a long draft of beer. "It was sort of a crazy day," he said. "Everything happened so fast. We'd had the best practice run ever and we were in high spirits. We were certain the team would finish in the top three, and you would win the downhill."

Beau sighed, forcing back the memories. "Yes, and rumors have been flying ever since, but no concrete information. That fall changed my life permanently. I want answers."

Miles set his beer down on a table. Water rings attested to the fact that it had served as a resting place for several bottles. He stood, working the kinks out of his neck, and took his time answering.

"Look," he said, "everyone on the ski team's speculated for ages that Peter and Josh were in this thing together. Both wanted a place on the podium. No one believes Peter's story about this strange guy lurking around the equipment. We think Peter was the one who did something to your skis. Just the evening before he was racing around looking for a screwdriver. Initially no one could figure out why he needed one."

"Why do you think he needed one?" Beau asked, making sure to keep his gaze fixed on Miles.

Miles circled the room flexing his strong neck muscles. "Of course whatever I say is hearsay. You'll need to keep my identity confidential or I'll deny it."

Beau nodded.

"All right, it's like this," Miles began. "A skier with your experience doesn't just fall. I watched that downhill race. You were in the lead; then all of a sudden you went crashing. Josh and Peter both wanted to place. Josh was the more solid skier. Why would Peter be looking for a screwdriver of a certain size? Why would he enter a restaurant leaving his wallet behind in his car? Then he comes back inside telling a bunch of the guys that he saw someone hanging around the skis. No one else saw anyone but him." Miles screwed up his mouth, his cynicism evident.

Beau didn't like the very vivid picture that kept popping into his head. It took all of his willpower to remain seated and listen to Miles finish. Unbelievable that he might have lost a race because of two people's ambitions. Not just a race either. The use of his legs for several months. He could have died. But he had no proof and he'd promised Miles not to say where he'd gotten this information from. Tough spot.

"Here's what I'm thinking," Miles said, finishing his beer in a gulp. "You know those little screws, the din settings on your bindings?"

"Ummm-hmmm."

"What if those screws were adjusted?"

"My foot would fall out. At high speeds I'd go toppling."

"Right."

"Thanks," Beau said, rising and picking up his cane. "You've been very helpful. I don't suppose you know what became of my skis or boots?"

"As a matter of fact I do. Josh volunteered to pack your things. We were surprised. You know he never puts himself out. We were in shock after your fall. No one started speculating until weeks after. A group of us met for drinks and then the stories kept coming out. Something smelled, big time."

"I really appreciate this," Beau said, leaning on his cane and slapping Miles on the back. "I'll be sure to keep your name out of it."

"I would appreciate that. And, Beau," Miles called, as Beau hobbled away. "Rumor also has it Josh shipped your skis and boots to his home. He wanted the evidence out of sight."

Beau didn't trust himself to answer. His mind was in

a whirl. If Miles was telling the truth, Peter and Josh were two conniving, dangerous people. But the fact that he'd survived his fall was testimony that he was stronger than they. He would fight back.

Beau got into his vehicle with one purpose in mind. He would catch Shayna at the Rehab Center before she got off work and persuade her to have dinner with him. He needed to discuss this new twist with her and strategize.

He pulled into the parking lot just as Shayna was exiting the building and sat for a while simply staring at her. She looked particularly attractive in a short mint-green skirt with dark green leggings under it. Her blouse was cropped, but not enough to show off her toned midriff or the little gold stud he found particularly sexy. A jaunty scarf was tied around her neck. She looked fresh, innocent, and pretty. And just looking at her made him happy.

Determined to show her he could walk on his own, Beau left his cane behind, and got out of the car. Shayna hurried across the lot, heading for employee parking. She appeared unaware of him sitting in the Saab. Beau limped trying to catch up with her.

"Shayna," he called, realizing it was an impossible task.

She appeared not to have heard him. She'd gotten her keys out, and the lights on her car flashed briefly as she punched the remote button.

"Shayna," Beau called again.

This time she turned to acknowledge her name.

"Beau, what are you doing here?" she greeted. "It's not your day for therapy. Where's your cane?"

He took her hand and pressed the palm to his lips. "I missed you. I figured if I just showed up you couldn't say no to drinks and maybe a little dinner."

"I'm not sure. . ."

"You're not sure, what? I know it's last minute, but I do really need to talk to you."

She softened. "Okay, I'll call home. Maybe I can convince my parents to go out to dinner and take Reggie with them."

"Good. We'll take my car."

"What do I do with mine?"

"Leave it parked."

He took her hand. "We'll get it later. Have you ever been to the Brown Palace Hotel?"

"Can't say I have."

"I see I have my work cut out for me, showing you Denver. Wait until you see the atrium lobby of Brown's. We'll do drinks there and decide what to do about dinner."

"Sounds like a plan." Shayna curled her fingers around his and followed him back to the car.

Beau put the Saab's convertible roof down, and held the passenger door open to let Shayna slide in. Revving the engine, he careened out of the parking lot.

She swatted his arm affectionately. "You really are a daredevil."

"It takes a good tactician with nerves of steel to be a downhill racer," he reminded her.

"And you were a very good one from what I read."

"The best."

"Modest too," Shayna said, knuckles gray as he took a hairpin curve on almost two wheels.

He drove somewhat more sedately when they arrived in downtown Denver. He had no choice. The traffic in a town that never slept dictated that. After he handed the key of the car over to a valet, they entered an airy, opulent lobby. Several people reclined on red velvet sofas or in high wingback chairs. Beau noted the older gentleman with the faded jeans and antique silver buckle. He wore a linen jacket and an expensive Stetson on his head. In the corner, a woman outfitted in an elegant suit and pearls held court with other ladies similarly dressed. Cow town meets Now town, a friend had once said, setting off a series of guffaws. It was true. Downtown Denver had turned out to be the place to see and be seen.

Shayna pointed out the stained glass canopy up above. "God, is that beautiful."

To their right was a bar, and Beau ushered her in there. They slid into a booth at the back, facing each other.

"So what's going on?" she asked.

"I'll tell you in a minute. Let's order." Beau motioned a hovering waiter over and without consulting Shayna, he said, "A bottle of Moet, please."

"Moet?" Shayna looked at him askance. "Are we celebrating something?"

"We're celebrating us."

"Us? What am I missing?"

He hoped this wasn't going to be an issue between them. He was a take-charge man and wasn't about to change.

The bottle of Moet was placed in a silver bucket and rested between them. The cork popped. Their waiter made a gigantic production of pouring.

Beau waited until the man had left before clinking his glass against Shayna's. "Here's to love," he said. "Love and getting to know each other better."

She smiled, but didn't say a word.

Insecurity kicked in. Shayna had recently admitted she loved him. They'd made mad passionate love together. Why was she backpedaling now?

"Something on your mind?" Shayna asked, interrupting his doubts. "You said you wanted to talk to me, so talk. I'm listening."

He sipped his champagne, savoring the bubbles, then swallowed. "I met with Miles Williams today."

"And what did he say?" She leaned across the table of the booth giving him an eyeful of cleavage. A light citruslike fragrance wafted his way. Now was not the time to think of holding her in his arms or of making love to her. Yet he wanted her with a ferocity that made no sense. Right now. Not later. *Focus, Beau.*

"And Miles said . . ." Shayna prompted.

"He made me promise to keep his name out of it. I'm violating his trust even telling you this."

"I wouldn't breathe a word. I swear." She held up a hand. Face flushed. Eyes shining in anticipation. "Come on, tell me what he said."

"He feels certain I was sabotaged. He thinks that Josh and Peter were in it together, that between them both they came up with a plan to ensure I would be disqualified. He thinks that maybe the tension on my bindings was adjusted. You know the screws on your skis—"

"Yes, I know what you're talking about," Shayna said, excitedly. "I do ski, you know. If someone adjusted those screws you'd crash and you'd never think to check. You'd just been skiing that morning."

Beau gulped his champagne. It was still difficult to believe someone would want to sabotage him. "I fell right out of my skis. I was going at really high speeds."

"You could have been killed. I can't believe people would be that evil." Shayna stared at him over the rim of her glass, tears of outrage glittering. "My God, what's wrong with the world?"

Beau shrugged. There had been one plus to this whole thing, he'd met Shayna.

"Bastards," she muttered, downing her champagne.

"I don't know for certain who did it," Beau reminded her, remembering his earlier conversation. "Maybe I can find out."

"Spill it."

Beau refilled both of their glasses before saying, "I met a man at the rehabilitation center. His name was Lenox. He was telling me all about how Hill Of Dreams had given him a second chance to moonlight as a drummer. He works for UPS during the day."

"Call him," Shayna said excitedly. "Give him an approximate date of your stay in Salt Lake City; then give him your address. Maybe he can even look up the shipment date in his computer."

"Good idea." Beau clinked his glass against hers. "What do you say to room service?"

"Room service? Why?" Clearly she didn't know where he was going.

"You'll have to go home tonight on account of Reggie and your parents. The drive back to my place is going to take time. We can take a room here. Have dinner sent up."

"Does dinner come with dessert?" Shayna leered at him.

"No with an appetizer. The DaCosta special."

"That might put you over the hill, Mr. Hill. You're not ready for me."

"Says who?"

Beau set his flute down, stood, and offered Shayna his arm. "Shall we put your considerable talents to the test, Ms. DaCosta?" he asked, escorting her out.

As they exited, Chandra pranced by with a tall, dark-skinned man on her arm. She glared at them, then made a production of kissing the man.

"You're too good to me, Franco," she said.

"Franco?" Shayna whispered as they hurried out. "Who's he?"

"Her Italian lover." He'd barely given his ex a glance. "Poor man has my condolences. The good thing is she's now no longer my problem, nor will she be yours."

Chapter Twenty-four

Six stories up in the Brown Palace, Shayna was stretched out under the covers. She watching Beau undress, enjoying the languid way he slid off his loafers, stepped out of his jeans, and carefully folded them over a chair. He remained clothed in only his black briefs and brightly colored shirt, sporting the Polo logo. Shayna's heart pounded as her eyes fastened on his strong thigh muscles and slightly rounded butt. He turned, smiled, and with his heart in his eyes, headed her way.

Shayna sat up in bed, deliberately letting the covers shift. Their entrees, he'd notified her, would be delayed. Appetizers came first. Beau's glazed gray gaze settled on her bare breasts. He looked as if he might leap at her any moment. She stretched, letting the sheets slide farther down.

As she'd expected, Beau came to her. He reached across to draw her close.

"I love you," he said, gathering her in his arms. "I even love the feel of you."

Shayna's palm moved across his shaved dome. It was smooth and perfectly shaped. Beau buried his face between her breasts, his wet tongue sliding down and around, tracing patterns. She fingered the lobe with the gold earring. "I love you, Beau," she said.

Vocalizing feelings didn't come easy to her. Love she'd come to associate with disillusionment and being hurt. Love she'd associated with Michael. Time to get over him. Move on. She began to unbutton Beau's shirt, to weave her fingers through his chest hairs, to find a nipple, and squeeze gently.

He'd fastened his mouth around one breast and now everything pulsed. Shayna drew his head even closer, allowing him to drink more deeply. One of his hands slid between her thighs and his fingers worked another kind of magic. She settled more firmly on his palm and began an exploration of her own. Her hands moved downward, sliding beneath the sexy black briefs, cupping his buttocks, moving forward to circle his sex.

He gasped. "Easy, girl, we wouldn't want a premature ending to this thing."

"You said you were ready for me, Mr. Over the Hill."

Beau kissed her, settling his tongue deeply in her mouth. She took hold of it, teasing him mercilessly, pressing herself against him, turned on by the friction of chest hairs rubbing against her breasts. Beau reacted by pressing a thumb into her and by finding the nub at her core and working it.

That cool, wintery voice of his said, "Tell me when you're ready, babe."

Oh, God, was she ready. Ready for him. She was hot, cold, and hot again. The Chinese red walls of the room quivered and vibrated with each stroke. He settled her on top of him again. Shayna squirmed until she found the right position, giving him access. He was at her breasts again, laving, sucking them. She gyrated her hips and clamped her thighs together, successfully trapping his hand. Taking his jaw between her hands, she kissed him.

Beau rolled on a condom and with a ferocity she didn't know he possessed, entered her. Shayna choked back a loud exclamation of passion. She shifted her weight and together they rocked back and forth finding a comfortable rhythm. She nibbed his earlobes and licked at his throat while he drove deeper. Wrapping her legs around his butt, she urged him to go faster.

The breathing she heard was theirs. The sighs of satisfaction hers.

"I can't hold back any longer, babe," Beau said, making a choking sound.

"Now," Shayna urged. "Let go, Beau. Let gooooooo!"

He did, emitting another guttural sound. The room exploded around her in sharp pinpoints of light. She hurled over the top, shouting his name. Smells, sights, sounds, forgotten. Sensory overload, she'd heard it called. Somewhere in this journey of exploration they'd formed a pact. It was she and Beau against the rest of the world. Beau and Shayna together and no one could break them apart.

Two days later, Beau decided a surprise visit to Peter might be in order. He'd debated just showing up on Josh Vanderhorn's doorstep but figured that, of the two men, Peter was more likely to break. The athlete's address had been obtained from Miles, who'd been a guest in Peter's home on more than one occasion. Beau had called Peter to verify he was home, hanging up when his teammate had answered. He parked the Saab half a block away and left his cane behind. Come hell or high water, he would make it there on his own two feet.

The door was answered by Peter himself. He gaped at Beau. "My God, Hill, you're walking."

Beau planted his feet firmly, despite the fact his legs ached. He was taller than Peter by several inches. "Aren't you going to ask me in?"

"Of course." Peter stood aside to let him by.

He entered a masculine living room, black and gray being the predominant colors.

"What brings you here?" Peter asked, his unease manifesting itself in the working of his lower lip.

Beau took a seat on the black leather couch and placed one loafer on a Levi-clad thigh. "I'm here for the truth, Peter."

Openmouthed, Peter stared at him. "What truth?"

"The truth about what happened to me on the day that I lost the downhill."

Peter went pasty white. "You were ahead, Beau; then you fell."

"Yes, I am painfully aware of that. I'm the one who broke my back, remember? I'm now being told that there was a cover-up, a conspiracy of silence, that everyone knew that you and Josh had something to do with sabotaging me. Did you, Peter?"

"I did not."

"Then where are my skis? My boots? I'm told you and Josh volunteered to send my things, but you conveniently had a memory lapse. You told me you didn't know who sent my personal items."

Although the room was not hot, Peter was visibly sweating. "I swear," he said, holding up one hand, "I did not volunteer to pack your personal stuff."

"Then who did?"

"Look, I told you I didn't know."

"I'll find out," Beau said, rising, "and if I discover that you're lying there will be hell to pay." He jabbed a finger at Peter and headed out.

"I'm telling you the truth," Peter called after him. "Miles Williams was the person I saw hanging around your equipment. I wanted to alert you but I didn't want to name Miles 'cause I didn't want to cause trouble. I figured if I told the guys I saw a suspicious person by the equipment they would tell you. Miles and Josh are friends, they've been for quite some time."

Seated again in the Saab, Beau punched in the Hill Of Dreams number. He got Malcolm on the phone and demanded he check old records to see if Lenox Frasier had left a number behind. After an eternity on hold, Malcolm returned to tell him he'd had no success. Time to put his thinking cap on. Lenox was a drummer for The Springs. The group still played at some of the popular LoDo nightspots. Beau made a second call.

"Meet Market," a boisterous woman answered.

Knowing that his name would produce a certain reaction, Beau identified himself. "How ya doing? Beau Hill here. I'm planning a party," he lied. "I'm friends with The Springs drummer. Would you have his number?"

"*The* Beau Hill!" the woman repeated, sounding awed. "Hot diggity dog! I'm talking to the skier."

Beau could hear her loud wheezing. *Damn it, please, no vapors.* He just wanted a phone number. He made himself sound civil. "That's me."

"Hold on a moment, I can't breathe."

Beau gritted his teeth. *Just gimme the damn number.*

A man's voice barked in his ear, "Hey, champ, this is a test, you claiming to be Beau Hill? How did he place in the World Cup and Chevy finals?"

Beau provided the appropriate response.

"No way to really be sure you're not jerking me around, but I'm going to have to believe you. Besides, you sound like him. I've heard that voice trillions of times on TV and that new commercial just aired."

The number. Just give me the number.

After more jabbering, the man finally gave Beau two numbers, a day and a night one.

His next phone call was made to Towanda and he waited for the housekeeper to check her files. She returned breathing heavily.

"I found the UPS slip," she announced.

"Good, give me the tracking number."

Beau scribbled the number down.

Next Beau punched in Lenox's day number. When a woman answered he quickly asked for Lenox Frasier and was then transferred to voice-mail hell. Frustrated, he identified himself, and left a message and phone number.

Beau careened down the road, going at least sixty miles an hour. He had no particular destination in mind. It was too early to head for Shayna's where he'd been invited for dinner. His cell phone rang and he narrowly missed sideswiping a Camaro when he reached to retrieve it from the console.

"Yes?"

"Lenox Frasier returning your call. What's up, man?"

"Hey, Lenox." Beau stated his purpose for calling earlier.

"I can probably help you if you have a tracking number," Lenox said.

"I do."

He heard the click-clicking of a keyboard and several muttered comments. "There it is."

"Is the sender's name listed?"

"Yup. Sure is."

"Read it to me."

Beau's stomach clenched in anticipation.

"Looks like the person sent several packages that day. The driver picked up seven from the address in Olympic village. Six were sent to 87 Scenic Drive. The other to an address in the Whispering Pines Country Club."

Eighty-seven Scenic Drive was Beau's address. He wasn't sure who lived in Whispering Pines but planned on finding out.

"The tracking numbers are linked. The one box went out insured. The contents reads skis."

"Who sent the damn packages?" Beau demanded, his rudeness taking him by surprise.

"Don't stress," Lenox said, "I'll tell you. The name's Miles Williams."

That rotten bastard. That lying piece of trash. Wait until I get my hands on him. He could have killed me.

But Miles didn't live in a country club, so what gave? Beau pulled off the road, took deep breaths, and carefully parked the car on a side street. He sat for a long time with his eyes closed, and his head on the steering wheel, until he pulled himself together so that he could make the next call.

He reached David on his cell phone and quickly explained what had transpired.

"Call your dad at once," his agent ordered. "If we can get hold of your skis and prove that they were tampered with, it becomes a criminal matter. We will probably need a search warrant to get into that place in Whispering Pines. Your decision. Call me back after you talk to your dad."

Luckily his father was in town. Beau took a full ten minutes to explain what he'd discovered.

"Williams would be pretty dumb to have your skis if

he did indeed tamper with them," Ed commented. "Try to reach him. Make him aware that you know the skis were mailed to this place in Whispering Pines." Ed paused. "Don't the Vanderhorns have a place there?"

Beau's thoughts raced. They did. The Vanderhorns were definitely the country club set.

"What do I do afterward?"

"That you'll have to decide. It's a pretty serious matter when someone sets out to deliberately hurt you. I would not allow them to get off scot-free."

After Beau hung up he decided to do one better, go to Miles's house and confront him. He called David back and his agent agreed to join him.

"You'll need support. Swing by my house and pick me up," David said, his tone containing suppressed outrage.

Fifteen minutes later they were on their way.

A Harley Davidson was parked in Miles's driveway when they pulled up. Beau and David hopped out and tromped toward the house with purpose. Music blasted from the inside, and over the music the sounds of a man huffing and puffing. Miles was working out.

Beau banged the brass knocker and was forced to bang it again when several minutes later they still faced a closed door.

"I'll be right there," an annoyed voice eventually called.

The door was thrown open, and a huffing, puffing Miles faced them. He wore a tank top and the evidence of his efforts was sprawled out behind him: weights and dumbbells.

"I wasn't expecting you." He eyed David suspiciously. "Did you forget something?" The last sentence was aimed at Beau.

"May we come in?" Beau's question was more of a statement as he pushed past Miles. David followed.

Miles trailed them in. "Is something wrong?"

"Plenty," Beau said, facing him. "You told me a story when I was here a few days back. It didn't check out."

"What do you mean?"

Miles looked flustered and uncomfortable. Beau moved in for the kill.

"I spoke with a UPS representative. I know where my skis and boots were mailed."

"What does this have to do with me?"

"Everything. You told me that Peter and Josh were the ones who mailed my stuff. I found out that's not true."

"I never said that," Miles said, backing up. "You misunderstood me."

"I don't think so."

David circled Miles, hemming him in from the back.

"Your name was listed on that UPS slip as the sender," Beau accused.

"Maybe Peter or Josh listed it," Miles sputtered. "Maybe they figured they needed to do that to take the heat off them if it ever came out."

"Then why not send the skis to your address? Why send it to the Whispering Pines Country Club? The Vanderhorn place?"

"Maybe they didn't know my address."

"You know what I think," David said, entering the conversation for the first time. "You're lying. I think you and Joshua Vanderhorn were in this together. I'm fairly certain that when we check this out we'll find out you and Vanderhorn were in cahoots and several skiers on the team knew it."

Miles visibly paled. Beau decided to press his advantage. "Weren't you the one looking for a screwdriver?" he bluffed. "That's what I heard."

"I . . ."

Beau went for the jugular. "You what? Didn't expect me to get seriously hurt?"

"Something like that."

Beau wanted to do serious damage to the athlete. "You evil son of a . . ." He lurched, going for Miles's throat. David stepped between them.

"He's not worth it, Beau."

Miles continued to blubber. "We volunteered to pack your stuff. Josh said we should send anything that might be incriminating to his parents' address, and he would get rid of it. So we did. We packed up the stuff together and I called UPS."

"That was dumb of you to list your name as the sender," Beau said, through clenched teeth.

"We didn't expect you to ever find out. I mean your skis disappeared. We thought it was over and done with. That you would never find out. Please . . ." Miles was crying openly. "Please don't involve the police. You'll ruin my career."

"You ruined mine," Beau said slowly and evenly. "You cost me a medal and you damn near cost me my life. Why should I care if you and Vanderhorn are locked up and put behind bars?"

Miles had gotten on his knees and was pleading. "I appeal to your decency. Your sense of sportsmanship. We were once a team."

Beau turned on his heel and beckoned to David. He shot over his shoulder, "You have a lot to learn about sportsmanship. Did anyone ever tell you that there's no *I* in team."

"What are you going to do?" Miles asked, crawling to them on his knees.

"What any sane person would do," David interjected. "Report your asses to the cops and let a judge handle it."

"You can't. Please, you can't. That will be the end of my career."

"You should have thought of that when you ended his," David said, an evil look in his eye. He exited, slamming the front door in Miles's face.

Chapter Twenty-five

The phone rang just as Shayna was about to chuck it in for the day. She'd been working with Earl, the quadriplegic. While there was little that she could do to improve his lot in life, his positive spirit and overall determination to work with his disability reaffirmed why she'd chosen to be a rehabilitation therapist.

"All right, Earl," Shayna said, "you did well today. I'll see you on Tuesday."

She gave him the thumbs-up sign and Earl blinked his eyes in acknowledgment. Shayna nodded to Mary Jane, who hovered at the entrance. She'd come to fetch her patient. The quadriplegic determinedly maneuvered his motorized wheelchair with the aid of the pencil in his mouth.

All of her patients should be like him, Shayna thought, positive and determined to beat the odds. Most weren't though. Most had to go through the usual stages before the breakthrough came. First there was denial, then anger, and later, acceptance. At some point, a decision had to be made to move on with their lives and work with or around their handicap.

So far it had been one harrowing day. She could use a good run, get that adrenaline flowing. Dealing with tense parents who were still awaiting the outcome of Reggie's situation was not easy. Dealing with her intense feelings for Beau and putting them in perspective only added to her stress. How did you get used to being in love with a person? How did you juggle the daily challenges? There were difficult patients, temperamental colleagues, and of course the politics that went with any organization. A busy weekend now stretched ahead. Memorial Day. Then later the trial.

The phone rang as Shayna picked up her purse and prepared to head out.

"Yes," she said, skipping the preliminaries.

"Hi, it's Colin. Good news, Shayna."

She needed good news. Shayna waited for him to go on.

"Are you there?" Colin asked.

"Yes, I'm here."

His voice sounded smooth as velvet on the other end. Seductive. Too bad he did nothing for her.

"Ed Anderson just called to apologize," he said. "He feels duped by his client. Turns out the whole thing was a hoax, staged for the insurance money. Mrs. Simpkins's husband punched her in the eye and with her consent gave her an overall pounding. They faked the vandalism and robbery. She started getting queasy with the trial practically around the corner. Remember I told you she was waffling about the boys' identities. Ed pressed her and she came clean. The judge of course threw out the case."

Shayna felt as if there were a load lifted off her shoulders. Anger soon took the place of relief.

"So you mean to tell me that she was willing to let my brother and those kids go to jail for something they didn't do? We should sue for slander."

"That's entirely up to you," Colin said. "Sleep on it. Meanwhile let's have dinner to celebrate."

"I'm sorry, Colin. I can't," Shayna said.

"Why not?"

"Because I'm dating someone and it's serious."

There was a pause on the other end. "Why didn't you say so before? Why get my hopes up?"

Good point. She'd known she wasn't interested in him. "This is a new development. We've only been seeing each other a short time," she said, as kindly as possible. "I tried my best not to mislead you."

"But you did." Another pause. "Look, I wish you the best of luck. Would this lucky man be Beau Hill?"

"It would."

"I'm not surprised. If it doesn't work out, call me."

"Thank you, Colin," Shayna said. "Thank you for everything you've done. You've been a good friend."

"I wish I could be more."

He hung up, and Shayna rested her back against one of the putrid green walls and took deep breaths. She held the phone, debating. After a while she dialed her home number, got her father on the phone, and told him the good news. Vincent was elated. Better than elated, ecstatic. Her mother grabbed the receiver and Shayna repeated the news all over again. She could hear Kara's sobs, but at least she knew these were tears of joy. Then Reggie was called to the phone. When the news was delivered he whooped in excitement. This was cause to celebrate.

Shayna then made a quick call to Beau.

"That's wonderful, hon," he said. "The best news I've heard all day. Why don't you bring the entire family over for dinner, say around eight? It will give me a chance to tell Towanda to toss another potato in to whatever she's making. How about you? Can you stop by now?"

Shayna debated. A quick call would take care of that. "Sure," she said.

She was able to get her family to agree to meet her at Beau's place. And for once she didn't have to cajole Reggie. He and Beau had bonded.

Whistling a tune, Shayna set off up the mountain road. Any thoughts of jogging had gone out of her head. She wanted to see Beau. Needed to see him. Independent as she might be, she relied on his support more and more.

Too much had happened in a short space of time. All sorts of different emotions now churned, threatening to spill over. She wanted to lay her head against his chest, have him wrap his arms around her, and tell her he loved her. Plain and simple she needed to be with him.

She parked her car behind an unfamiliar-looking sports utility vehicle and, using her key, entered the house. Voices came at her from the terrace. She'd thought they'd be alone. Wasn't that why Beau had asked her to come over early?

Shayna stepped onto the terrace with some trepidation. She was still not used to seeing Beau managing on his own. Walking. The cane he used primarily for long distances.

"Hello," Shayna greeted the small party that gathered. She flashed a smile in the direction of his mom, dad, and Kelly. But the only person she was really interested in stood just a few feet away. His eyes lit up when he saw her.

A young man that she didn't recognize stood with the group. Shayna nodded at him absently.

Victoria greeted her joyfully. "Hi, Shayna. I'm so glad you're here. You're all Beau talks about these days." She kissed Shayna on both cheeks.

Ed Anderson, whom Shayna had never met in person, introduced himself, then kissed her hand.

"I'm sorry and a bit embarrassed," he said. "Sorry your parents had to go through such an ordeal because my clients were deceitful, and embarrassed because I took them on."

Shayna said nothing. Ed had said it all. The stranger, who, judging by his hair color and coloring, must be a relation, interrupted.

"Is anyone going to introduce me to this beautiful woman?"

"We're getting around to it, Jason," Beau said.

Jason was a handsome man meticulously dressed like a preppy. He wore chinos, a buttoned-down oxford shirt, and loafers, not a hair out of place.

"Come meet my brother," Beau said, kissing Shayna soundly on the lips, branding her as his. He took her hand and guided her toward the starched-looking blond man who could easily have stepped off the cover of *Horse and Country*.

A warm embrace ensued, and a drink was shoved into her hand.

"I've heard quite a bit about you," Jason Anderson said. "You're actually one of the few people who can manage Beau."

"It's more like Beau manages me," Shayna muttered.

"I wouldn't even try." Beau's arm circled her waist.

Shayna pretended to glare at him, and he tightened his hold on her, and fitted her snugly against him. The group stood for a while engaging in more small talk.

After another few minutes elapsed, Beau said, "You'll have to entertain yourselves, Shayna and I are taking a walk. If the DaCostas show up before we get back, keep them entertained."

Beau led her down the steep terrace steps and toward the vicinity of the stables. Shayna could hear Scotch's, Vodka's, and Whiskey's snorts as they got closer. She wondered if Beau envisioned a late evening ride. She was hardly dressed for it. Besides, that would be so rude, no one else had been invited. But he walked past the stables, leading her down a path that soon would be moonlit. They came to a wide tranquil lake before he stopped.

He turned to Shayna. "I figured this might be the only time we would be alone tonight."

"Too bad we can't change that."

Beau gathered her in his arms, staring into her eyes. He kissed her soundly. When they eventually came up for air, she cuddled against him. The pinks and purples of a setting sun painted the distant mountains in a dreamy hue. Water dippers skimmed across the lake's surface, putting off a soft buzz. Summer was definitely in the air.

"Shayna, I love you," Beau said. "More than I thought I could love another person."

"And I love you." This time it came easily.

Beau turned her around, cupping her chin in his hand. "We should talk about us. What we want to do about this beautiful and unexpected relationship that has developed."

"What do you want to do about it?" Shayna challenged, putting the ball firmly back in his court.

"I want it to go on forever. You're all I think of. I'm incomplete without you. Life is meaningless."

Shayna sighed. Beau was letting all his barriers down, telling her how he really felt.

"We've only known each other a short time," she said. "And there's no rush. You've got decisions to make, like whether you'll want to ski again. Like what to do about Miles and Josh, now that the others on the ski team ratted them out and Josh was forced to admit he got rid of your skis. You also need to decide what you want to do with Hill Of Dreams."

"Yes, I know all of that and I know what I want. What I want is you. No amount of time is going to change my mind. And I've already thought about all the things you've mentioned. We'll take it nice and slow. I'd like to ski again. I'll never be Olympic caliber, but I'll hold my own. I can always coach young hopefuls.

"As for Miles and Josh, they've both been kicked off the ski team. That's justice enough for me. Their reputation is tarnished in the industry, and no one wants anything to do with them. Athletes as driven as they are need to ski. There isn't a more fitting punishment."

Beau kissed her again and the whole world tilted. She no longer saw the tranquil lake, the rapidly darkening sky, or heard the horses in the background neighing.

Shayna closed her eyes, kissing him back. She leaned into him, trusting him to support her.

"So I thought," he said, when he stopped kissing her, "that a vacation might be in order. Maybe go to Paris, Rome, see London. When we return I'll focus my attentions on Hill Of Dreams, and continue to develop it into the place I want it to be."

"I have vacation time coming up," Shayna said, stars in her eyes.

"I know. I checked. What do you say?"

"I say, yes. Oh, Beau, yes."

"Shayna," Beau said, taking her face between his

hands. "You were my dream come true. I knew that from the moment I met you."

"And you were my worst nightmare," she said, holding his gaze, "a handsome nightmare, and a very sexy one, but a nightmare no less."

"Kiss me and tell me that again."

Shayna fastened her arms around his neck and gave him the full DaCosta treatment.

When the kiss ended, Beau held her away from him.

"Shayna," he said, "I love you so much it hurts."

"And I love you more than I thought was possible. I'm trusting that you'll eventually make an honest woman of me."

"I'm ready to do that now."

"It's too soon," she said, kissing him again. "Ask me in, say, six months."

His kiss made her forget about the family waiting. About reality, and its habit of dousing cold water on dreams. Reality thinking wasn't about now what. Reality thinking was about when. About having hopes and dreams. About realizing them.

"I'm asking you now," Beau said again, holding her close.

She squeezed her eyes shut and took the plunge. "Okay . . . Yes."

She knew in her heart it would always be Beau and Shayna forever. She challenged anyone to try breaking them apart.

Dear Readers:

Have you ever had a change of heart? Were you ever involved in a relationship that seemed as if it had no place to go, or simply couldn't grow?

My hero and heroine are two people meeting because of happenstance. Beau, a proud athlete, is humbled when his accident leaves him vulnerable and dependent on others. He is as prickly as they come. Shayna, a once famous athlete, has had a similar experience. She knows what it's like to be a has-been. Her adjustment to the world of real people was not easy, and she's not about to be intimidated by Beau. He represents a personal challenge, and Shayna loves challenges. She is determined to get beneath the layers and find the real Beau.

I really enjoyed writing this story, because I believe that falling in love requires delving beneath the layers to find the real person and their vulnerable side.

If you liked Beau and Shayna's story, please let me know. Your support keeps me writing meaningful stories that make you think. My E-mail address is: Mkinggambl@aol.com. You may also write to me at: P.O. Box 25143, Tamarac, FL 33320. Be sure to include a self-adressed, stamped envelope.

Stay blessed,
Marcia King-Gamble

ABOUT THE AUTHOR

Marcia King-Gamble is a Caribbean-American author who relocated permanently to the United States at the tender age of fifteen. She has since lived in New York, New Jersey, Seattle, and Hawaii. Currently she resides in Florida.

Marcia is a world traveler. She has spent time in exotic locales such as Saudi Arabia, Istanbul, and the Far East. She is a graduate of Elmira College, Elmira, NY, hometown of Tommy Hilfiger. She holds degrees in psychology and theater. She is now a travel industry executive.

Marcia is the author of two novellas and six novels, two of which were nominated as *Romantic Times'* Picks of the Month.

"Writing is my passion," she says. "I write because I have to."

More Sizzling Romance From

Marcia King-Gamble

__Reason to Love	1-58314-133-2	$5.99US/$7.99CAN
__Illusions of Love	1-58314-104-9	$5.99US/$7.99CAN
__Under Your Spell	1-58314-027-1	$4.99US/$6.50CAN
__Eden's Dream	0-7860-0572-6	$5.99US/$7.99CAN
__Remembrance	0-7860-0504-1	$4.99US/$6.50CAN

Call toll free **1-888-345-BOOK** to order by phone or use this coupon to order by mail.

Name_____

Address_____

City_____ State_____ Zip_____

Please send me the books I have checked above.

I am enclosing $_____

Plus postage and handling* $_____

Sales tax (in NY, TN, and DC) $_____

Total amount enclosed $_____

*Add $2.50 for the first book and $.50 for each additional book.
Send check or money order (no cash or CODs) to: **Arabesque Books, Dept. C.O. 850 Third Avenue, 16th Floor, New York, NY 10022**
Prices and numbers subject to change without notice.
All orders subject to availability.
Visit our website at **www.arabesquebooks.com**.